Not the Only One

Not the Only One

lesbian and gay fiction for teens

edited by

Jane Summer

alyson books
los angeles

MANUFACTURED IN THE UNITED STATES OF AMERICA.

THIS TRADE PAPERBACK ORIGINAL IS PUBLISHED BY ALYSON PUBLICATIONS,
P.O. BOX 4371, LOS ANGELES, CALIFORNIA 90078-4371.
DISTRIBUTION IN THE UNITED KINGDOM BY TURNAROUND PUBLISHER SERVICES LTD.,
UNIT 3, OLYMPIA TRADING ESTATE, COBURG ROAD, WOOD GREEN,
LONDON N22 6TZ ENGLAND.

FIRST EDITION: SEPTEMBER 2004

04 05 06 07 08 **a** 10 9 8 7 6 5 4 3 2 1

ISBN 1-55583-834-0

LIBRARY OF CONGRESS CATALOGING-IN-PUBLICATION DATA
    NOT THE ONLY ONE : LESBIAN AND GAY FICTION FOR TEENS / EDITED BY JANE
    SUMMER.—1ST ED.
        SOME STORIES APPEARED PREVIOUSLY IN COLLECTION EDITED IN 1995 BY TONY
    GRIMA.
        CONTENTS: MRS. HOUDINI'S WIFE / ANGELA BROWN — GUARDING THE PUNCH–AND
    ALICE / BONNIE SHIMKO — IT FEELS GREAT / PAM MCARTHUR — SARA / MICHAEL
    THOMAS FORD — FOOLING AROUND / CLAIRE MCNAB — THE WIDEST HEART / MALKA
    DRUCKER — SOMEBODY'S BOYFRIEND / LAUREL WINTER — HER SISTER'S WEDDING /
    JUDITH P. STELBOUM — RAIN / CHRISTINA CHIU — NEW YORK IN JUNE / BRIAN
    SLOAN — CROSSING LINES / JUDD POWELL — TWO LEFT FEET / JANE SUMMER — HAPPY
    BIRTHDAY / NAN PRENER — JUST LIKE A WOMAN / LESLÉA NEWMAN — THE HONORARY
    SHEPHERDS / GREGORY MAGUIRE — GOD LIES IN THE DETAILS / DONNA ALLEGRA —
    THROWING ROCKS AT CATS / BRENT HARTINGER — GAY / MELANIE BRAVERMAN —
    SHE WON'T BITE / WILLIAM MOSES — FORENSICS / STEPHEN GRECO.
        ISBN 1-55583-834-0 (TRADE PBK.)
        1. YOUNG ADULT FICTION, AMERICAN. 2. GAY MEN—FICTION. 3. LESBIANS—FICTION.
    [1. SHORT STORIES. 2. LESBIANS—FICTION. 3. HOMOSEXUALITY—FICTION.] I. SUMMER,
    JANE, 1954– II. GRIMA, TONY, 1967–
    PZ5.N66 2004
    [FIC]—DC22   2004047690

CREDITS
COVER PHOTOGRAPHY BY FARHAN BAIG/PHOTODISC RED.
COVER DESIGN BY MATT SAMS.

Contents

Introduction

The first edition of *Not the Only One: Lesbian and Gay Fiction for Teens* was published nearly ten years ago. When Alyson Publications invited me to edit the 2004 edition of the anthology I hesitated, wondering, *What exactly is lesbian and gay fiction?*

My question was somewhat disingenuous. I knew from my correspondence with the publisher that lesbian and gay fiction is defined as "fiction with gay content." But to my mind, excellent literature transcends content: Shouldn't a novel be judged by the author's level of storytelling mastery and not whether its leading ladies are gay or straight? What librarian or bookseller classifies fiction according to content? By this system of categorization, for example, the consummate novella of alienation, Franz Kafka's 1915 *The Metamorphosis,* in which the protagonist Gregor Samsa is transformed into an insect, could be considered "bug fiction."

If we classify books by content, don't we vastly limit their readership as well as diminish their integrity, their power to teach, transfigure, and enthrall? Why should a love story where the characters are the same sex be shoved aside to the special-interest (i.e., gay) bookshelves? It's segregation pure and simple, and as we know from the civil rights era, separate rarely means equal. Books in the gay section of the library or bookstore seem to receive less serious critical attention or national publicity, and their authors tend to be paid advances far below those whose books are published by more "mainstream" presses. This is largely because few publishers other than those catering to a gay audience are willing to take on stories with gay protagonists. Thus, those of us who write from a gay perspective or about gay characters often have no choice but to go with the smaller specialized publishers who generally haven't the financial muscle—or inclination—to reach out to a larger audience.

Does this matter? If the best of literature surpasses issues of content, is the characters' sexuality of any real importance? Can't gay readers relate to the doomed love of Romeo and Juliet as well as heterosexual readers?

It angers me to think how many generations of high school students have been instructed in the Romeo and Juliet matrix, leaving their gay classmates without any literary reflection just as it angered me as an eight-year-old to be fed stories about white kids exclusively. This kind of narrow literary diet devalues everything "other." It becomes the cultural norm. It leads leading publishers to decline manuscripts with "gay content."

Another thought: I don't even know if "gay literature" and "lesbian literature," once you subtract their minority status, have all that much in common. What do you think?

Here's my solution, my big dream: We change the subtitle of this anthology from *Lesbian and Gay Fiction for Teens* to *Fiction for Teens,* and we make it standard reading for high school kids—*all* high school kids.

These stories, as in the best anthologies of any category, contain a wonderful variety of voices. They are excellently crafted and united by the perennial questions of adolescence: Who am I? What human qualities do I value? How do I survive in this madhouse?

Angela Brown's fabulous fabulist tale, "Mrs. Houdini's Wife," evokes New York in the late 1800s. Also journeying back in time is Bonnie Shimko's "Guarding the Punch—and Alice," which, though set at the close of the intolerant 1950s, offers an auspicious ending. The ecstatic feeling of self-definition is fully captured in "It Feels Great" by Pam McArthur. "Fooling Around," from Australian writer Claire McNab, tells a tender story about getting caught—with a twist.

The poignancy of retrospective understanding is the subject of Malka Drucker's "The Widest Heart." Laurel Winter's "Somebody's Boyfriend," in which boy meets boy, is sparsely told yet full of possibility. "Her Sister's Wedding" by Judith P. Stelboum reflects what society makes of us, living lives of secrecy and guilt. "Rain" by Christina Chiu explains both the necessity and the perils of secrecy.

Brian Sloan's affecting "New York in June" unspools a story of abiding love and self-knowledge. In "Sara," Michael Thomas Ford writes about an unusual boy, who, fully aware of his otherness, creates a safe world for himself. In the excerpt from his novel of the same name, Judd Powell's "Crossing Lines" examines the decisions his character must make as he grows into his self and acknowledges his blossoming sexuality.

"Two Left Feet," which takes place in a rural town in the 1960s, depicts the mystery of love and the fatal consequences of prejudice. The electrical charge one gets from making a human connection is perfectly rendered in Nan Prener's dramatic "Happy Birthday." Lesléa Newman in "Just Like a Woman" intimately reveals the strange world of parents and its effect on adolescents.

Another love story is Gregory Maguire's brilliantly written "The Honorary Shepherds," in which two students struggle "to identify their growing friendship with something outside themselves." Donna Allegra's remarkably understated "God Lies in the Details," set in Guinea, tells of an African-American girl verging on her "dream strong enough to draw blood." "Throwing Rocks at Cats" by Brent Hartinger conveys those bright and shining moments of understanding that arise from loving another person. Melanie Braverman's "Gay," the only poem in the anthology, stunningly pinpoints moments of passion and self-discovery.

William Moses in minimalist style evokes the unstoppable, regenerative powers of love and lust. And finally, Steve Greco's hugely original "Forensics," an excerpt from a forthcoming novel, presents, as the author says, "different ways of taking power into your own hands" and a new kind of justice sure to arouse debate.

Our voices are loving and boisterous, mournful and seductive, compassionate and fierce, as are these unique tales—and this anthology itself. Long may we continue to drown out the awful silence of the past.

—*Jane Summer*

Mrs. Houdini's Wife
Angela Brown

Harry Houdini didn't know a thing.

Sure, he knew how to produce a flower out of thin air. And he could pull a tape through his neck before an audience of gaping, cork-faced men at curio halls. It was no problem for him to sprint five miles along the Hudson River in one stretch, and later that day backstroke three more and barely lose his breath. But when it came to his wife, Bess, he didn't know a damn thing.

It was 1895, and as twenty-year-old Bess lay in bed next to Harry that sticky August night, a stew of odors wafted through the open window and kept her awake: beer, cigar smoke, various colognes and perfumes, sex, possibility. Their small, cluttered apartment sat at the corner of 6th Avenue and 29th Street, smack in the heart of what the New York City clergy had taken to calling Satan's Circus. In the afternoons, Bess often strolled along the Ladies' Mile, an area between 23rd and 9th Streets, which attracted armies of elegantly dressed female shoppers with its enormous cast-iron and brick department stores like B.

Altman and the 200-foot-wide, seven-story Stern Brothers, which Harry scornfully called "That Monster." Bess was especially fond of R.H. Macy's, with its elaborate Christmas displays; she'd stare with delight at the flickering green-and-white lights and rosy-cheeked mechanical Santa. But at night, the Ladies' Mile transformed itself into a boisterous, brightly lit whores' promenade, where rowdy johns, reeking of liquor and sweat, filled horse-drawn landaus, broughams, and coupes. Perfumed prostitutes lined the avenue like dolls at Coney Island game booths, waiting to be picked. Not all of them were pretty, but all were good at what they did. And the men didn't mind. "A hole's a hole," Bess had heard more than one loaded john exclaim, when she and her husband ventured out at night, arm in arm, Harry always on the lookout for trouble. A block west of that blighted strip, swarms of black prostitutes choked 7th Avenue, which residents and visitors alike flatly called "African Broadway."

"Satan's Circus, indeed," Bess muttered as she wrapped one of Harry's thick black curls around her slender index finger, careful not to wake him. But something besides busy 6th Avenue kept Bess awake that night, and it had nothing to do with the devil.

In just two days, Bess and Harry would be leaving the city, to tour their act in small Pennsylvania towns. How would she—could she—say goodbye to Tom? She closed her eyes, recalling the May afternoon when they had met.

Twenty-one-year-old Harry—a mere babe in the magic world—had been working small-time theaters and circuses, an exhausted Bess in tow, barely making ends meet. He supplemented their income with what he called "The Graft": magic and how-to booklets he penned himself and hawked outside their venues for ten cents a pop. That day, Bess had been standing in the lobby of Huber's Palace Museum in Union Square, reading one of Houdini's pamphlets, a poorly cut-and-pasted tract called *Dogs and How to Keep and Train Them.*

Harry had dashed out a few minutes before to round up some lunch for the two, when a gentleman approached Bess. His first words upon greeting the five-foot, ninety-pound woman were, "Like a bird, you are. So small, such a *bisel freyd!*" His voice was like honey, thick with a Yiddish accent.

"A *bisel freyd?*" a wide-eyed Bess replied.

"A little joy!" the man said, grinning devilishly and tossing his hands into the air.

He was perhaps a head taller than Bess, with a handsome olive-skinned face that was rugged but not hard. He was around thirty years old and dressed to the nines, Bess thought, in a freshly pressed black suit, with a gold watch fob running from a vest button to a pocket. A shiny top hat was perched on his head, and his brown eyes gleamed—nearly laughed, Bess now mused—in the mid-afternoon sun that streamed through a window in the shabby dime-museum lobby.

When the man removed his hat, masses of dark-brown curls tumbled out. "Berta Thomashefsky," the man—now woman—said, placing a firm hand at the small of Bess's back, in a manner that was not so much forward as fatherly. "But everyone knows me as Tom," she went on. "And you?"

"Bess Houdini," Bess replied, perplexed and very curious. In fact, she felt more than a little intimidated; she was practically frozen in her spot. Why in heaven's name was this woman dressed in such a way?

"Your face is very sweet," Tom said, brushing her hand against Bess's cheek. "And look at those eyes. So big! You'd think I was the King of Egypt!" She grinned again. "Loosen up, *khaver*. You're stiff as a board. My outfit?" she said, reading Bess's mind. "It's part of the act," she whispered, and poked Bess playfully with her elbow.

Bess felt a little more at ease now. How could she not? Tom was an absolute charmer. And never before had she met a woman so forthright and sure of herself. Bess was envious.

"You're waiting for someone?" asked Tom.

"My husband and I have a magic act," Bess explained. "We started here today, a three-month run."

"How nice," she replied, but Bess noticed a change in Tom's expression when she mentioned Harry. Still, she didn't think much of it, at least then.

"I've been here five years," Tom continued. "*Meshuggeh* work, but it pays the rent."

Bess laughed softly, and Tom explained her post at the dime museum: She ran an animal act, one in which she repeatedly allowed rattlesnakes to bite her on the arm. "But before they dig their fangs in," Tom told her, "I show the crowd how deadly the venom is."

"How?" Bess asked.

"I take a long needle and inject it into a rabbit. And those bunnies don't like it a bit! Their eyes pop out of their heads. Oy, they writhe. At home I have a heap of rabbit skins knee high. Someday I'll make a lady a nice fur coat. Maybe for you, even!"

Bess was aghast. "You watch those animals die day after day?"

"It's not so bad, really." Tom smiled. "There are worse things a woman could do for a living."

"And how do you get the venom out of the snakes?"

"What *tsouris* that would be!" Tom chuckled. "It's not real venom, *khaver*. I use kerosene!" She doubled over in laughter, and Bess smiled faintly, horrified by Tom's story but taken with her strong cheekbones and thick lips. She saw a long scar running from Tom's left ear to her chin.

"How on earth do you survive the bites?" Bess asked.

"You're a magician, *nu?*" Tom smirked. "You should know better than to ask a girl for her secrets."

When Tom offered her a tour of the museum, Bess protested—"My husband will be back soon," she said—but Tom would have none of it.

"Just a few minutes, dear. It's not so big a place." And they walked arm in arm through the empty, musty corridors; paying customers were few and far between in the warm late-spring and summer months.

As they strolled, Bess noticed a slight limp in Tom's gait. The place was crammed with oddities, anything that might draw in the river of 14th Street pedestrians: shrunken heads, wax figures of African pygmies, a model of Niagara Falls with running water, biblical dioramas, stuffed and preserved creatures that had been painstakingly patched together: a half-dog, half-fish, for example. Even after P.T. Barnum's death several years before, humbug was alive and well in New York City.

"There's so much more here. This place is a world of its own," Tom said, her eyes lighting up again. "And you'll make friends, I'm sure of it. William, the human windowpane? You can practically see his heart beating, the poor thing. And my buddy Harriet? God bless her. Forearms as big as a boxer's! She can lift fifty pounds with her pinky finger! Some call them freaks, but I call them my tribe, good people. I'll introduce you to them."

"I would like that." Bess smiled, enchanted by Tom's enthusiasm.

No matter how many dime museums she and Harry worked, these sorts of places always fascinated her; she was just a nice Catholic girl from Brooklyn, and while she'd grown tired of performing over the months, the museums' wonders continued to surprise and delight her. Now she stood silently before an expertly crafted wax dummy of Napoleon, admiring the artistry of its furrowed brow and serious expression. When the mannequin winked at her, she jumped back and covered her mouth with her tiny hands. "Oh, my!" she squealed.

"Frank, you should know better!" Tom chided the man through a quiet laugh, then put her arm around a clearly shaken Bess. "It's called living statuary, *shayna maidel*. Relax."

"What's *shayna maidel*?" Bess asked, a little calmer now.

"Pretty girl," Tom said, and Bess blushed.

Over the next few weeks, Bess stole away from her act with Harry whenever possible to spend time with Tom. Although her husband got along with the "freaks" employed by the museum, he showed disdain for Bess's new friend. "Too manly," he'd tell her. "I don't know what's wrong with her, but she gives good Jewish women a bad name." And then he'd bury his broad handsome face in his hands.

Bess didn't know what Harry meant. "And you give good Jewish men a bad name. Talking like that!" she'd say.

Many times she'd join Tom and the other performers out back when they'd slip away for a cigarette or swig of whiskey. Her favorites were Nell—a humorless, rail-thin, bearded woman—and Jerome, a midget with Chiclet teeth who performed in a variety act with trained chimpanzees. One afternoon he brought one of the chimps outside and put on a show especially for Bess.

"Watch this," he said, and lit a cigarette. When the monkey squawked raucously, Jerome handed him the cigarette and the creature started puffing away. "How about that!" Jerome chuckled, and when he did, his face screwed up into a twisted little walnut. When Bess kneeled down to pet the animal, the chimp reached out and grabbed her left breast, squeezing it hard; Tom quickly slapped the paw away.

"He's as bad as I am!" Tom said with a wink, and everyone laughed except Bess, who didn't understand the joke until later that night. And when she did, a slow smile spread across her face.

After that afternoon, Bess thought a lot about Tom, and a lot about Harry, too. Even though they'd been married less than a year, she felt a divide in their relationship. Many nights after dinner, Harry would leave the house, walking along the riverfront for hours, creating new and better acts in his head. "The Metamorphosis...it isn't right," he'd say, referring to an act in which he'd enter a large cabinet and Bess would secure him in a black sack.

She'd then draw the curtain shut, come around the back, and in a matter of moments, Harry would appear, pull open the curtain, and there Bess would be, bound in the same bag. "We're taking too long. We've got to shave off a few seconds," he'd say, and off he'd go along the Hudson.

This isn't to say Harry Houdini wasn't a decent man. He protected Bess. He made certain she was taken care of and well fed. He loved to have her by his side, with her silky dark hair, cherub face, and big hazel eyes. And he sweetly referred to her as his "large wife." But even more, he treasured the adulation of the crowds, the thrill of performing. He loved the way ladies looked at him when he pulled Buffalo nickels from behind their ears, loved the way gentlemen envied him with Bess on his arm. Bess was certain she didn't want to be loved like this, knew that love could be more than self-fulfillment. And then one night, when Tom invited her over for *Shabbos* dinner, she began to think her curiosity might be love in disguise.

They had taken the Culver Line from the Bowery to Coney Island, where Tom lived in a hotel by the ocean. Even though Tom was wearing her suit and top hat, no one had given the couple a second glance; they looked for all the world like man and wife. In fact, Tom had told Bess that no one ever gave her trouble when she dressed like a man; it was her form of self-protection, and she felt more comfortable in men's clothing anyway. Tom lived in what was called "The Elephant"; shaped like a giant pachyderm, the hotel was a wood-framed, tin-skinned building—more than a hundred feet long and a hundred feet wide—that housed thirty-four rooms in its head, stomach, and feet, and various shops in its trunk and one of its forelegs. Outside the hotel, the smells of clam roasts, ice cream, and lager hung in the warm air; the area was just as seedy as Bess's corner of 6th Avenue, but it had a prettier, more festive appeal.

Bess had told Harry she was visiting her mother overnight in Brooklyn, certain he wouldn't approve of her plans. "Send Mama my love," he had said, a bit sarcastically, since Bess's mother continued to object to the marriage simply because Harry was Jewish.

"Why do you live in such a strange place? There are plenty of apartments in Manhattan," Bess said, as they rode a cramped elevator up to Tom's room.

"That kind of life is so ordinary," Tom replied, trying to manage the two bags of food she and Bess had picked up from a delicatessen along the way. "And I'm not an ordinary girl, *shayna*. You know that. Sure, it costs a little more, but the worthwhile things in life always do."

When the couple entered Tom's room, Bess's eyes grew wide. Yiddish theater posters plastered almost every inch of her walls, a red velvet–covered bed took up a great deal of the small room, and the sweet smell of jasmine floated in the air.

"What are all these?" Bess said, pointing to the posters.

"Oy," said Tom. "Those are from my previous life."

"Were you an actress?"

"For a time." Tom placed her bags on a small oak table in the corner of the room. "Before the trouble."

"The trouble?" Bess asked, her eyebrows raised.

"Let's put it this way: I was a damn good actress—and a looker. *King Solomon,* I was in, at the Thalia Theater. Goneril in *The Jewish King Lear* at the National Theater. The lead in Jacob Gordin's *Sappho,* even."

"Sappho?" Bess asked.

"Sort of a Greek princess," Tom mumbled.

"What happened?"

Tom and Bess sat on the bed, and Bess summoned the courage to place her arm around Tom. Her back felt strong and firm.

"I had just finished up a melodrama at the Bowery Garden," Tom sighed. "You know, the kind where poor shlubs win out over rich villains, and sweet, pure shop-girls escape their advances? And you know how the Bowery is, *nu*?"

Bess nodded. Harry had taken her to a production of *Thomas Edison, Amazing Electrician,* and even though the play was purported to be "educational," she could barely make out the actors' lines over the spectators' drunken hollering and hooting.

"After the show," Tom went on, "my boss says, 'There's some men who want your autograph.' And I thought nothing of it. People always wanted my autograph. With a face like this, why not?" She let out a small laugh, but Bess could hear the sadness in it "So I went out back, behind the theater, where actors gather, and there they were."

"There who were?" Bess said, her hand now slightly rubbing Tom's back.

"Three men. *Shmutsiks.* Greasy, they were. And I wanted to run, but instead I said, 'You want my autograph?' What did I know from anything? I was young, you know, like you. And they said, 'Yes.' And I said to them, 'You've got something to write on?' And one of them said, 'Write on this.' And then they grabbed me…and they had their way with me. *Gotenyu,* so much pain I was in afterward."

"Is that what this is from?" Bess ran her hand down the scar on Tom's cheek.

"And the limp. You're sweet for not asking before. And then I quit. '*Genug.* Enough,' I said. I needed it for nothing. Like they would want a cripple onstage anyway."

"Thank you for telling me," Bess said.

"I never told anyone before," Tom answered, looking at

the floor. "But enough about me. Let's celebrate! It's *Shabbos*!" She jumped to her feet and raced to the bags in the corner of the room. "What's this, a roasted chicken? Oh, my! And a bottle of good red wine! And sweet little green beans and a cherry cheesecake! But first we will light the *Shabbos* candles, *mein shayna*!"

Tom placed the food on the oak table, along with dinnerware and glasses, and then retrieved two brass candlesticks from a closet. "Do you and Harry light the candles together?"

"Oh, no," Bess said. "I mean, my husband was raised religious. His father was a rabbi. But Harry turned away from all that when he left home. I'm not Jewish, but it makes me sad that he doesn't follow his tradition."

"What about you? Do you go to church?"

"Not since Harry and I married. But don't get me wrong—I do believe in God."

"Well, sweet girl, you're going to believe in God a little more in a moment."

Bess raised her eyebrows, unsure of Tom's remark.

"Here, I've written out the blessing. We can say it together. But first you light the candles."

"It looks so foreign. What if I mess up the words?"

"God won't mind. Go ahead, *shayna*."

Bess tentatively struck a match and lit the tapered white *Shabbos* candles, and the two read the blessing together: "*Baruch atah Adonai, eloheynu melech haolam, asher kidshanu b'mitzvotav vetzivanu lehadlik ner shel Shabbat.*" Blessed are You, O Lord our God, Master of the universe, who has sanctified us with your commandments and commanded us to light the Shabbat candles.

When Bess looked up and saw the glow of flames, she

understood what Tom had said about believing in God.

"They're so lovely!" she exclaimed. "Not like other candles. It's like seeing God before my eyes."

"And if you close your eyes, you can almost hear God," Tom whispered in Bess's ear. And as she did, Bess let her head drop back, and Tom kissed her lightly on the neck. Bess turned toward her and stared into her soft eyes. She took Tom's hand in hers and silently led her to the bed.

One by one, their articles of clothing slowly came off and were tossed to the floor. First Bess's button-up boots, then her petticoats, her bustle, her knickers and corset. Tom's polished black shoes, trousers and suspenders, crisp white dress shirt and tie, her undershirt. Wordlessly, the two lay side by side on the bed, naked, wanting. Bess leaned over Tom's lithe, muscular body and began kissing her from head to toe. Gentle kisses, tiny licks, butterfly kisses, starting at her forehead, running down the slope of her nose. Dotting her cheekbones, resting on the long scar on her face, lingering on her chin. Down her smooth neck and breastbone. She ran her tongue lightly along Tom's clavicle, which was lovely and defined; like a Rodin sculpture, Bess thought. Tom's eyes were open, her body calm and receiving, her chest slowly rising and falling. Bess focused on Tom's arms, which were badly scarred with snakebites; with each kiss, she healed Tom's body, transformed her wounds into something beautiful. When every section of Tom's front side was kissed, Bess whispered, "Turn over. I don't want to miss a spot."

Tom did as told, and Bess began all over again, until she had finished her work. "No one's ever kissed me like that before," Tom said.

"No one's ever let me before," Bess smiled.

So it went all evening, the two making love in the bright light of the *Shabbos* candles, stopping occasionally to eat and drink, to whisper words that lovers do. And it was that night Bess first noticed how Tom's voice changed when the two were alone together, how her tone grew softer, more urgent, tinged with what can only be described as prayer, as if she were saying, "I love you" every time she opened her mouth. "You make love like a Jewish woman," Tom said, as the two were curled in each other's arms, Tom's hand on Bess's soft belly.

"What's that supposed to mean?" Bess said through a quiet laugh.

"You know what you want and don't stop until you get it." She lowered her voice a bit. "Maybe you're a *gilgul*."

"A *gilgul*?"

"Legend claims there are those who are born in a *goyishe* body but have a Jewish soul. They say Jewish souls always come home."

Bess just smiled and closed her eyes.

"My sweet *gilgul*," Tom whispered in Bess's ear. "Welcome home." And they drifted off to sleep as the last flickers of the candles died out.

Every other Friday for nearly two months, Bess spent *Shabbos* evening with Tom, each time telling Harry she was visiting her mother in Brooklyn, each time surprised he believed her. But now, as she lay in bed next to her husband on this hot August night, knowing she'd be saying goodbye to Tom the following evening, it wasn't her lying to Harry that bothered her; it was her lying to Tom: her sin of omission. Even though they'd been spending the night together, lighting the candles in joy and wonder, speaking to each other from their hearts, she hadn't told Tom she loved her. But was that necessary? Did Tom not know? *Of course, she knows,* Bess thought. *But she also knows I can't leave Harry. It would kill him. And what kind of life could I live with her?* Still, she made up her mind to tell Tom how she felt. That's the worst sin of all, Bess thought, to keep your heart locked up, to not say the words you need to say, because you're too proud and maybe afraid.

The following night, both Bess and Tom knew, would be their last together. The Pennsylvania tour would be followed by a Midwest run through Milwaukee, Chicago, and St. Louis, and who knew where the husband-and-wife team would go from there. The sky was the limit, especially since Harry had been receiving so many favorable notices in the city papers.

That Friday morning, Tom had asked Bess to bring her bathing suit; she had a surprise in store for her. Bess would have to ride the Culver Line alone, since Tom had taken the afternoon off from Huber's. "I've got something special planned," she'd said, and Bess had something in mind as well. When Bess knocked on Tom's hotel room door that evening, she was taken aback by the sight before her: Tom's hair was shorn into a stylish men's cut.

"Oh, my!" Bess said. "How handsome you look! But why?"

"Just for you, *shayna,*" Tom replied. She was wearing a striped one-piece men's swimsuit, and Bess stood there admiring her toned physique, thought for a brief moment that Tom really might be a man, with her flat chest and tight biceps. But to Bess, she was unmistakably a woman.

"You'll see," Tom said. "You brought your suit, *nu?*"

"It's in my bag." Bess gestured toward a small valise at her side, then entered Tom's room, where she quickly changed into her bathing suit. She didn't know what Tom had up her sleeve, but she was willing to play along.

"All done?" Tom said, and Bess nodded. "We're going Electric Bathing, my sweetness."

Bess had heard about Electric Bathing, although Harry had refused to take her on more than one occasion. "Lovebirds swooning in the ocean!" he'd say. "Makes a mockery out of a decent sport like swimming. No wonder they call it Sodom by the Sea." Coney Island retailers had pitched in a few years before and installed arc lighting at the beach, and for the first time, people could swim at night and actually see where they were headed. Of course, more often than not—especially in the past few years when the beaches had become integrated, as opposed to years prior when men and women adhered to separate swim schedules—couples took advantage of Electric Bathing to become intimate with each other, away from prying eyes, albeit in public.

Now Tom's new haircut and outfit made sense, Bess thought. If they were going Electric Bathing—which meant only one thing—they couldn't go in as two women, now could they? At this moment, Bess loved Tom more than ever.

When they got to the beach, Tom asked Bess to sit down for a moment, and Tom wrapped her arm around her lover. "I've got something to tell you," she said, reaching into a paper bag she'd brought along.

"No," Bess interrupted. "Let me go first."

Tom smiled and waited for Bess to speak.

15

"I just want to say…" Bess paused, trying to find the words. "I love you."

"Is that all? I know, *shayna*," Tom said, and placed a kiss on Bess's forehead. "Now, *sha*. Listen. Remember how I told you about the *gilgul*?" Bess nodded. "Well, here's another story. And maybe it's true and maybe it's not. What do I know? They say certain people meet for a reason, they're soulmates. You've heard this, yes?"

Again Bess nodded, and smiled a little, seeing Tom's sad eyes shine in the electric lights. "Some say that two *neshemahs*—two souls—who come together in this life were standing side by side at Sinai when the Israelites received the Ten Commandments. Maybe it's shmaltzy, a *bobbeh meyse*—you know, a tall tale—but maybe there's a little truth there. So I'm giving you this, just in case."

Tom reached into the paper bag and withdrew two silver rings. "Nothing much. But something. I picked them up at the drugstore." She placed one of the rings on Bess's pinky finger and the other on her own. "So when we're apart, you just look at this, and there I'll be, always with you. And when I get sad, and maybe a little lonely even, there'll you be with me."

"Like your wife?"

"*Mein khosen*. My chosen. And me yours."

When Bess reached out to wipe a tear from Tom's cheek, Tom just smiled and said, "So you want to go swimming or what?"

Hand in hand they waded into the ocean, surrounded by a multitude of couples. They walked out as far as they could until the water reached Bess's shoulders. She looked up at the dark sky littered with dozens of bright white stars, and then at the shoreline, where she saw hundreds of blinking lights—blue and green, red and yellow—and the Loop-the-Loop and the towering Coney Island Roller Coaster and the massive trunk of the Elephant in which Tom, her tender lover, lived. And as Tom's hands made their way down the curves of Bess's body and she whispered, "My sweet *gilgul*" in her ear, Bess knew, at least for the moment, she was where she was supposed to be.

Guarding the Punch—and Alice
Bonnie Shimko

As far back as I can remember, I've felt as if God put me together wrong. Like He got sidetracked when He was assembling my brain, and the wires got crossed. I didn't figure out what my problem was until the middle of sixth grade.

"This is Alice Weinstein and her twin brother, Mark," the teacher announced when we returned from Christmas vacation. "They've moved here all the way from New York City, and I'm sure you'll make them feel welcome."

I had never wanted to make anyone feel welcome so much in my entire life. While the other girls were having heart attacks over Mark, I was fantasizing what it would be like to kiss Alice. It scared the heck out of me. But it was also the most amazing thing I'd ever experienced. It was as if a gigantic swarm of friendly bees had invaded the most private part of my body to celebrate a huge event—one of their birthdays, maybe—and they had invited me to join them.

That's when I decided I'd better keep my distance from the other girls for fear I'd let my guard down and they'd know what I am. And when boys asked me out, I said, "No, thank you" so many times, they've given up trying. So this year, while the normal girls counted the days until the senior prom, I tallied them like a prisoner on death row, waiting to be led to the electric chair.

That's me over there, standing under the CLASS OF '59 banner, collecting tickets. The tall strawberry blond in the god-awful turquoise dress. The strapless number with the rhinestone trim and the big fat bow on the butt—the one Roxie picked out and spent a week's wages on.

"Charlotte! This is it!" she said, as she pulled it off the rack, away from the long-sleeved, high-necked black one I had my eye on. She loves anything froufrou—the flashier the better. Probably because her life is so dull.

Roxie's my mother, but she thinks if I call her by her first name, people will think we're sisters, which is pretty dumb because we've lived in Highfalls, New York, population close to nothing, since before I was born. The whole town knows about the memento a redheaded jackass named Lonnie Kraft left after he got tired of my mother's affection and moved on. I'm the bastard who lives in the dilapidated house at the edge of town with her wild-eyed mother and her grandfather who thinks he's President Roosevelt and on really bad days wears his underwear on the outside.

I learned about the foundation of my life—brick by brick—from Grandpa Thomas and some big-mouth kids at school who thought it was their job to make other people miserable. Grandpa Thomas usually handed me the bricks gently, adding a fib or two to make what Roxie did seem okay. But sometimes he'd slip and drop a sharp one on my foot when he was drunk; before Grandma Francie died and he checked out of life permanently—took to the big green La-Z-Boy in the corner of our front room, sitting there ever since, somber as a shadow. The bottom-feeders at school threw the bricks at me, aiming to kill. Like when that grease bucket, Buddy Seymour, took pleasure in announcing in gym class that my father was a convicted felon—armed robbery. And that Roxie saw his picture in the paper, thought he was too good-looking to have committed a crime, and started taking him cookies and cigarettes on visiting days at Dannemora.

I've never asked my mother straight out about Mr. Lonnie Kraft, or where he might be now. The way I feel is—why bother? I'm sure he's the same creep loser he was then, only sixteen years older. Besides, Roxie's about one aggravation away from joining Grandpa Thomas in outer space, and I don't want to be the one to send her off. I've already disappointed her enough. It's hard on a mother when she's trying to live life through her daughter. Especially when the mother's always dreamed of being a famous fashion model and the daughter wants to be an anthropologist—has actually landed a full scholarship to Vassar and feels guilty about it, but not guilty enough to let some other low-income girl scoop it up.

I suppose you're wondering why I didn't kick up a fuss about the dress and wearing the idiotic tiara Roxie dug out of the trunk in the attic—the one she would have worn to her own prom if she'd been invited. The fact is, I don't really care. There's nobody here I want to impress—except Alice—and what's the point of that? She's been going steady with Jeff Harper since freshman year. Besides, if you'd seen the look on Roxie's face when I came out of the dressing room at Marquette's Bridal Salon and Formal Wear, you would have done the same thing.

"Ah, Charlotte," she said, her eyes overflowing like the dam in her heart just broke. "You'll make the other girls look like weeds." And before I could stop her, she reached down the front of the dress and hauled everything she could find upward. "A woman has to show off her assets," is how she put it. Then she patted and adjusted as if she were kneading two hunks of bread dough. "You'll drive the goddamn boys crazy with that figure. Jesus! What I would have given to look like you when I was in high school." She fished a Kleenex out of her purse, wiped away the rivers of mascara that were flowing down her cheeks. "If I was you," she said, blowing her nose hard, "I'd go after that Jeff Harper boy. His father's got more money than Elvis." She planted her hand on her waist and jutted her hip out so far it looked as if it had come unhinged. Then she took in a huge breath of air and let it out slowly; as if what she was about to say was making her tired. "Now, I know you're more interested in your studies and all, but it wouldn't hurt to send out a few signals, get things headed in the right direction."

"*Roxie,* he's already taken," I said, rescuing a runaway bra strap—a limp, gray wormy thing that had made its way halfway down her arm. "I've told you that a million times. And I promised Mrs. Hanover I'd take the tickets and pass out refreshments. She needs somebody she can depend on." When I saw the look of desperation on Roxie's face, words escaped that I didn't mean to let out. "Besides, I've got my eye on somebody else." Then I added, "But that one's spoken for too," so she wouldn't start quizzing me.

A ray of sunshine lit up her eyes and then a storm cloud. "Not a married man, I hope. You might as well get yourself mixed up with a nest of rattlesnakes as walk into a mess like that. He'll maul you and promise you the world so he can get what he wants." The muscles in her jaw tightened and her voice dropped a notch. "And you know what that goddamn son of a bitch Lonnie Kraft did to me."

It's embarrassing the way Roxie curses as easily as most people breathe, but I can't really blame her. Her life's not exactly what anybody would sit up nights wishing for. If I told her what was in my heart—that the only person I'd love to be mauled by is Alice Weinstein—she would have fainted dead away. Then, when she came to, she'd probably call me the ugly name she uses when she talks about Miss Drew, my typing teacher, and her roommate, Annie Pine, the town librarian and the kindest lady in the entire world.

It seems strange that Roxie would make fun of people just because of who they love. You'd think she'd know better, having been the brunt of cruel jokes for loving my father. Maybe that's why. Maybe she thinks calling two perfectly nice women queer freaks is the only way she can get back at the world. But under the anger I feel toward her is a smidgen of pity. A person shouldn't have to sink that low to build herself up.

✪

I'm guarding the punch bowl so it doesn't get spiked and our school won't get sued by a bunch of angry parents, like what happened last year. The crowning is about to take place, so I'm alone in the lobby, sitting at the refreshment table. I'm watching a ball of pale-green foam that used to be lime sherbet float around the puddle of Hawaiian Punch and pineapple juice in the bottom of the bowl. The coconut cream pie Roxie made is sitting there untouched amid the almost empty plates of finger sandwiches and tea cookies. The fact that the note I took home specifically asked for two-dozen lemon bars didn't faze Roxie one little bit. "This is a special occasion," she said, running her voice up an octave on the word *special* to make her point. "Lemon bars won't do. Besides, this is the night a girl waits for her whole life, so I'm going to make your favorite."

Once Roxie gets something in her head, it's stuck there like cement, so I knew nothing I could say would make a difference. Plus, it could have been a lot worse. She could have baked a wedding cake like the one she learned how to make in the cake-decorating class she took when she was getting ready to marry Harvey Malt, the butcher she works with at the A&P. He had most of his belongings moved into our house before he remembered to mention that his battle-ax of a mother and his old maid sister with the hand-washing problem were coming, too.

"What the hell's the matter with you," Roxie said, poking her finger into Harvey's chest so hard I thought he was going to fall over backward. "What'd you think, I wasn't going to notice?" Harvey stood there mute with his hound-dog face, clutching a box of wrestling trophies he'd won in high school, waiting for Roxie to run out of steam. "Damn it all, Harvey, I could handle your mother, but if you think I'm going to spend a king's ransom on soap, you've got another think coming."

So she helped him return his stuff to his mother's apartment, and they went back to their Saturday-night routine. Supper at Leona's Diner and then Harvey's attempts to fix the clanging radiator in Roxie's bedroom while I watch TV with the volume turned up full blast so

I don't have to hear the bedsprings squawking and my mother squealing with delight.

✪

Last year's king is about to place the crown over Jeff Harper's ducktail, while I'm wearing out my eyes, staring at Alice's long, dark hair streaming over her shoulders like a flood of black satin. Of course, she's the queen. She's the most popular girl in our class, the whole school even. There isn't anything about her that's not perfect, and the only person I've told how I feel about her is Grandpa Thomas.

✪

Mama was still at work, and the sitter the county pays for woke up from her nap on the couch and went home. On her way out the door, she rolled her eyes and sighed huge when I asked if Grandpa Thomas had a good day. I'm not sure what her problem is. He's like a stuffed animal, calm and easy to be around. I take care of him when I'm not in school because Roxie uses any excuse she can think of to stay away. "Sick people make me nervous," was her answer when I finally asked her about it. I was ready to tell her how lame I thought that was when I realized that I used him as an excuse to escape the well people in my life.

I sat on the arm of his chair, laid my head on his shoulder and took hold of his hand. I pour out all my tenderness onto him, because syrupy stuff makes Roxie fidgety. Maybe because of the shield she wrapped around her heart when Lonnie Kraft walked out—the shield that keeps people at a safe distance so she won't get hurt that badly ever again.

24

But anybody can walk away—even your own daughter when she goes off to college and leaves the people who depend on her to fend for themselves.

Grandpa Thomas smells like moldy bread. He stares straight ahead, blinks once in a while. And his silence lets you imagine what he might say.

"You know the girl I've told you about a million times?" I asked, examining the patch of whiskers below his ear that the county woman missed when she shaved him.

You mean Alice Weinstein? The smart girl who plays the violin and can beat her brother in tennis? The one who's wasting her time hanging out with that blowhard Jeff Harper when she could be with you?

"Right. Well, she touched my hand today." I sat up, looked straight into his eyes. "We were changing after gym, and she asked me to toss a towel over the shower stall. And when I did, she grabbed my hand instead of the towel, even waited a second before she pulled hers away. Do you think it could have been on purpose?"

Of course it was. She had the whole thing planned. Nobody forgets a towel by accident.

I noticed for the first time that he has green specks in his velvety brown eyes—clear eyes like you see on a much younger person. "That's what *I* thought. But then I figured maybe it was just me being a jerk."

No way! She was definitely trying to tell you something.

"Tell me what?"

That she's had the hots for you since the first day she saw you.

My heart started banging against my ribs and I could only take in half-breaths. "Maybe you're *right*. And there was that other time, too—in biology lab when we were

25

partners and had to dissect that poor little frog. When she saw my face, she put her arm around my shoulder, told me to sit down that she'd do the cutting and I could take notes. Said she's going to be a doctor and that she had to get used to that kind of thing. And I'm pretty sure she gave my shoulder a little squeeze before she let go."

Well, see, that proves it.

"I love her so much, Grandpa Thomas. I think about her all the time. How perfect it would be if we could spend our whole lives together. Maybe in a cabin in the woods where nobody would even know about us."

Good idea. You could go to your jobs during the day and then live the rest of your lives as mystery women.

"That's exactly what *I* was thinking. That way nobody would make fun of us." I take his hanky from the end table, wipe the bit of drool that's traveling down his chin. "There's just one other thing I want to ask you."

What's that?

"Do you think I'll go to heaven when I die?"

I wait. Nothing from him but a tiny sigh. I lay my head back down on his shoulder. Tears burn my eyes, and the lump in my throat makes me feel as if I'm being strangled.

✪

"I'll be right back," Jeff Harper says, tapping the bottom of the pack of cigarettes he's holding until one pops out and he puts it in his mouth. "I'll just be in the parking lot." He's talking to Alice Weinstein who's standing in the middle of the lobby in her black taffeta floor-length gown, classy plain. Her only jewelry is a gold Star of David on a chain around her neck.

"Take your time," Alice says. "I'm going to see if there's any punch left."

I didn't pay any attention to the music that's been wafting from the gym until now—Bobby Darin's "Dream Lover."

"Hey, Charlotte, how's life treatin' ya?" Jeff calls over in his big-deal voice. He doesn't even look at me on his way to the door. Just waves the Marlboro package in my direction.

I can't think of anything to say besides fine, so I just smile, wish I could fall into a hole and disappear.

"Charlotte!" It's Jeff again. He's holding the door open with his back, lighting his cigarette with a Zippo. "Keep an eye on Alice for me, okay? I don't want the other guys getting ideas because she's alone."

"I will," I say, glad that he doesn't know about the ideas that are tripping over each other inside *my* head.

After he's gone, I look over at Alice, wait for her to say something, think how dry my mouth has suddenly become. The Fleetwoods begin to sing "Come Softly to Me."

"It's like an oven in there," she says, walking in my direction. Her cheeks are flushed pink, which makes her blue eyes stand out even more. "My feet are killing me. I'm not used to high heels. Do you mind if I sit down?"

"Oh, sure," I say, too fast and too eager. I drag the folding chair that's next to me around to the front of the table.

She drags it back where it was. "Is it okay if I help with the goodies? He won't be back for a while. There's a bottle of vodka in his car."

"That'd be great. There's not much left, though, so business is slow."

"Yeah, I know. Everybody's using the water fountains in the locker rooms. What kind of pie is that?"

"I'm not really sure," I lie. "I don't even know who brought it."

"Well, let's cut into it and see." She picks up Roxie's silver-plated pie server that's lost most of its silver, slices through the whipped cream and says, "Oh, my gosh! It's coconut—my absolute favorite food in the whole world. Do you want a piece?"

"Sure. It's my favorite, too. If I'd known that, I'd have gotten into it earlier." I take paper plates and plastic forks out of the bag I hid under the table and hand them to her.

✪

"Here...just a sec. Stay still," Alice says, leaning toward me. Frank Sinatra's belting out "High Hopes," and we're working on our second helpings of Roxie's masterpiece when she reaches over, runs her hand across my mouth, then licks her fingers. "You had some whipped cream on your lip."

Holy shit! My mouth germs are actually mixing with hers. Then I close my eyes, try to slow my breathing. *Oh, please, God. Don't let Roxie's filthy words slip out of my mouth. I don't think Jews are allowed to swear.* "Thanks," I say, touching my lips. I'm a little surprised that they're actually still there. I thought they might have melted away under her warm smooth touch.

"No problem. You don't want anything to spoil your perfect face. Did anybody ever tell you that you look a lot like Sandra Dee? "

I look over to see if she's serious. Her face says she is. "Sandra Dee? Really?"

"Did you see *Gidget*? She reminded me of you the whole time I was watching it."

"No, I haven't seen it yet." I don't add that the last movie I saw was *Bambi*. That I cried so hard when his mother was killed I wouldn't leave Roxie's side for days, and how I'm still angry with the movie people for pulling such a rotten stunt on a bunch of little kids. But I see Sandra Dee's picture on the cover of movie magazines in the drugstore every time I pick up Grandpa Thomas' medicine. And the fact that Alice Weinstein is comparing me to one of the prettiest girls ever makes me light-headed. I change the subject, because being the center of attention is twisting my stomach into a knot.

"So," I say, all matter-of-fact. Have you decided where you're going to college yet?"

"Vassar."

Dear sweet Jesus! "Really? I'm going there, too." Connie Francis—"My Happiness."

"I know. The guidance counselor told me. Maybe we can be roommates."

Oh, my God! Thank you, Lord. I don't know what I did to deserve this. But I'll try to make it up to you.

"That would be nice," I say, like she's just told me the price of bologna might drop. If I acted the way I feel inside, I'd pounce on her and French-kiss her so hard she'd have me arrested for assault. She'd explain to the police officer that she was just being friendly to poor Charlotte Zublonski when she was attacked. Then she'd mumble something under her breath about my whole family being nuts.

"Oh, I'm sorry," she says with embarrassment in her voice. "Do you already have a roommate picked out? I just thought..."

"No! I don't have a roommate picked out. That would

be great. I'd love to have you be my roommate!" *Ah, jeez, Charlotte. Rein yourself in.*

Dion starts to sing "A Teenager in Love," and neither of us says anything. We lean back in our chairs and stare at the wall as if we're waiting for a movie to start. *Well, now I've done it. I've scared her off by being too excited.* I put my hands in my lap, pick at a hangnail, bite the inside of my lip.

"This is my favorite song," she says, almost in a whisper. I feel her staring at me, and then I watch as her hand moves toward mine.

The bees are back in my belly, only this time they've brought another swarm with them. I close my eyes, squeeze her hand, wait until I can breathe. "I love it, too. When's Jeff coming back?"

"I don't know. Pretty soon, I guess."

I turn, face her. "What's the deal with that, anyway?"

She looks at me with sad eyes and her shoulders sag. "My parents are the deal. They can never find out about me. It would absolutely kill them."

"I know what you mean. I've been dancing around my mother for years. But if she finds out, I'll be the one who gets killed."

She shakes her head, laughs a little. "At least you've been true to yourself. Didn't try to fake it, like I did."

"Are you kidding?" I grab the tiara off my head, run my fingers along the rhinestones on the neckline of my dress. "You think this getup is being true to myself?"

"I was wondering about that."

"This is my mother's idea of date bait." I'm mustering up the courage to tell her about my train wreck of a family when we hear the front door open.

Brook Benton's singing "It's Just a Matter of Time" while Jeff walks toward us. Alice and I give each other's hands a goodbye squeeze and let go. "I see you took good care of her," he says when he gets to the table. "Anybody try to make a move on her?"

"Just me," I say.

"Mm-hmm, *right*," he says. "Don't even joke about that kind of shit. Those freaks make me sick."

Silence hangs in the air until Conway Twitty croons the first few notes of "It's Only Make-believe."

"Hey, Alice," Jeff says. "They're playing our song. You don't mind if I borrow my date, do you, Charlotte?"

"Nope, not at all. As long as you give her back."

"Damn it, Charlotte, stop kidding around."

"Sorry, couldn't resist. Go! You're going to miss your special song."

While they're walking toward the gym, I think how sometimes life unfolds in your favor and you really don't know whom to thank. But then I see Roxie's pie and her tiara, and I think how important tonight was to her. And if she hadn't been her offbeat, pushy self, I wouldn't even be here. I owe her a lot for that.

It Feels Great
Pam McArthur

This is why I don't like driving. Everyone has my life in their hands and they treat it as carelessly as a smoked-down cigarette. A throwaway. Here I am in the middle lane of the highway, my needle steady on 55, and cars are flying by so fast they're a blur. The traffic is heavy enough to be scary, but it doesn't slow anyone down. My heart stops with an electric jolt when a big blue truck roars up to my rear bumper, then swerves at the last minute and squeezes in front of me. I hit the brake pedal and pray to a god I don't even believe in.

People must feel immortal as they hurtle down the pavement, most of them not even buckled in, and I don't understand it. They must not have the vivid imagination that I do, because I can see it all: cars in flames, tangled metal, twisted bodies. I can hear the crack of my eggshell skull against a shattering windshield. Long gone is the time when I felt safe in a car—curled up in the backseat, half asleep under a starry sky, my father solid and square in the front, bringing us home. And my mother in front, too?

Doing what? Yelling, "Look out! Oh, that car came awfully close. Look, the light is red. Stop, stop!" And she would slam her foot impotently on her rubber floor mat.

Oh, yes, my mother. She gave me my imagination. A big gift for a young girl, all those bright pictures of disaster dancing in front of me day and night. She taught me everything in life *not* to do. Sometimes I hate her for stealing away my childhood with all those tales of danger. To hear her talk, life is a porcupine with the quills turned inward, ready to prick your insides at the slightest misstep. She has the whole world wrapped up in rules of dos and don'ts. Mostly don'ts. Don't stick you hand out the car window: You'll lose your fingers. Don't wash your underwear at the Laundromat: Strangers will see it. Don't dive into water without checking for rocks first: Even if it's the same pond you swim in every day, still, you never know.

"Mom," I said the summer I was ten and sick of dog-paddling around, checking the same water over and over. "What do you think's gonna happen? A rock grew here last night?"

"Don't talk smart to me," she snapped. "All I know is, when your uncle Howard was younger than you, he cracked his head open—right open so the insides could spill out—and ever since then he thinks he's a squirrel. Sits under Grandma's trees looking for acorns. He broke her bird feeder once, trying to get at the seeds. Broke her heart."

I couldn't tell if it was the broken skull or the bird feeder that had broken my grandma's heart, and I didn't ask. I dog-paddled along the shore, checking for rocks. More and more, I was learning to keep my mouth shut— storing up Mom's pictures of death and destruction until sometimes it's almost too scary to get out of bed in the morning. That's why I'm surprised to find myself here, on the highway with all these maniacs. But I had to come, after I heard Gina's lecture.

Gina—now there's danger for you. If Mom knew about her, she'd have plenty to say, believe me. Gina is the first woman I ever heard say the words "I am a lesbian." I wish you could've heard her. "My name is Gina Rollins, and I am a lesbian," just as matter-of-factly as I might say, "I'm sixteen years old," or "I like pizza." As if it didn't matter that she was talking to my entire high school, kids who would never say the word themselves. "Lezzie," yes; "queer," yes. "Lesbian"—no, I don't think so.

But Gina just gave us a clear, confident smile as she went on to say that everybody—gay and straight—deserved respect, deserved a chance at love. Standing relaxed on the stage, as calm and articulate as any of our teachers, she spoke what had always been unspeakable. And then she looked right at me. My heart froze. I didn't know how she could know what I was only beginning to guess about myself, but she knew. She knew. I was sure that she knew. And if she knew, then anyone could know. The kid sitting next to me, my teachers, anyone.

Gina began speaking again. "There is no way to identify a person who is gay or bisexual. No special way that we walk or talk or dress." I began breathing again. Maybe she didn't know about me, after all. Though it would almost be a relief if she did—just her, no one else.

"Your best friend could be gay and you might never know it." Looking out at us all, Gina seemed to speak directly to the clusters of kids who were whispering and snickering. "I say that not to create a climate of suspicion and accusation. I say it to remind you that gay and lesbian youth are normal—and as diverse—as the rest of the population. I charge you to build a community that is strengthened by your diversity, a community that represents each of you as you truly are."

I stared at Gina. Where had she found her pride? I wished I could soak it in through my skin. I was still staring when she finished her speech and the oak floorboards of the auditorium roared under the feet of 200 stampeding kids. A lot of them ducked past the teachers who were handing out flyers at each doorway. Keeping my face carefully blank, I accepted the handouts, just as I always did the homework, always showed up for class, always kept my mouth shut.

Ducking my head, I slouched down the hall toward my second-period class. The special assembly, part of a week-long program called "Diversity Within Community," had the hallways humming with talk and laughter, and I didn't want to be a part of it.

As I slipped into my classroom, a girl named Carly grabbed my arm.

"Hey," she breathed softly, and I looked at her in surprise. I backed away from her as I shook my head, but she followed and bumped me gently with her hip.

"One hundred lezzies escaped from a psych hospital this morning."

Carly's hip brushed mine again and she barred her eyes before delivering the punch line. "The police caught ninety-nine of them."

A burst of laughter broke out, and I realized that all of Carly's friends had been watching. I shouldered past her, trying to ignore the jokes that were flying around the room.

"How many lezzies does it take to screw in a lightbulb? You idiot, lesbians can't screw!"

"Hey, did you hear about the Polish fag—"

I couldn't take anymore. The years of keeping my mouth shut came to an abrupt end as I shouted, "Hey!" My fury rose like smoke over the room. "Why don't you all grow up?"

Suddenly, I knew what Uncle Howard must have felt in that breathless moment between land and water, no turning back, no telling what lay just under the pond's familiar surface. I had launched myself into clear air, and the fishbowl silence of the classroom gave me no cue as to what my landing would be. I rebelliously told myself I didn't care, but I didn't look up from my desk until our teacher entered the room.

I did not take it out until later that night. Then, lying in bed, ready to turn out the light if I heard my parents in the hall, I read the handout. A brief discussion about sexual preference. Some questions and answers about AIDS. And at the very bottom, mention of a Gay and Lesbian Youth Alliance that met in the city. Every Tuesday night.

Folding the paper back into my book, I clicked off my lamp and lay down in the darkness. Remembering my outburst at school. Wondering if everyone would think I was gay, would push me over the line before I myself was sure. Knowing that I was facing one of those dangers my mother had been preparing me for, all along. I thought about the one time my mother had talked with me—I think—about homosexuality. I must have been about fourteen. There are two women who live together across the street from us, and I often see them in the yard. Raking leaves, planning a garden, whistling for the cat.

"They whistle for that cat like it's a damn dog," my mother complained one evening as the familiar sound trilled through our open windows.

"Now, what's the harm in that?" my father questioned good-naturedly.

"It's not normal, that's what. Nobody whistles for a cat!"

"Cat comes, too," I couldn't resist observing.

"Well, it's not natural," my mother repeated, glaring at me. "Whole house goes against nature. Don't you go near them."

I knew even then that Mom was upset about more than just whistling for a cat, but it took me a whole year to figure out just what it was that those women represented. And another year to realize how important that might be to me.

So there I was, staring into the darkness of my room, trying to picture myself at a meeting of gay youth. For once, my imagination failed me. All I could conjure up were questions. What would these kids be like? In spite of Gina's lecture, I couldn't quite believe that gay kids would really be just the same as everyone I grew up with. I imagined them as dressing differently, having their own language—codes by which they identified themselves, a special group. And what if I walked into their meeting and found that I was different, even from them?

Turning my face into the pillow to muffle the sounds, I tried out the words: "I am a lesbian." The pillow tasted like shredded cardboard in my mouth, and I had no idea if the words were true.

Truth was hard to recognize in my house. It was observed in my mother's dark warnings of danger, as if life could be that one-sided. I suddenly realized that the other side of life is adventure, excitement, freedom; and I longed for that freedom. Before falling into an anxious sleep, I plotted my first move: borrowing the car under the pretext of going to the library.

And that is how I came to be here tonight. Part of me still flinching as cars flash their headlights at me, cut me off, remind me that some dangers are real. After all, it is not just in my mother's gun-shy mind that Uncle Howard sits under the oak tree, chasing acorns. But I can't live forever in the shadow of the human squirrel, burdened with my mother's fears, I have to take the risk. As I drive down the highway I know that I am leaving home, and yet somehow it feels like coming home.

✪

"Elemental Lentil," Barbara says. "A health food store."

"Planter's Worts," Jeri counters as she bends over the oven. "Garden supplies."

Laughing, Barbara adds. "For gardeners with bad feet."

Barbara is the taller of the two. The other, Jeri, is the one who whistles for their cat. When I asked her about that, she launched into an enthusiastic explanation about a dog she used to have, and how the cat loved the dog—something else my mother would call unnatural—and she concluded with a shrug, "Peebles just always comes when I whistle."

Right now Peebles is curled in a tortoiseshell lump on a sturdy kitchen chair. Her ears twitch as she listens to the women inventing new businesses for themselves.

"Let's see," Barbara muses, "how about Bosom Buddies—we'd sell bras."

I blush and hope they don't notice. Their sun-dappled kitchen has become familiar to me over the past weeks, but I am not yet at ease here. For one thing, there is always the sense of danger as I slip across the street whenever my mother is running errands. If she catches me, if she catches me—well, I don't know what would happen, but it wouldn't be pretty. That knowledge beats with the blood at my temples until I have a headache the size of Idaho.

And then there are the women themselves. The first day I stood on their doorstep with an empty measuring cup, my need as transparent as clear water, I had a whole list of questions memorized. Questions designed to get a conversation going, no matter how reluctant they might be. While Barbara measured sugar into my cup, I got out the first question—"What's your cat's name?" but I never got any further. Encouraging these women to talk is like asking a weed to grow—totally unnecessary. They play with conversation like Peebles bats at a catnip toy, sending it all over the house, even into dusty corners and the darkest hiding holes. There is nothing they won't talk about. Nothing. It's frightening—and immensely attractive.

Seems like I spend half my time here blushing, and today isn't starting out any different. My cheeks feel hot enough to start a forest fire. I turn away from Barbara and see Jeri coming toward us, big oven mitts cradling a pan of brownies fresh from the over. With the words "bosom buddies" ringing in my ears, I look at her breasts. I can't help myself. And then I think about Jeri and Barbara together, and I blush straight up to my scalp. "Dirty," my mother's voice hisses. "Dirty, dirty, dirty."

Suddenly I swing dizzily back to the time I was three years old and hearing those words for the first time. I was in the ladies' room of a bus station, sitting on a toilet, when the door of the bathroom stall slammed open and my mother rushed in.

"What are you doing?" she yelled as she jerked me up by the elbow. "Don't you know that's dirty?" She yanked me out to the cracked sink with a green streak under the dripping faucet. I was immobilized by the twisted wad of pants and underpants around my ankles. "Dirty," she said as she grabbed a fistful of brown paper towels and ran water over them. "Dirty," she repeated as she scraped my bare bottom raw. Strangers walked past us, but she kept right on.

"Lord knows who's used that toilet!" she hissed in my face. "You could get any disease. You could die!"

Die. From that day on she told me about the ways I could die—toilet seats, a stranger with candy, a jar of mayonnaise left out of the refrigerator too long. I learned from her that the way to survive was to risk nothing, question nothing, do nothing. Sitting in Barbara and Jeri's kitchen, caught between their honesty and my mother's threats, I realized that I am fighting for my life. I mean, fighting to make it really mine, to be active instead of just watching the world go by, hoping it doesn't trample me.

Suddenly, I realize that the room has grown quiet. Jeri is watching me as she sets the brownies on the table. She sits down, nearly squashing Peebles on the chair. The cat slips onto the floor and gives one hind leg a disdainful shake before sitting in a splash of sunlight. She spreads her toes and licks them aggressively, one by one.

Jeri looks at me thoughtfully. "You're awfully quiet," she says softly as she hands me a huge square of brownie. "What are you thinking?"

Oh, Lord. I hate it when people ask me that. They expect

to hear some really deep thought, when usually I haven't been thinking anything in particular. Or else it's not something I can talk about. But I know that Barbara and Jeri talk about anything, and maybe—maybe—I can learn to do that, too. I realize that I've been to their house three times now, and I haven't said anything about why I'm there. They talk and talk about their lives, and I just soak it up and don't say anything about mine. As I wolf down my nut-filled brownie, I think about how it began.

"Well," I stammer, then reach for another brownie. I take a bite and start again. "I guess I want to tell you about this meeting I went to."

And so I start to talk. I've been to only one meeting of the Gay and Lesbian Youth Alliance so far—I don't want my parents to get suspicious—and my first feelings are still clear and strong. Excitement, yes—exhilaration at taking my life into my own hands—but also a clutch of dread when I walked through the door. I felt cold water close over my head, and I realized that even if I didn't split myself open on some hidden rock, I still had a long, long swim ahead of me. Less melodramatic than my uncle Howard, but in its own way just as hard.

I sank down into the first chair I found and watched as the small room filled up. There were about fifteen people seated in a ragged circle when a short, dark girl cleared her throat.

"Okay, okay," she said. "Let's get started. Hello, everyone, and a special welcome to anyone who is here for the first time. Okay, we always start by saying our names and something about ourselves, so I'll go first. I'm Katherine, and I'm the co-leader of the Gay and Lesbian Youth Alliance. And in preparation for our topic tonight, which is

41

'coming out,' I came out to my parents yesterday." There was a rustling around the room, some clapping, and a loud cheer. Katherine smiled and did a mock bow. "More about that later. Okay, next?"

One by one around the circle, people gave their names while I stared in fascination. Here were all these people, mostly looking like the kids in my high school—and they all were gay? As each person spoke, I imagined them in a group of my classmates. Was there anything about them that would stand out? Mostly, the answer was no. Although there were a few exceptions, most notably a tall, thin boy who said his name was Lawrence. He spoke in an improbable falsetto, had two earrings in one ear, and I swear he had on makeup. He made me really uncomfortable.

When it came my turn to introduce myself, I wasn't going to say anything more than my name. But after a moment I heard myself adding, "And I think I'm a lesbian." What a dumb thing to say! I could've bitten my tongue off. But people nodded and grinned at me, and Lawrence stood up and clapped, and suddenly I didn't feel so dumb. The word "lesbian" hung in the open air, not sounding at all like it had when I muffled it into my pillow. Saying it in public made it less frightening. It began to sound like something I could accept.

After we had all said our names, the attention turned to Katherine. "So, what did your parents say?"

She was quiet for a minute before answering. "Well, my mother just cried."

Cried? If I told my mother I was a lesbian, she wouldn't cry. She'd crack open my head herself and set me out under a tree next to Uncle Howard. And tell me it was for my own good. Just thinking about it, I got a roaring in my ears: my lifeblood pounding through like a diesel locomotive. Pounding out *I'm alive. I'm alive.* Alive like I'd never been before, alive to who I really am. Exhilarated and scared.

Katherine went on talking. Others joined in, and soon the room was thick with stories: people who had been found out, some who chose to keep their lives secret. Whenever things got too tense, Lawrence would jump in with a joke.

"Hey, what do gay athletes drink?" he would ask, totally out of the blue. "Gaytorade."

Or, "Where do blue-collar homosexuals work? In a fagtory!"

Everyone would laugh, except for me. I didn't like the jokes. They reminded me too much of the jokes and nasty comments I heard at school. But in the weeks after that meeting, I thought about Lawrence a lot and I began to understand him better. I realize that everything about him that made me uncomfortable—his voice, his earrings, his jokes—are his own way of saying yes to his life. Maybe when I get braver, I will like him for it.

Barbara and Jeri have been sitting in uncharacteristic silence, but when I get to this part of my story, Barbara interrupts. Raising her brownie as if proposing a toast, she says, "Sounds to me like you're plenty brave already."

"Yes," Jeri chimes in. "Going to that meeting took courage. So did telling us."

At this unexpected praise I feel myself blush. Blushing again! But this time I don't mind. I tell them, "Well, at least I'm swimming now."

Barbara raises a quizzical eyebrow at Jeri, who just

shrugs. I grin recklessly and it feels good. Someday I'll explain about Uncle Howard and the threat of disaster that stifled me for so long. But right now, all that matters is that I am swimming. I'm swimming and I'm learning to love water. I'm saying yes to my life and it feels—great.

Sara

Michael Thomas Ford

for Tove

"Islands are foolish," I say to her. "They just sit in the sea all of their lives getting in the way of ships and being teased by the waves."

Sara laughs. She does this a lot, which is one of the reasons I like her.

"The veranda shouldn't be blue," she points out. "It should be yellow."

"I know," I tell her. "But it's all I could find."

Sara climbs onto the veranda railing and swings her legs through the flowers that grow along the side of the porch. "I just think an island would be nice sometimes, so we would have somewhere to take the boat. What's the fun of having a boat if all you can do is float around in it?"

"I'll think about it," I say.

The bedroom door opens. It's my mother.

"Thomas, come down to dinner now. I've called you four times already."

"I'll be right down," I mumble.

"Now," my mother says again.

I follow her downstairs.

"Hi, sport," my father says as I sit down at the table. "How was school?"

He says this every night.

"Same as usual," I answer. "Stupid." I don't know why he always asks. I guess he thinks that one night the answer will be different.

My father takes some peas. "It can't be that bad." He smiles.

"It's worse," I say.

My father won't give up. "Mrs. Wilkins says you wrote a wonderful report for her."

I forgot about conferences. They were this afternoon. I pretend one of the peas is Mrs. Wilkins and cover it with an avalanche of potatoes and gravy.

My mother joins in, trying to sound cheerful. "That's great, Thomas. I'm really proud of you. What was the report about?"

"Robin Hood," I lie. It was really about sheep, but that doesn't sound very interesting. Besides, I really did want to do Robin Hood. Mrs. Wilkins told me he wasn't real, though, and that sheep would be easier. When I told her I was going to tell Robin Hood that she said he wasn't real, and that she better watch out the next time she was in a dark forest, she told me I read too many of the wrong kinds of books.

"She also said," my father continued "that you still aren't getting along with the other kids very well."

I take the Mrs. Wilkins pea and feed it to Max, who is sitting under the table. Mrs. Wilkins screamed horribly as the wolf messily devoured her, I think.

"She says you won't play kickball during recess or team up with anyone for science projects." My father is still going on from across the table. "And that all you do is sit under a tree and read."

I make a tree out of some broccoli and plant it in the potatoes. I decide that Mrs. Wilkins is buried under it, and I'm not sad.

"Why don't you try harder?" I hear my father finish.

I push some potatoes onto my fork and the broccoli falls over. Timber, I think.

"Do we have any green paper?" I ask.

"Thomas," my mother says, exasperated, "your father is trying to understand you. The least you can do is listen."

"I am listening," I say. "Don't we have some of that wrapping paper left over from last Christmas?"

"Thomas, this is important," my father says. "You don't seem to be getting along well at school. Your grades are fine—excellent as a matter of fact—but you come home every day and lock yourself in your room. You never do anything with the other kids."

I put the entire fourth grade onto my fork and swallow them. "I'm fine," I say. "Really." I smile for extra effect.

My mother looks at me. "Well, why don't you ever have anyone come over, or go to anyone else's house?"

"I don't want to," I tell her. "I don't like any of them."

She sighs. "You must like some of them."

"Why?" I ask her, interested.

"Because it's normal to have friends," my father says

tiredly. "People to call on the phone, go to movies with, that kind of thing. You can't always be alone."

"I like to be alone," I say, for about the millionth time. "And anyway, I'm never all alone. Usually, Max is with me." Max pokes his nose onto the table to prove this. I feed him a piece of steak.

"Hey, that's good food," my mother shrieks. "Don't waste it on the dog."

"He's not just a dog," I say angrily. "And I like him better than most people around here." I think to myself, *He doesn't ask stupid questions.*

I put the broccoli tree in my mouth like a cigarette. I'm Bette Davis. "Besides," I drawl like Bette, "the children at school are awful. Simply awful." I love Bette Davis. I know fourth graders are supposed to like movies where about a billion people get blown up and the hero drives around in a big truck, but I don't. I rent Bette Davis movies from the video store all the time. They think I'm weird, too. Of course, no one else will watch them with me. My mother says she's the wickedest woman she's ever seen, and my father says she gives him a pain and asks why I don't like Arnold Schwarzenegger, like everyone else.

But Sara and I love her movies. Our favorite is the one where Bette looks around this room and then says, "What a dump." Sometimes we sit around saying "What a dump" and laugh so hard we can't breathe.

"Put the broccoli down," my mother orders.

I ask to be excused and carry my plate into the kitchen. Max comes with me, and I feed him everything but the broccoli. We hate broccoli. I name it Mr. Schrader and behead it with my steak knife; it's a guillotine. Mr. Schrader is our principal. At least once a week Mrs.

Wilkins sends me down to see him, and he tells me I have socialization problems.

At the top of the stairs, I sit and listen to my parents talk about me. This is nothing new; they usually do it after dinner. More often than not, they end up saying they just don't understand me. I could have told them that, but they never bother to ask me.

Once my mother said she thought I should go see a counselor. This was after I told her that there were ghosts in the second-floor clothes cupboard. Now I don't tell her anything. Her or my father. They don't really understand much of anything that's important, although my father can take apart the tractor and put it back together. Sara says that's worth something.

I don't tell them about Sara. I started to once, but my mother got the same look she got when I talked about the ghosts, so I asked for a peanut butter sandwich instead.

When I get back to my room, Sara is busy picking roses off the bush by the window.

"There you are," she says. "Did you get an island?"

"I forgot," I answer and fall onto the bed. Max jumps up and lies down next to me. I rub his back hard, and hair flies all over.

"Look," I say to Sara, "a blizzard."

She laughs. She thinks this is hysterical. She laughs so hard she falls over the rose bush. I notice that one of her feet is torn. There's some black paper on my desk. I get a scissors and cut out a new foot. It's a little different from the old one, and Sara says thanks after I tape it on. She likes to be different.

The door opens again. It's my mother.

"Thomas, here's the green paper you wanted," she says and sits on the edge of the bed. She looks at Max and starts to say something, but then she stops.

She looks around my room. "This is really creative," she tells me. "You've made a whole world in here." She points to the house near the closet. "Why is the house blue?" she asks. "And why is there such a pointy roof on that tower?"

"They like it that way," I tell her. "Besides, we had lots of blue paper left over from art class. Miss Roberts said I could have it."

"That was nice of her." She points toward the window. "What's that over there?"

"The sea," I tell her. "And maybe an island," I add, looking at Sara, who is lying on the bedside table.

My mother picks up Sara. "What a funny shoe." She laughs.

I take Sara and put her near the boathouse.

My mother sighs. "If only you would put this much effort into making friends," she says. "We only want you to be happy, Thomas."

I don't say anything, and she goes out. She shuts the door behind her.

"I think the dinghy has a leak," Sara is saying when I turn around. She is standing on the beach and throwing stones into the water.

I pick up the green paper my mother has brought and cut furiously. Soon I have a rough round shape. I take my dark green marker and scribble a little, then I put the paper on the wall with tape.

"Look," Sara says excitedly, "an island. And it has trees on it. Let's go explore."

I get in the dinghy, and we push off. The sea is calm, and we row quickly. The island gets bigger and bigger. Finally, we slide onto the beach, and I pull the boat away from the waves.

Sara gets out and looks around. "Beautiful," she cries, and runs through the sand.

I chase her. She shrieks and hides behind a tree. I find her and we collapse, tired and happy, on the ground.

"I like it here," I say, and Sara smiles.

"So do I," she says.

We explore all over the island. We pick up shells and flowers and three kinds of bird eggs, one of them pale green. We find a dead crab, but Sara says it's too sad and we let the sea have it.

Then it begins to rain. It falls on the sea and sends spiderwebs across the water. It hits the rocks and makes them look like marble.

Sara points to a spot in the trees. "A cave," she says.

We run to the cave. Inside it is dry, and there are soft piles of leaves to sit on. We sit and watch the rain come down. The leaves crunch when we move. Pretty soon it starts to thunder.

Sara goes to the mouth of the cave and yells into the wind. "Isn't it wonderful," she screams. "So big and terrible and beautiful."

The rain comes down harder, and lightning crackles across the sky. In our cave, Sara and I dance. We take flowers we have picked and throw them into the air. The wind scurries them around and around. We dance in a circle, holding hands and swinging each other around until we are dizzy. Sometimes we stop to watch the rain. Once when we look out we see the dinghy floating far out on the sea. We look at each other and laugh.

We dance until we are tired, then lie down on the piles of leaves and go to sleep.

Sometime during the night I wake up. My mother is

shutting my window. She asks me if I am frightened by the storm. I look over at Sara and she is sleeping quietly.

"No," I say, and go back to sleep.

Fooling Around
Claire McNab

"Brett—how could you!"

"Mum, we were only fooling around."

"Fooling around? Fooling around!"

"Give me a break—"

He could have smiled at the emphatic way she was slamming cupboard doors as she put the groceries away, if he hadn't felt so sick with apprehension. She swung around to face him. "Do you know how it looks? Do you care? It's bad enough for you to do such a thing, but to have Doug Blanchford find you with his son..."

Brett shrugged, wanting to downplay the whole thing. "Mum, it was nothing."

She was flushed with anger. "Look, I can understand a joke, something to make people laugh. I've got a sense of humor like anyone else. But you two were sneaking around in the dark"—her mouth twisted—"kissing."

"It doesn't mean anything. I told you, we were just fooling around." Brett wanted to sound unconcerned, but he could hear the tension in his voice.

His mother opened the fridge so hard the door banged against the kitchen bench. "It's not as if you haven't got a girlfriend. What do you think Emma's going to think about this?"

"Leave her out of it."

Last night already seemed as though it had happened weeks ago. Loud music had been pulsing through the windows open to the summer air. Brett remembered standing in the darkness looking into the lighted room where his friends were dancing, drinking, laughing. He and Steve hadn't been talking, just standing quietly together. He'd been so aware of Steve's breathing, of the heat that rose from his skin. Brett had tingled, tightened, known he was on the edge of something. It wasn't the drink. He'd had a couple of beers, that was all. It was Steve and the darkness and the promise of the warm night.

He was brought back to the present by the sound of the front door shutting. Brett's father was the manager of an electronics store and had to work on Saturdays. His mother confronted him as he came into the kitchen. "Where in the hell have you been, Martin? Didn't you get my message it was urgent?"

In contrast to his mother's brittle vitality, Brett's father was moderate, calm, subdued. "What's up?" he said.

She was direct. "Helen Blanchford called this morning. Doug was still too angry to talk. At the party last night he caught Brett and Steve kissing...Each other."

His father raised his eyebrows, but didn't comment. Her mouth tightened. "Aren't you going to say anything?"

"Well, they'd probably had a bit to drink—"

She cut him off. "For God's sake, Martin! If this gets out..." She glared furiously at Brett. "You say you were

fooling around, but you can't afford to let people think"—
She gestured with stiff fingers—"that you're..."

"Gay?" Brett said, as though he didn't care. The word
whispered in his ears, compelling and dangerous.

"That's the kindest thing they'll say!" She turned back to
his father. "How are we going to face Doug and Helen next
Saturday?"

"It'll have blown over by then."

His lack of concern infuriated her. "Trust you to take
that attitude! I might have known you wouldn't support
me." Brett stared at his mother. Now she seemed more
angry with his father than with him.

"What exactly do you want me to do?" His father said
patiently. "See Doug? Tell him the whole thing's blown out
of proportion? I'll be doing that anyway."

She leaned toward him. "You of all people should know
where this could lead."

Brett saw his father's face grow cold. "Netta..." he said.

"Talk to him." She pointed a shaking finger. "You talk to
him." The air vibrated as she slammed the door behind her.

His father leaned against the bench. "Tell me what
happened."

Brett rubbed his forehead. The dull throb of a headache
was beginning. "We were just being stupid."

"Where did Doug Blanchford find you and Steve?"
His father seemed interested, rather than accusatory.

"Outside, in the garden. It was hot..."

"You'd been drinking?"

"Yeah, of course." Brett was tempted to say he was
drunk and didn't remember anything, but his father's mild
questions deserved the truth. "Not much. A couple of
beers."

"And Steve?"

"I don't know—the same, I guess."

"And you sort of accidentally kissed? Is that all?" His tone was dry.

Brett nodded slowly, wondering why his father wasn't pissed off with him. "That's all." He added hastily, "It'll never happen again."

Never, he thought, already feeling a sense of loss.

"Do you want it to?"

Brett felt a vibration of longing for something that he couldn't even allow himself to imagine. "Of course not."

His father smiled wryly. "And I suppose Doug Blanchford was pretty upset?"

"Yeah. Pretty upset." Brett could still hear the flat slap as Steve's father backhanded his son and the loathing in his voice as he told Brett to get off his property.

"Not surprising, since Doug's a real man's man," his father said sarcastically. He gave Brett a rough half-hug. "It won't be a big deal, as long as you make a joke of it."

"A joke?"

"It'll get around—this sort of stuff always does. Don't say it isn't true. Just make out it's a big laugh, okay? Don't ever let anyone think you're worried about it."

"Jeez, Dad..."

"Look, Brett, almost everybody experiments a bit when they're young."

Brett thought of the personal development lessons at school. "Just a stage I'm going through?" he said sardonically, surprising himself with his nonchalance.

His father grinned. "Something like that."

"Mum's pretty mad."

"She'll cool down."

Brett felt closer to his father than he had for years. "What do I say to Emma? Someone'll tell her, and we're supposed to go out tonight."

"The same story." His father suddenly looked grim. "Always tell the same story."

The phone rang out in the hall. The closed door didn't muffle the angry satisfaction in his mother's voice as she called out, "Brett, it's for you. It's Emma."

When Brett hesitated, his father said, "Get it over with. And don't wait for her to bring it up. Say something straight away."

Brett felt as though he was watching himself act on a stage. He opened the door, walked over to the phone and picked up the receiver, then looked pointedly at his mother until she disappeared into the kitchen. His father patted his shoulder as he passed him. Brett licked his lips and said cheerfully into the receiver, 'Hi. I was just about to call you." It wasn't so hard once he'd started. He even made Emma laugh with some mocking remarks about Steve's father, implying that the two of them had known he was there and had deliberately hammed it up to outrage him. When he put down the phone, he allowed himself to feel a cautious hope that he could get out of the situation without too much damage.

He went to pick up the phone again, suddenly wanting to hear Steve's voice. He needed to know what was happening with Steve's family, what he felt, and what he was saying to people. He paused with his hand on the receiver. How could he talk with Steve, knowing that they would both have to play dumb, pretend to each other it was nothing.

And maybe it was nothing to Steve. Maybe that's all it really was: Steve had had too much to drink last night.

Brett took his hand off the phone. Kissing Steve had been different from kissing Emma—so much more important, more exciting, disturbing.

Raised voices broke into his thoughts. His parents were having a full-scale fight in the kitchen. His mother's voice penetrated like an industrial drill. "Jesus Christ! I might have known you'd side with him."

"Don't take it out on Brett," said his father savagely. "He has no idea why you're carrying on like this."

"No idea? He can't think it's normal to kiss another boy."

"You know what I mean, Netta."

"This time, Martin, this time maybe he'll get away with it. But what about next time? And don't shake your head at me! We both know there'll be a next time."

Brett wanted to get away from their furious voices, but he was suspended, listening. Next time? He walked quietly down the hall and stopped outside the kitchen door.

His father said softly, regretfully, "It isn't fair, is it? It must seem to you that it's happening all over again."

"It's never stopped, Martin. We both know that."

Brett leaned his forehead against the door frame. What were they talking about? Not him. There was a long silence, then his father said, "I've done the best I can."

"It isn't good enough." Her voice was hard. "It's never been good enough."

"I've got to get back to the store. We can talk later." His father sounded weary.

His mother didn't reply. Brett walked quickly back toward the front of the house, the words he'd overhead spinning in his head. He waited until his father had driven off, then went back to the kitchen. "Mum?"

She seemed exhausted, all her rage used up. "What?"

"I heard what you and Dad said to each other."

She smiled grimly. "Did you?"

"It wasn't about me."

"Only indirectly." She gave a short, bitter laugh.

He frowned at her. "What do you mean?"

"You father'll have to explain. I'm not going to."

The afternoon dragged. Brett gave up on surfing the Net and switched off his computer. He couldn't concentrate on anything. He kept waiting for the phone to ring, for someone to call him a fag, a queer, a poof—or worse. Or Steve might ring. Brett wanted to talk with him, but he was both relieved and disappointed when all the calls had to do with the charity bridge evening his mother was arranging for the next weekend.

His father came home late in the afternoon, low-key as usual. "Want a beer?" he said to Brett. "Let's have it in the study." This was his grand name for a little room packed with electronic gear, an untidy desk and an ancient wooden swivel chair.

He came back from the kitchen, tossed a cold can to Brett, then settled into the old chair, which creaked under his weight. Brett propped himself against the desk and opened his beer. "Mum said we should talk."

"I've spoken to Steve's father." He ran a hand through his short, graying hair. "Fortunately, Doug's cooled down and he's more than ready to forget the whole thing."

"I heard you and Mum arguing."

"And?"

"She said you'd explain."

Tracing patterns in the condensation on his beer can, his father said somberly, "We all have to make decisions in life." He looked up with a slight smile. "I think you're working up to making one now."

"Mum's off her head, so why aren't you angry with me?" Brett hadn't known he was going to ask the question.

"Look, you know I love both you and your mother, don't you?"

"Yeah, I suppose." Brett moved uncomfortably under his father's steady gaze. "So?"

"Netta's angry about what's happening. She's been through it before."

Brett felt cold. His father was going to tell him something he didn't want to know. He took a long swallow of beer to postpone asking the obvious question. At last he said, "How?"

"Your mother and I had known each other for years. We were dating, about to get engaged." He shook his head. "This is bloody hard…"

"What? Just tell me."

"I got caught with another guy, my best friend from school"—His father let out his breath in a long sigh—"and we were doing a lot more than just kissing."

"Shit!"

"Rather more than that hit the fan."

Brett ignored his father's painful attempt at humor. "But you married Mum. Did she know?"

"Everyone did. And Netta stood by me. I knew I had to decide between her and…" He shrugged. "So to everyone's relief, Netta and I got married."

Brett stared at him. "Shit," he said again. "Is it someone I know?"

"No. He dropped out of my life." His voice was harsh. "I promised your mother, and I kept my side of the bargain as best I could."

Brett thought of Steve. He said, "Did you want to see him?"

"Yes."

Brett met his father's eyes directly. The silence stretched between them until Brett said, "Was it the right decision?"

"I have you and your mother. I love you both."

"That's not an answer."

His father spread his hands. "That's all I can say."

Another long silence. Brett said, "Dad, about Steve and last night…"

"Yes?"

"I don't think I was fooling around."

"I know," his father said.

The Widest Heart
Malka Drucker

Maybe it's not right to talk about other people, but what happened between Marcia and me was so long ago. Besides, I keep thinking of things I never told her. So, forgive me, Marcia, wherever you are, and I hope you read this.

We met in Spanish class the first day of school at Granada Hills High on a typical, oven-hot, smoggy San Fernando Valley morning in September. The school had just opened, and everything was in wild confusion— nobody, not even the teachers, knew where their classrooms were, or even where to find a piece of chalk. I was kind of glad for the heat and chaos, since it would probably slow down the teaching process.

"*¡Buenos días, clase!*" Mr. Applegate screamed. No one seemed to understand him; our boisterous English grew only louder.

I pulled at my straight skirt, which was riding up my thighs. As I feared, I'd gained some weight over the summer. But it didn't matter, because I didn't see any of my junior high pals in the room. They were too gutless to take a foreign language.

I searched for an interesting face. A fat girl with a bulbous nose and full lips caught my eye and smiled. I flattened my lips into what could be mistaken for a smile and looked away. She was not someone I wanted to be friends with.

Applegate started to pass out copies of *El Fríjolito Saltón,* a skinny red book with a leering jumping bean on the cover. The class filled with sniggers until a tall blond girl sailed into the room as though she owned it. She spoke privately to the teacher, and then he asked the class, "Who here is Marcia Moore?" The fat girl who had smiled at me earlier half raised her hand.

"Marcia Moore," he said, "meet Marsha Moore. She has your registration packet." So the blond girl and the fat girl had the same name. The class looked from Marcia to Marsha and a few people giggled. Even though I didn't know her, I felt sorry for Marcia Moore. Marsha could have been a model, while Marcia could have been a poster girl for Overeaters Anonymous.

But Marcia was a good sport about the mix-up. "Oh, so that's why I got that weird invitation to a party from people I don't know. I thought they'd spelled my name wrong, but it was for you."

The blond nodded, unsmiling. "Right," she said. "Now, do you have my reg packet?" Marcia fumbled through her backpack, spilling pens and paper. Finally, she pulled out an envelope marked "Marsha Moore." The blond grabbed it from her quickly, as though she wanted to get away from someone so ugly who shared her name. Marcia smiled at her as she walked out.

I found Marcia in my next class, English—in fact, we were in all the same classes. At the end of the day, I grabbed my backpack and ran for the bus. With luck, I could get a seat all to myself. But Marcia got on the bus, spotted me, and asked if the seat was saved. I shook my head and squeezed over to the window to make room for her. *Oh, well*, I thought. *At least it will be just the two of us. A third person will never fit.*

"Nice scarf," Marcia said, pointing to a soft blue silk scarf I'd tied into a cravat. It was my grandmother's, and she had just given it to me. I adored it.

"Thanks," I muttered, squeezing closer to the window. She continued to stare at my scarf. To end her fixation, I offered her a corner to touch. She gently massaged the creamy fabric between her fingers.

"I've never felt anything so wonderful," she said. Somehow I knew she wasn't exaggerating, yet I wondered how that was possible.

"Boy, that was really embarrassing in Spanish today," Marcia laughed. "At least the other Marsha Moore was only beautiful. If she'd been nice, too, I'd really hate her." Despite my resolve not to be friends with this girl, I laughed. She had a nice, twisty sense of humor.

We were an unlikely pair: me, cynical and proud of my perpetual gloom; Marcia, seemingly sunny and easy-going. But we immediately saw behind each other's masks and discovered how alike we were. We both loved reading, we hated cheerleaders, and we thought a Latino should teach Spanish. "I don't want to speak Spanish with Applegate's Iowa accent," Marcia wailed. We both wanted to leave La-La Land, as we called Los Angeles, and go east to college, where we believed the focus was more on the mind, not the body.

We also shared an unspoken desire. I didn't want to know her troubles, and she didn't want me to know them. Why I ran from her pain, I don't know. Maybe I thought I couldn't do anything about it. The truth is, I didn't know right away that Marcia's life was hell. Only too late did I see how hard she worked to keep that knowledge hidden from everyone, including herself.

I went to her house for the first time on Halloween. She had to take her little brothers out trick-or-treating. Her house was bigger and fancier than mine, but I didn't like it—it felt cold. I stood in the hall waiting for Marcia. A man with steel-rimmed glasses, brushed-back white hair, and a widow's peak like Dracula's let me in. He nodded when I asked if Marcia was there, and then abruptly left me in the hall while he went into the living room and turned on the television.

"Meet my dad," Marcia said, coming to get me. The old man—this social retard—was her father!

"A pleasure," Mr. Moore slowly articulated in a thick accent, barely glancing at me before returning to the football game in front of him. I knew Marcia's family originally came from Greece. Marcia was always doing youth group stuff at the Greek Orthodox Church. Marcia smiled and whispered, "He's shy." In my family, we didn't call it shy, we called it rude.

Her little brothers were wearing incredible alligator costumes, which was not surprising to anyone who lived in Granada Hills. Mr. Moore owned a fast-food restaurant called the Gator Shack, which had a pit of live alligators in the middle of the parking lot to attract customers. I could never understand why anyone wanting a burger would go out of his or her way to eat one in the presence of an alligator. In fact, I always lost my appetite when I looked in the pit and saw those poor creatures piled on top of each other with no room to move.

The two-legged alligators in the living room were restless and having a tail-fight. "Let's go, Teddy and Freddy," Marcia said. She put on a big black coat, the kind my grandmother wore. Catching my eye, she laughed. "It's a hand-me-down, but it's warm." She looked like she was wearing a tent. Even though I was a good twenty pounds too heavy, as my mother constantly reminded me, I never felt overweight around Marcia.

We were almost out the door when Mr. Moore's voice cut like a knife: "Marcia! Don't take your eyes off the boys, not for a minute! Am I clear?"

"Yes, Dad, I know," she answered, smiling. "Don't worry." We walked down the sidewalk and stopped in front of the first house of the night.

While Marcia's eyes never left the children, I asked her, "Did you wear an alligator suit when you were little?" I tried to imagine her as a plump reptile.

The smile, then, "No, I never went trick-or-treating."

When I was little, I couldn't wait for Halloween. Candy, costumes, and roaming outside at night. I still get excited with the memory of it. "You're kidding," I said.

"No," she said slowly. "See, Mom isn't my real mother. My mother died when I was four, and Dad married this mom a couple of years later. She had just come from Greece, and she didn't know about what kids do here."

Anger burned in me, as though I were the one who hadn't gone trick-or-treating. I knew better than to press her, but I couldn't help myself. "Marcia, didn't they watch TV or read the newspapers? They must have talked to other parents! And what about the kids that came to *your* house?" No smile from her, just a shrug and eyes that begged me to shut up.

After that, I avoided talking about her parents—I thought my silence made me a good friend.

We spent much more time at her house than mine because she always had to baby-sit her brothers. This was okay with me, because whenever I brought Marcia home, my mother scarcely spoke to or even looked at her. To my mother, Marcia represented the enemy—fat. This wasn't only an aesthetic objection; it was character. Marcia's weight showed she was out of control, without discipline. My mother was a size six, and she intended to die that size. My being friends with Marcia represented her failure as a mother.

All my life, my mother told me to make something of myself so I could choose my friends. No one had to tell me that in my mother's eyes, Marcia—at five foot one and 150 pounds—was not a good choice. When my mother asked, "Who is that girl?" I told her we were working on an assignment together. My mother would never understand how Marcia was the best friend I'd ever had because she was the first person who liked me just the way I was.

Marcia began working after school at the Gator Shack. When she turned sixteen, her father bought her a car right away, but she was only allowed to use it to get to school and work. I missed riding the bus with her, so sometimes I'd hang out at the restaurant while she worked. I'd bring my homework and not bother her, because her father watched her every move. If he caught her talking to me, she'd get grounded during her precious free time.

But after a while I stopped going to the restaurant because I hated listening to the way people talked to her. There she'd be, her moon face glistening from the heat of the kitchen, her fine hair hanging like limp spaghetti, taking orders with a smile from kids who wouldn't look at her in school.

Suddenly she became their pal. "Hi, Marcia! Jeez, I forgot to bring my money. Give me a Coke and fries and I'll pay you next time?" Or, "Marcia, how about going heavy—heh heh—on the fries?" When she tried to explain that she couldn't do that, the kid would sneer and say, "What happened? You eat them all?" or "You're cheap, just like your old man." She never lost her smile, but sometimes I'd see her eyes well with tears.

Marcia was working twenty, sometimes thirty hours a week. I almost asked my mother if that was legal, or if it was child abuse, but I was afraid she'd get into it and Marcia would freak. Anyway, Marcia wasn't complaining.

One Sunday before Christmas I helped her make goodies for the holiday. Marcia loved Christmas like a little kid. Maybe it triggered memories of a happier time. Whatever the reason, we had a great time cooking and singing and laughing that day. Following a recipe of Marcia's grandmother from the old country, we kneaded dough into little balls that we dropped into spitting hot oil. After they fried, we rolled them in honey and nuts. It was the stickiest, sweetest food imaginable, and Marcia and I ate tons of it.

Mrs. Moore checked on us from time to time to be sure we were keeping up our production and to tell us we were not to eat any of the sweets—they were for the family and the church. Besides, she'd say, looking us over, we didn't need it.

Between work and school, I don't know how Marcia found time to get ready for Christmas, but she did. Besides the cooking, she went to the mall and spent all of her money on gifts. I still have the blue woolen hat she gave me, which matched my grandmother's scarf perfectly. How did she remember the scarf's exact color? If I only knew then how special she was.

I gave her a volume of Edna St. Vincent Millay's poems. I adored Millay's passionate verse and wanted to share it with Marcia. Within a week she was quoting parts of the poems to me. When I'd complain that life sucked, she'd throw her head back and recite:

> The world stands out on either side
> No wider than the heart is wide;
> Above the world is stretched the sky—
> No higher than the soul is high.

I'd shrug, scowling, with my narrow heart and flat soul, but she'd just look at me, patient, waiting. And pretty soon I'd lighten up and we'd both laugh.

After Christmas, if Marcia wasn't working, she was sleeping. She even nodded off in class. She was fatter than ever, with dark circles under her eyes, and her skin seemed to absorb the grease from the restaurant. I thought of the alligators in the parking lot—who was worse off? Still, I never said anything, not even "Are you okay?"

It wasn't much fun for us to be together anymore. We used to talk for hours, now we didn't have much to say. Marcia still listened to my latest woe or my newest strategy for snaring some guy, but she seemed far away. She no longer had the luxury of having "problems." If a teacher gave her a D when she thought she deserved better, she shrugged. If someone cut in front of her in the food line, she ignored it. If she didn't have a dress to wear for a party, she laughed it off and stayed home.

One day at lunch she told me she was switching from an academic to a business curriculum. "I just can't keep up," she said, her eye so sad I had to look away. Of the two of us, Marcia was the better student. Furthermore, although she was too smart to say it, she loved studying. We had planned to go to the same college and room together. We dreamed of opening a bookstore in New England; Marcia had wanted to call it Sisters.

It wasn't only *her* life that was being ruined. Marcia's father had destroyed my dreams, too. "Why don't you tell your father you can't work so many hours?" I asked, my voice rising. "Why don't you tell your father to go to hell?" Marcia's face went white. "Sorry," I said. But I couldn't keep quiet anymore. "Marcia, you're just a kid—it's not fair!"

Marcia sighed. "It doesn't matter. *My* dad won't pay for college anyway—he says it's more important for boys. He's old-fashioned. He wants me to graduate from high school and work until I get married."

If I had to work at the Gator Shack, I'd get married the next day to anyone who was willing. And that especially included Albert Levy, whose muscled body stopped my heart when he swam at varsity meets, but who was more boring than a rock. My mother, valuing his lineage of lawyers, totally approved of him.

Between my being with Albert and Marcia's work schedule, we rarely saw each other anymore. She didn't even come to school regularly. When the English teacher passed out copies of *Pride and Prejudice* to read during spring break, I took an extra copy to take to Marcia.

If felt strange going to her house as a guest when I used to spend nearly every day there. I rang the doorbell, half hoping she wasn't home. My heart pounded as I heard the knob turn. She opened the door and let out a scream when she saw me. "Come in," she said, laughing and dragging me into the living room. This was a first—Marcia and me in the living room.

"Mom and Dad are in Las Vegas for the weekend," she said. Her eyes smiled.

"Great," I said, feeling shy. Marcia looked so different. She'd lost weight, she had a good haircut, and she was wearing eye makeup again. But the biggest change was in her clothes. Instead of the old-lady clothes Mrs. Moore made her wear, she was wearing narrow-legged jeans and a white silk tunic. I didn't realize until that moment how much I'd missed her. I wanted to hug her. But I only said, "You look terrific."

"Thanks." We stood there smiling at each other and nodding, each waiting for the other to speak.

At that moment, a spectacular-looking young woman walked into the room, green-eyed and raven-haired. She thrust out her hand to me and said, "Hi. I'm Dannie Walker." Her voice was musical.

We all sat down, no one saying much. I felt out of place, as though I didn't belong. I felt jumpy, maybe jealous, and I wanted to leave.

Marcia said, "Dannie goes to UCLA and works for Mom and Dad as nanny for the boys—I'm too busy working to watch them." She smiled at Dannie in a way I'd never seen before. "She's earning money for opera lessons."

Dannie was looking at Marcia, too, the way I dreamed someone would look at me someday. But I pictured a guy, not a soprano.

No. No way. I'm imagining things. They're just good friends.

Dannie went into the kitchen and came back with three cups of peppermint tea. After handing me a cup, she sat down next to Marcia—and I mean next to, even though it was a big room. She handed a cup to Marcia and let her hand linger on Marcia's for a second.

I stared at their hands and then at my own, which had begun to tremble. The tea burned my lips as I tried to gulp it down. I had to get out of there.

God, we'd shared beds with one another! How could I not have known? How could she not have told me? But if she had, I wouldn't have liked it. I had too much of my mother in me—fat was one thing, gay was another. If we were friends, everybody would think I was like her.

Marcia asked me, "So, how's Señor Applegate? I'm going to try to study Spanish on my own this summer— Dannie's going to help me."

I nodded vigorously and stood up. My voice sounded like Minnie Mouse's. "Spanish is totally boring—you're not missing a thing." I looked at my watch and squealed, "I have to leave—this minute! I totally forgot that my mother needs the car. Hey, give me a call, okay?" I edged toward the door. "Oh, and nice to meet you, Dannie."

I was halfway down the steps when I remembered the purpose of the visit. "The book!" I shouted, bounding up the steps. "How can I be so dumb—I almost forgot to give it to you!" Marcia took the book from me with a question in her eyes. I looked away, without an answer. I ran to my car as fast as I could without falling. On the way home I thought about how she and I used to joke about the butch gym teacher who used to stroll through the showers.

I never called Marcia again. She called me once, but I was only polite to her. I didn't understand that love comes in lots of ways. And I was afraid.

Whenever I think about Marcia, I imagine her living with Dannie far from the alligators of Granada Hills, the two of them smiling at one another as they did on that day long ago.

I miss you, Marcia—you and your wide heart.

Somebody's Boyfriend
Laurel Winter

The day Maggie brought her new boyfriend home, I was splotching the walls of my room. Mom and Dad let us do pretty much anything with our own personal space, as long as it doesn't involve major structural changes. Last year, when Maggie was fifteen, she painted her entire room—including the windows—matte black. I helped her use a razor blade to take the paint off the glass a few months later, when she got tired of living in a black hole. Who says a guy can't learn from his sister's mistakes?

Anyway, I was wearing prehistoric shredded jeans and a shirt that was completely ripped up the back when she brought him into my room, "Jeff, this is my little brother, Alex."

I rolled my eyes at the "little brother" part, which Maggie had delivered with a giggle. "Hi," I said, shaking hands with the air in Jeff's direction, since my hands were covered with six or eight different colors of paint.

Most of Maggie's boyfriends regarded me as if I were about four years old and covered with frog slime—which isn't the case, because Maggie's only thirteen months older than I am, and about six inches shorter. It didn't bug me too much, though, because the guys Maggie dated always turned out to be conceited jerks.

Jeff actually took hold of my psychedelic hand. "You don't look much like a little brother," he said. His hand was warm. He looked at the half-finished walls and the model helicopters hanging from the ceiling. "Great room."

Then he quit looking at my room and looked right at me. "Thanks," I said. His eyes were a weird bluish green. Almost like one of the colors I was dabbing on my walls.

Then I said something that made my sister glare. "You're better than Maggie's usual boyfriends."

Jeff gave me a strange look, like a smile, but not quite. "I'm not usual," he said.

Maggie pushed him into the hall, pausing only to mutter, "That was brilliant." Then they were gone and the room was empty.

What does a person mean by "I'm not usual"? Something like, "I'm a psycho ax-murderer"? Or "I'm an alien from another planet"? I could tell it meant something, though; the half-smile had convinced me of that.

I painted for a few more minutes, but I was sticking the splotches too close together or too far apart or something. "Screw it," I said, dropping a chunk of sponge on the old sheet that covered my bed. I poured the little jars of paint back into their respective cans.

Then I clattered down the stairs to the kitchen, wondering if Maggie and Jeff were still there. My shirt flapped behind me. For a second, I thought about changing but decided that was dumb. I was going to paint more after I had a snack.

They were at the table having a snack. Jeff raised his

hand, palm toward me. "Look," he said. "You left a mark."

There were streaks of paint on his hand and fingers, yellow and orange and the bluish green. "Sorry," I said. My face flamed up. "I didn't mean to." *And you're the one who shook my hand,* I added silently.

"No problem," Jeff said. "After all, you could become a famous painter." He studied his hand, squinting one eye as if appraising a work of art. "Maybe I shouldn't wash it off."

Maggie laughed. "You guys are ridiculous."

I nabbed a couple of potato chips from the bowl in front of her. "Ridiculous and proud of it," I said, shoving the chips into my mouth. "Right, Jeff?" That was the first time I'd said his name. My face reflamed.

"Right," he said.

I've read that the Mona Lisa's smile is "enigmatic." Well, that was the sense I got from the expression on Jeff's face. Of course, *he* had eyebrows—and he was a guy—but the smile was the same. I shivered.

"You should put some more clothes on, little brother," Maggie said. "Your jeans are so holey they're practically sacred."

"It's the shirt I like," said Jeff.

"Lay off it," I said. My jaw tightened.

"Just a joke, son," Maggie drawled. She winked at Jeff. "He's so sensitive sometimes."

I raced up the stairs to my room. The skin on my back where the shirt gaped felt exposed and vulnerable. "Shit, shit, shit." I slammed the door.

I didn't' feel like painting anymore, but I opened the can of blue-green—kind of a sea green, really—and stirred it slowly. So what. Big deal. What should I care if my sister's boyfriend made fun of me?

Someone knocked on the door.

"Yeah," I said.

Jeff slipped into the room and shut the door behind him. "Alex," he said. "I'm sorry. I didn't mean to make you mad."

"No big deal," I said, still stirring. the paint swirled in the can like melted ice cream. I could see Jeff from the corner of my eye.

He just stood there and looked at me for a minute. No smile this time. "Well, I'm still sorry."

"Okay," I said. My skin started prickling up into goose bumps.

"Friends?"

This time I looked up. He was holding his hand out to me.

I had a basketball in my chest. I let go of the paint stick. It wobbled, tilted to one side. I took his hand, but the word "friends" stuck in my throat. I just nodded and gave his hand one shake.

When I let go, he once again displayed his palm to me. "You got me again."

"Sorry," I said.

"It's okay."

We stood there for a second. "Where's Maggie?" I asked.

He tilted his head. "Changing into different clothes," he said. "We're going for a bike ride."

"Oh."

As if our words had created her, Maggie ran through the hall and down the stairs, calling, "Jeff! I'm ready."

"I'd better go," he said.

"See you," I said.

"Yeah." He stopped on his way out. "I really do like your shirt." The door clicked shut behind him.

The basketball in my chest expanded. I looked at my hands, at the open can of paint. "Oh, shit," I said softly to myself.

I had a crush on my sister's boyfriend.

✪

Background: I don't like girls. I mean, there are some girls I like, and I don't necessarily dislike too many of them, but they don't turn me on. I mean, I have friends who are girls, but no girlfriends in the friendliest sense of the word. Maggie tried to set me up with her friends for a while, but after a few blind-date disasters, she gave up on me.

For a long time I thought I was just slow or something. Lately, I've known it's more than that. Not that I've told Maggie or my parents or anyone—I guess I first had to finish telling myself.

✪

After that, it seemed like Jeff was over constantly. He wasn't really, but I had this afterimage burnt into the backs of my eyes or the back of my mind or something, so it seemed like he was. I kept seeing him. Every time I looked around my bedroom, the bluish green spots reminded me of his eyes. Funny how the last part of the room had its fair share of sea green.

Yeah, real funny.

I also kept almost asking Maggie about him: how much did she like him, how far had they gone, did he ever ask about me. "Almost" was the key word there. Depending on her answers to the questions, I wasn't sure I wanted to know.

But Maggie and I were too close for things to stay on that level. One night after supper, when Mom and Dad were watching CNN in the living room and we were doing our homework in the kitchen, I put on my most casual tone and asked, "How's Jeff?"

"Okay," she said. "Fine, really. Oh, I don't know."

"What do you mean?" The basketball was back in my chest.

"Well, you remember the first time he was here and you said he was better than my usual boyfriends?"

I remembered so well that all I could do was nod.

Maggie went on: "Well, he is nicer, except he says we're just friends. I think he might like me..." She was playing with her pencil now, doodling in the margins of her Algebra II homework. "He hasn't really done anything about it, though. Not that I'm ready to jump into bed or anything, but I wouldn't mind getting an occasional kiss from him."

The basketball was practically choking me. "Oh," I said.

"Besides," she continued, "all he ever wants to do is come here."

I couldn't remember how to breathe.

Maggie erased her doodles, because her math teacher graded down for messy work. She cocked her head. "Hey, do you suppose you could talk to him sometime? See how much he likes me?"

"I don't think—" I started.

"Sure you can," she said. "The next time he comes over, I'll get Lisa to call me and pretend it's an emergency. You can grill Jeff."

"Maggie, that isn't a good idea."

"Sure it is," she said. "And you'll do it for your sister, won't you?" She jabbed at my ribs, my most ticklish spot. "*Vee haf vays* to make you talk to Jeff."

"Okay, okay," I said. How could it be the thing I most wanted to do and the thing I most dreaded?

Of course, her question wasn't my top priority, but I would ask it. Partly because she had asked me to—she was my one and only sister—and partly because it might be a roundabout way to ask *my* questions: How did Jeff feel about *me*?

★

Either Maggie and Lisa had synchronized their watches, or girls just have a sixth sense about things like this. We were sitting around the kitchen table having pretzels and pop when the phone rang. "I'll get it," Maggie yelled, practically knocking Jeff over. She gave me a meaningful glance over his shoulder. "Hello...Lisa! What's up? Oh, my God, really?"

The conversation seemed fake and lame to me. I hoped it was just because I knew it actually was fake and lame.

"Sure, if you really need to talk." Maggie cupped one hand over the receiver. "Uh, Jeff, Lisa is desperate right now. Why don't you talk to Alex for a while?"

"Okay." He turned his chair toward mine. Maggie grimaced at me.

"Uh, maybe we should go up to my room," I said. I nodded toward Maggie and the phone. "I doubt that we want to hear this."

Jeff laughed. "Good point." He gave a courtly bow, with one arm outstretched. "Lead on."

The stairway seemed a thousand steps long, but it only took us a few seconds to reach my room.

Jeff closed the door. "We wouldn't want to accidentally eavesdrop," he said.

It was the first time he'd been in the room since I'd finished the walls. My hands slicked up as he looked around; I was sure he would notice the overabundance of sea green on the last section. And know why it was there.

"So," I said, immediately feeling stupid. My tongue tripped all over itself. Actually, it was my brain being clumsy; the words never even made it into my mouth.

Jeff didn't seem to notice. "This is a great room," he said. "You're really artistic."

"Thanks," I said. "I notice you washed you hand, though."

He laughed again. "No, I didn't. It wore off naturally."

"Oh." Suddenly, I had become Mr. Monosyllable.

Jeff looked at me steadily. "So, what's with Maggie?"

"What do you mean?"

"I overheard her reminding Lisa to call at four sharp." He held out his wrist. "My watch says 4:03 now."

"Shit," I said, and sat on the bed. There was entirely too much sea green in the room. I was on the verge of drowning.

"So, what's with Maggie?" he repeated.

"She wanted..." My voice felt tight. "She wanted me to find out how much you like her."

Jeff let his eyelids drop for a second and took a deep breath. "Oh," he said. "So you volunteered?"

"Not really." There wasn't room in my chest for air. "I told her it was a bad idea."

He took another gulp of air. "Maybe it wasn't."

I had to stop looking at him. I closed my eyes. "I don't think I want to know."

"Maybe you do." His voice sounded closer. I opened

my eyes, and Jeff was right next to me. He sat down on the floor.

"Maggie's okay," he said carefully. "We're friends. She's a nice person—for a girl."

For something that felt like an hour, neither of us said anything.

"Oh," I said. I could barely hear myself. I started to shake.

Jeff held out his hand to me. I practically strangled his fingers. After a while, the shaking stopped. "Man, this is weird," I said.

He gave that look that was almost a smile. "Agreed," he said. "But we'll get used to it."

"I suppose." I looked at our hands, clasped together. With my free hand, I touched one of the blue-green splotches on the wall. "Did you know your eyes are almost exactly this color?"

"Did you know that I really did like that shirt you were wearing the first day we met?"

We both laughed. My laugh felt pretty wobbly. I didn't know what I was going to tell my parents. And what about school? I mean, I just couldn't ask a guy to the prom. "This is going to be weird."

At that point, Maggie apparently lost her patience and burst into the room. I was still holding hands with her— with *somebody's*—boyfriend. It was like the time Mom caught me behind the garage with a box of matches, except that time I was alone. And that time involved just a few scorched G.I. Joes and some burnt twigs.

I didn't have time to wish that Jeff would let go—or that he wouldn't. Maggie's face went from fake-casual to totally stunned. I couldn't tell if she was mad or upset or what. She didn't say anything. She just spun around and left.

This was going to take some getting used to for all of us. There were parts I wasn't looking forward to—talking to Maggie, for example. At the same time, though, I knew who I really was—I really knew, after all that guessing.

Jeff's grip tightened, as if he knew what I was thinking. He didn't let go of my hand.

And I didn't let go of his.

Her Sister's Wedding
Judith P. Stelboum

The organ music was peaceful. Veronica closed her eyes and pretended she was at a concert, shutting out the excitement in the church, the shuffling relatives, their nervous murmuring above the music. Actors, she thought, must feel this way while waiting for their cue before stepping out onstage.

So she was an actor, waiting here with the rest of the cast, rehearsing and planning their moves for the big march down the aisle. She watched the others, how easily they could talk to each other, start up small talk, chitchat. Damn it! Why was she always on the outside, looking in? Did she make herself an outsider? Could she once—just once—be a part of this world? On the "happiest day" of her sister's life, she was unable or unwilling to join in with the others, and she hated herself for being different.

Ever since her third year in high school, this tension—this difference—had intensified, separating her from her family. Marie would come home from school and talk about Frank, her feelings and passions and hopes for the future, but Veronica knew she couldn't talk about Leslie that way. So she started biting her lower lip, swallowing these feelings and her need to talk about them, to share them with her family. She guarded her behavior, carefully selected her words, whenever she was with them. She lost her ability to be spontaneous—this one part of her life had started to undermine her self-confidence and self-esteem.

And her family was always assuming things about her. They assumed that she wanted to go to the prom with Tommy. They assumed that all those nights at Leslie's house were spent studying. (*Well*, she thought, *we did study some!*) But all those nights were just part of the plan: she and Leslie would study hard, get good grades, go to the same college (far away from home), and live together as roommates. And no one would know the truth.

Now, visiting home, she saw that everything about her relationship with her family was an act. She played the little girl they always wanted her to be and kept the real Veronica hidden away from view. She was an impostor here, at her sister's wedding. She was in drag—wearing the itchy dress her sister had picked out. This facade was costing too much, sapping all of her energy. But what could she do?

Veronica walked over to her sister. "Marie, I have to tell you again how beautiful you look."

Marie put her arms around Veronica and hugged her warmly. "You're beautiful, too, Ronnie. Oh, I know that someday soon you'll be as happy as I am right now. My little sister!"

Veronica pulled back and looked at her sister. "I'm— I..." She bit her lip and nodded.

She was tired of dealing with all these assumptions! But this was not the time to challenge them.

Marie squeezed her hand and looked into Veronica's eyes. "Veronica, we all love you so much! Frank, too!"

"It's time, everyone! Get in order! Mr. Santini, you'll have to check—just before you start walking—check that Marie's gown is straight in back, so we can all see it. I'll try to come back to help, but just in case..."

"Sure. I'll check it. Don't worry."

"Remember, everyone, to listen to the music, and just follow the tempo. Don't walk too fast. Just relax and smile, and you'll all do fine. You all look lovely."

Veronica started to walk down the aisle, alone. Everyone was looking at her. She couldn't remember ever feeling so nervous and shaky.

She imagined that everyone could see through her act. She thought she heard:

"That's Marie's sister. She'll never get married."

"That's Marie's sister. She's a lesbian."

"That's Marie's sister. She's a pervert."

But Veronica willed herself into confidence; no one could see her secret. "Let the performance begin."

With a simpering perfect smile on her face, Veronica continued her walk toward the altar. The "Wedding March" began, and she turned her head to watch her father and Marie come toward her. Everyone oohed and aahed as the bride passed them.

Veronica tried to look interested as the priest spoke, but she was barely hearing the ceremony. In sociology class at college, she had dismissed this religion as primitive drivel. Leslie had been shocked by her vehement attack. Leslie still had fond memories of the nuns at their high school, but Veronica was angry at the subtle and unsubtle ways they'd tried to shape her mind. Sometimes Veronica would get angry with Leslie, for not being strong enough to resist this religion that said they were sinful.

But now, here at Marie's wedding, Veronica was forced to be a part of Marie's acceptance of the Church. Marie had always believed in it. She, Frank, and their children would be part of it. Preserve it. Perpetuate it.

And how did you escape? she thought. *I don't know. Did I?*

"I do."

The ceremony was going by so fast. The priest blessed them. They exchanged rings. Frank kissed Marie.

And soon they were walking back up the aisle.

Veronica was relieved that it was over—but now came the social part. The sequel to the church ceremony would be equally horrendous for her. The matinee performance was over; now, for the evening crowd. She was the second female lead in this piece, and she would really play it up.

She shook hands with someone from Frank's side of the family and then leaned forward to kiss her cousin Connie and her husband, Brian.

"Oh, you look so beautiful, Ronnie. Doesn't she, Brian? You look really grown-up."

"Thanks, Connie, you look good, too. I love your dress."

Veronica watched her sister and Frank laughing and talking easily with their guests. *Marie really does look beautiful today,* she thought. *Everyone's so happy to be here—sharing their happiness. There will never be a day like this for me. I don't want it. Or do I? I don't think I'd want a wedding—just some kind of recognition and acceptance. Can Leslie and I ever have this? No—all we have is fear. Secrecy. Guilt.*

She tried to imagine her wedding to Leslie. Who would wear the tux? No contest—Leslie would look beautiful as a bride. *No! I don't want a wedding like this. I don't want to imitate them. I just want to exist—to exist in their minds. To exist in a world of my own. Of our own. But that world doesn't exist. That's why there can never be a day like this for me. There are no ceremonies like this to make me feel happy, good about myself. No one would stand around, praising my love. They'd throw bottles, not rice. There'd be insults instead of toasts.*

Thinking about this, Veronica was getting angry and felt like she had to run out of this place. Sweat trickled down her armpits and beaded up on her forehead.

She felt trapped. She had to get out, move from this place. But her feet felt nailed to the floor, and her smile was frozen to her face. She was wearing a mask, a dress, a smile. She was a fake. She had been lying to herself—this was her world. She didn't belong anywhere else. If they couldn't accept her, accept her with Leslie, what would be left for her?

Even though Veronica knew she had her whole life ahead of her, the thought that she might have to live without the love, support, and approval of her family filled her with a fear so strong that it seemed, for the first time in her life, to threaten her very existence.

She had never really thought about living without her family before. She had read and heard such stories at college. She and Leslie had gone to some women's meetings and dances, and some of the women there had come out to their families. One girl had to leave school because her father refused to pay her tuition after he found out. Leslie had warned Veronica to keep quiet about their relationship.

This was the price—the price of independence. Was she able to pay? Was Leslie?

I won't think about this now. How can I stop this anxiety? Take deep breaths. Think of pleasant things. Look at Marie and Frank. Veronica tried to focus on them, but they started to blur together. She bolted from the line and ran to the ladies' room. She was nauseated and felt like she'd throw up. Her forehead was wet with sweat as she leaned over the toilet. She retched for a while, then leaned back against the cool stall door. Her breathing was shallow and she felt faint.

At the sink she put cold water on her face and looked at Veronica Santini in the mirror. Her reflection was rouged, lipsticked, eyelinered, moussed—completely fake and unnatural.

She realized that everyone had been telling her how beautiful she looked. Like this? This was beautiful to them? She looked like a wax figure, a mannequin. But that was the point—be what they want, not what you are.

"Okay. I'll just think of this as a costume party. I'm dressed as a femme tonight. Actually, I've always resisted being so femme; let's see how I like it."

She patted her face dry and returned to the celebration, just as her brother, Terry, was toasting the bride and groom. Everyone applauded.

Veronica was cornered by Aunt Sally, one of the relatives on her mother's side.

"Veronica. I saw Sister Irene the other day. She asked about you. I told her what you were doing, you know, with school and all. She seemed pleased—you were one of her favorites." Aunt Sally gazed toward the head table. "Oh, Marie is so wonderful, don't you think? And Frank is so nice. They should have a wonderful life. You'll find the right boy, too, when your time comes. Don't settle! Take your time. You have all the time in the world. All that school—high school, now college and a scholarship—it makes it harder to find the right guy." Aunt Sally stroked Veronica's cheek. "We're all so proud of you, Veronica. The first one to go to college, the brains in the family."

Veronica couldn't tell if Aunt Sally was complimenting her or lamenting her fate, but she thanked her anyway.

"I guess I should walk around and talk to the guests."

"Yeah, sure, Veronica, that's good. Oh, you look so beautiful!"

Music started and some couples got up to dance. Veronica walked around speaking to friends and relatives.

"Hi, aren't you Veronica?"

"Yes."

"I don't know if you remember me. I'm Buddy—Buddy Riggio. Frank's cousin. We met a few months ago at Frank's mother's house."

She had no idea who he was. "Sure, I remember. Hi. Nice to see you again. Great wedding, isn't it? Are you having a good time?"

"Yes. You really look great tonight. I like that dress. Your hair looks different, though. You know, after we met, I asked Frank for your phone number so I could call you, but he told me you lived out of town."

"Yeah, Connecticut. I started college there."

"Oh. What do you study?"

"Forest ecology."

"Now that sounds different from the usual stuff people study."

She questioned him: "You mean subjects that girls study?"

Buddy laughed. "Okay. Yeah, I picture all of those hard hats and heavy boots. Guys tramping through the forest cutting down trees. You know, lumberjack types."

"I'm studying how to save trees, not cut them down."

Buddy's expression became very serious. "Oh. I know. I know that."

Veronica started to walk away. Buddy followed her.

"Veronica, would you like to dance? Would you dance with me?" He opened his arms, ready for her to walk into them.

She couldn't believe this. This was not in the script she had studied for this evening. She smiled. "It's been a while since I danced with..." She couldn't finish the sentence, and decided to let him fill in the blanks.

He held her around the waist, and they joined the other dancers on the floor. He was an old-fashioned boy, this Buddy. She could tell by the way he held her that she was in the "Madonna" category, not "whore." But she knew that if she married him, she'd quickly become the ball and chain. He was so predictable. She had grown up with guys like him and all the others—Frank, her father, her brother. She knew how they thought. She had known all of these stereotypes instinctively and only now was starting to talk about them in classes, write about them in papers.

The band was playing a Dean Martin song: "When the moon hits your eye like a big pizza pie..." Everyone was singing and dancing with the band. Buddy looked at her, smiled, and sang, "That's *amore*." She looked at his big, broad, happy grin and returned a weak smile.

She didn't want him to notice that she wasn't enjoying this dance. She looked at his black wavy hair, with one curl coming loose and clinging to his forehead. His palms were moist with perspiration, and a small line of sweat glistened on his upper lip. Was he nervous? What was he thinking? Veronica noticed the stubble of his beard beginning to show and looked away.

She saw her mother and Terry looking at her. They spoke to each other, and then Terry gave Veronica the thumbs-up signal. He thought she was in good hands, that she was doing the right thing. He approved.

Despite her feelings, Veronica was pleased to have her family's approval. She tried to forget that she felt awkward and uncomfortable in Buddy's arms. His hand was on her back, pulling and pushing her across the dance floor. This dance, she thought, is just like married life. His direction, his desire, his strong arm pushing and pulling her.

Panic crept over her again. How could she continue this? Her throat clenched up, and she knew she wouldn't be able to talk. When the dance ended and he offered to get her a glass of champagne, she could only smile and nod.

He led her by the arm to the bar, and started to talk about Terry, and being a fireman. She nodded and smiled.

He didn't seem to notice her discomfort. He was probably used to girls who let him ramble on, listening passively to his thoughts, dreams, ambitions, feelings. This is what a girlfriend was supposed to do.

But Veronica was panicking, clenching her teeth and trying to maintain some outward composure. Leslie could always tell when this was happening. When they were alone, Leslie would hold Veronica, whisper in her ear, soothe her. Veronica always felt safe with Leslie. She could be herself, breathe easily.

In public, when Veronica started to lose control (like she

was doing now), Leslie would grab her arm and give her hard candy. Veronica didn't have Leslie or hard candy right now, so she had to make do with the champagne. She sipped it slowly through clenched teeth.

She thought, "If I drink more, I'll relax and be able to continue with all this." She took another sip, and Buddy offered her a second glass.

Veronica felt like Buddy was taking control of her, and was frightened by the thought that he wanted to be something more to her than just a stranger. A stranger who had danced with her at her sister's wedding.

He guided her over to some chairs and continued talking. *God*, she thought, *he must think I'm shy or something because I haven't said a word.*

She tried to will herself out of the panic attack, breathing slowly and deeply. She felt trapped by her own insecurities and by this boy who wouldn't stop talking to her. She wanted to escape, but she couldn't open her mouth enough to excuse herself.

The breathing worked, and the attack passed slowly. She smiled, but worried that Buddy would think she was flirting. He took her hand and asked if he could come up to Connecticut to visit her.

"Uh, um…" She was taken by surprise. What could she say? She didn't want to encourage him, but she didn't want to be rude. She thought that maybe he'd forget about her after tonight, so she mumbled, "Sure." She didn't think he would really travel all that way just to see her; they had just met, after all, and she hadn't done much to encourage him—except for the smile. And the dancing.

Veronica began to worry that Buddy would become a problem in her life.

"Veronica! Veronica, come! Marie's going to throw the bouquet."

Veronica walked to the door, where Marie and Frank were kissing everyone goodbye before leaving for their honeymoon flight. Veronica's mother appeared and stood next to her.

"You stand here, Veronica, and Marie will be sure you catch it. It's good luck, you know, and I just know you'll be the next Santini bride."

"But, Ma. Ma, I don't want—" She couldn't finish the sentence because her throat had tightened again. Her mother held her by her waist and waited for the toss. Veronica had never seen such intensity in her mother's face. She had to have that bouquet for her daughter, especially after seeing Veronica dancing with Buddy...

Her mother wanted Veronica to become one of them, a married lady with children who went to church. How could Veronica protest against that? It was what her mother lived for—it was the way her mother lived.

Marie turned to glance at the gathered single women, and her mother waved at her, as if to say, "Here we are, Marie! Make sure we get it!" Marie saw them, blew them a kiss, and tossed the bouquet over her shoulder. Mrs. Santini pushed Veronica at it, and Veronica noticed that all the other girls had stepped away. Everyone wanted her to catch it.

Veronica's athletic instinct made her raise her arm and catch the projectile that was aimed at her face.

She inhaled the scent of the flowers as people congratulated her. Her mother grabbed her in a big hug. Veronica saw Marie and Frank coming over to them. They kissed her, and Frank said, "You know, Veronica, Buddy never forgot you from the last time he met you. He was excited about coming here today and seeing you. He's such a great guy."

So this had all been planned: Buddy, the bouquet, another wedding, a few kids. Veronica felt the sweat trickle down her armpits again.

"Sure, he's very nice," she blurted, to pacify Frank and the others.

This was all happening so fast. She had thought she was in control, but she wasn't. She wanted to run, but that was impossible. She felt trapped—she had to think.

This is not your wedding. They are only hoping for your wedding, and that's natural. They want to plan your wedding, but you don't have to go through with any of it.

Veronica calmed herself again. Her mother was still holding her by the waist, wiping her eyes with a handkerchief. Across the room, Veronica watched as her father and brother talked to Buddy. The three men started walking toward her. Again, she was trapped.

The three men kissed her on the cheek and congratulated her on her catch. They were all smiling. Terry held her hand and kept patting it. He looked proud of her.

"Terry," she said, holding out the bouquet to him, "I think these should be for you. You should be the next." But he turned away and continued talking to Buddy. The band started up again, and her father led her mother out to the dance floor. Everyone applauded as they danced. Terry pulled Veronica out to the floor, and everyone applauded more as they began to dance.

For the rest of the evening, Veronica and Buddy danced together. She felt that everyone's eyes were on her. She knew that she was allowing them to believe that she was interested in Buddy. She hated herself for the pretense.

Later, Buddy led her outside. Veronica still held a glass of champagne, and things were starting to get hazy. But at least she felt relaxed.

"Veronica, this night has been real special for me." He was holding her hands and turning them over in his. "I like you so much, Veronica. I hope we can see more of each other. I know you live far away, and it's hard to date like that, but I'd like to try to make it work. What do you think?"

She was frozen. "Buddy, you're a nice guy and all, but—"

He put his hand up to stop her from finishing the sentence and shyly looked down at the ground.

"Yeah, well, I know we really don't know each other. But I really want to get to know you. I want to see more of you. I'm serious. I want you to think of me as a serious contender here. I know someone with your looks probably has lots of guys hanging around. Me—I'm just a fireman. You should be used to that, I mean, with your father and brother and all. Maybe that's in my favor? Although you probably know a lot of smart college guys…"

He looked at her closely. Her eyes were wide-open now. She was speechless.

"Have I come on too strong?" He was pleading with her.

Veronica felt sorry for Buddy. Sorry that he had chosen her. Sorry that he probably wouldn't understand when she told him the truth. She didn't want to encourage him. She didn't want to hurt him. She would have to choose her words carefully. Suddenly, she thought of Leslie and how she'd tell Leslie the story later.

"Buddy, no. No, you've been fine. It's just that I'm not interested in—"

Buddy stopped her again. "I know you want to finish

school. Even if we dated, I would never interfere with that. I'm not one of those old-fashioned guys who thinks a woman should sit at home with the kids. Please don't think that."

This was so hard! She wanted to scream it so he wouldn't doubt her: *"Buddy, I'm a dyke. A dyke. I don't want you, I want Leslie."*

Instead she said, "Buddy, listen to me. I—I don't want to get married. I'm not the marrying kind."

He laughed. "Oh, is that all? I thought you were going to tell me you had some special guy in Connecticut. Well, listen." He squeezed her hand, and shook his head as if relieved. "We can take it slow. I used to feel the same way. I thought I'd never want to settle down. I guess I just needed to meet the right girl. You know what they say— you gotta grow up sometime."

She took her hand out of his and walked away a little.

"Don't say anything now, Veronica. Let's just see what happens. Don't stop this before it even begins."

"But that's just it. It can never begin. I don't want it to happen."

He quickly followed after her. "Some bozo must have really hurt you. Right? Well, things like that happen. I've been hurt lots of times, too, but I think it's worth it to keep looking. We're not all so terrible, you know. Veronica? Veronica?"

He turned her around to face him, and he saw the tears running down her cheeks. He took out a handkerchief and gently wiped them away.

"This must be a hard day for you. Your sister getting married. Catching the bouquet, all of those people looking at you. I should have known."

He lifted her chin and kissed her on the mouth. His lips were soft. He pressed his cheek against hers, and she could feel the roughness of his shaved face.

"I'm sorry, Buddy. I'm sorry."

He pulled her close to his chest and stroked the back of her head.

"It's okay. It'll be okay."

Exhausted, Veronica let her head rest on his chest and quietly allowed the tears to flow.

The band started playing Italian favorites again. After a few minutes they walked back inside to join the celebration. She hoped that no one would notice that she'd been crying. Buddy looked longingly and protectively at her for the rest of the night. She danced and did not object when he pressed her close to him.

People were finally leaving, and Buddy had to take his parents home. He squeezed her hand. "I'll call you soon."

She did not respond, just nodded her head weakly.

She followed him outside, and he lifted his arm to wave goodbye. And in that moment she realized she had to stop the panic attacks, the lying, the pretense. If she didn't do it now, there would be a million excuses not to do it later. She turned back to the party and looked first for her brother, Terry.

Rain
Christina Chiu

Just like that. Rainy and me—our lives banged open for each other.

Sitting in front of my house, I stared at a crack that would soon be hidden by ivy. Pink soaked into the gray sky. The Chang house was sleeping still.

Rainy will be home soon.

We were the kind of twins who should have known these secrets about each other. We had never been the type to wear the same clothes, but we thought enough alike to finish each other's sentences. Not because we had ESP or anything, but because we had known each other from the beginning. In diapers, we'd exchanged babble talk, bursting into laughter or rocking while we sang:

> "Rain, rain, go away,
> Come back another day..."

We shared candies and chocolate, jumped rope two at a time, drew the same cartoons. After winter blizzards, we would build igloos with cake pans, or make angels in the snow. We spent afternoons mapping hideouts, rescuing victims like heroes, planning adventures. Sometimes, when we were mad at Mom and Dad, we'd pack garbage bags, and imagine that we were going off on a dangerous mission. There was always a mystery to solve.

Now, Rainy felt as far away from me as the fading moon. How could twins become so different and feel so far apart?

Mom used to call us her double blessing, since we were born on the day of the Chinese New Year. We were supposed to be a sign of good luck. But on our tenth birthday, Mom was joking with us, and it slipped out that although we were born only three minutes apart, we were born on different days. I had come too early.

"I told you to wait," she said, laughing. "But you didn't listen—you never listen."

The strangest thing popped into my head: by the Chinese New Year, did that make me a monkey and not a rooster?

"No difference," Mom insisted, but I knew there was. Maybe I was the Curious George type and not one to cock-a-doodle after all.

When I left without eating a piece of my birthday cake, Mom came to find me.

"It's bad luck to be sad on New Year's," she said.

"It's Rainy's day," I told her. "Not mine."

"Ah, yeah," she muttered. "Such a little thing and you have to be so sensitive?" I sucked in my lip, careful not to welcome bad luck for the New Year. There is a difference, I wanted to argue.

Learning to hate Rainy came easily. First came the check marks in school—pluses or minuses. Rainy was a check-plus kid. I don't remember how, but no matter how hard I tried, I always fell into the minus group. With straight B's, school became the biggest minus in my life.

"Work harder," Mom always said. "You're not trying hard enough." She never had to say, "Look at Rainy, and how well she's doing."

When the grades came, Mom clicked open her purse.

"I'm proud of both of you," she'd say, but a promise is a promise, and Rainy would be the one to get ten dollars for every A. My B's weren't worth anything.

"You don't love me," I complained. "You love Rainy more than me."

"That's not true," Mom said. "If you had listened to me and worked harder, you would have A's just like Rainy." I started to study in the closet so that Mom and Dad wouldn't know that I was stupid.

Rainy spent her money on mint-chocolate-chip ice cream. Bringing two spoons, she'd come to find me between the sneakers and the shoes, hidden behind my pink, fluffy dress.

That was before the real trouble happened. Our older brother, Stephen, was already at college. Rainy and I were in the eleventh grade, and things had definitely changed between us. Rainy cut her hair into a bob; I permed mine. She had her friend, Jade—Mom loved Jade. I thought it was because she took advanced courses; she was smart, like Rainy. Or maybe it was because Jade was Chinese, like us. Sometimes Rainy and Jade seemed more like twins than Rainy and me.

I had my boyfriend Jimmy, my friends who always threw the coolest keg parties, and a killer body that guys loved.

One night, after coming home with beer on my breath, Dad announced the news: "Next year, you two should think about community college. You can live right here at home with your mom and me." I remembered the way he cleared his throat. "Stephen's tuition is all I can afford, and besides"—he turned to me—"I don't want anything bad happening to my girls." This was his warning to me: Do not shame the family name.

It didn't make a difference to Dad that Rainy always had straight A's. He had expected Stephen to go to an Ivy League, but for his girls, community college was good enough unless we proved we deserved better. "School is school, after all."

Rainy couldn't look me in the eye that night. Still, we hugged tight-tight under a blanket and cried into the mattress so that Dad wouldn't hear.

"Don't cry—we'll find a way," Mom whispered to us when we wouldn't come out from under the blanket. "You can get a scholarship." I wasn't sure what a scholarship meant, and I didn't check Mom's face to see if she meant we'd "find a way" for both Rainy *and* me.

It was then that Rainy simply disappeared. She studied hard and, when that seemed enough, harder still. She stopped talking to Dad, then Mom, then me. When she stopped showing me her report card, I knew for sure that she was getting straight A's. Rainy was tunneling her way through to college, without me to slow her down. I grew desperate. I studied, too—harder and harder, like Rainy. I wanted A's. I wanted a scholarship. I wanted to go away. College meant freedom.

"How can I make this an A next time?" I asked my English teacher, when she showed me the red B written next to my name. She told me to wait after class.

"I know that it must be hard for you, but, you see,

sometimes there are A people, and sometimes there are B people. Maybe you are just one of those B people."

"No," I said, shaking my head. "I'm an A person." But it was useless to explain to her about A's, scholarships, and college; she had heard it all before, and I was starting to look like a grade-grubber.

Finally, at the end of our senior year, the news arrived, bound in a thick envelope. Mom announced the news.

"Scholarship."

"Congratulations," Dad said, thinking Rainy wasn't the troublemaker he'd imagined.

"I hate you" almost slipped from my mouth. I swallowed it and disappeared. Rainy came to find me, but this time, there wasn't enough room for both of us in the closet. I wasn't in the mood for ice cream anyway.

"I'm sorry," she said through the door. I shut my eyes.

It didn't matter. I had Jimmy—a guy that every girl would die for. When Jimmy and I were alone, I was in a different world. A world all mine—and safe from Mom and Dad.

Rainy knew I was Jimmy's girlfriend—everyone knew, except Mom and Dad. They would have packed my bags and thrown me into the street if they knew. So what if Jimmy was a football player? So what if he liked me?

"Those American boys, they only want one thing," they'd say.

"And so do I," I wanted to tell them. But in this house, there was to be no "funny" business, no tramping around.

Rainy looked at me with pity. I figured she had made up her mind about what I was doing with Jimmy. I imagined Mom's voice escaping from her lips: "Tramp." I belonged in hell. Maybe it was that look that drove me deeper into Jimmy's arms.

But then, tonight, Rainy and I collided.

I'd been slipping out of the house for months. Right out from under Mom's nose. With shoes in hand, I'd make my way past Rainy's room, past Stephen's, past Mom and Dad's, and out the back door. It was routine. I grew to be unafraid of shadows stretched by moonlight. I was Superwoman. Mom could usually sense anything—a drop of beer on my breath, a puff of smoke from a cigarette in my hair. But this time, I had pulled one over on her and Dad. With night came arms and kisses and everything more.

So it was the usual Friday-night two-in-the-morning after-curfew thing. Dad's snoring was gut-deep and perfectly on schedule. With my shoes in my hand, I went down the stairs and out the back door. I did it with my eyes closed.

As I crept outside, I opened my eyes, ready to run. That's when I saw them, kissing.

They jumped apart the way people do when they've been busted. Rainy and I didn't say anything. We just stared, bug-eyed, at each other, as if looking into a mirror. She could have been me: the curve of the eyes, the bridgeless nose, the black straight hair. I smiled; we were both tramps. I glanced at the stranger with the baseball cap, wondering who the Romeo was.

Oh, my God.

Jade?

Rainy and Jade were always together, but I'd figured they were only best friends. No wonder they had planned to go to the same college.

The truth moved through me like thunder, and my smile followed gravity. I wanted an explanation.

"Rain?" Her gaze fell to the ground.

Jade reached for her hand and gave it a squeeze.

"Be out front," she said.

"Is it so horrible?" Rainy whispered, when Jade was gone. My throat went dry as a flood swarmed into my head.

"No, I just—why didn't you—"

Jade appeared again.

"Hey, someone's waiting down there," she said.

Quickly, I checked my watch: 2:06 A.M. One minute late. One more minute and Jimmy would be gone.

Rainy focused on her feet, wiggling her toes, I noticed her sandals in her hand and realized that maybe it wasn't her first time either.

"Going out?" I asked. Rainy nodded.

"Uh—talk later?"

"Later."

I didn't look back until I was in the car.

"Let's go," I told Jimmy.

"Hey, who's the guy in the cap? Bo-peep finally found her sheep—who's the fella?"

"Yeah, she has. So?" I snapped, like, *What's it to you?*

"Whoa," Jimmy muttered, hands up as if in surrender.

"Sorry," I kissed him on the cheek. He turned, catching me on the lips. I pulled away.

"Just go, okay?"

"Whatever," he answered, shrugging, We drove up the street, and he pulled me closer to him. I wondered why Jimmy hadn't recognized Jade, but then I remembered that I had needed an extra look, too.

As the car turned the corner, I watched Rainy and Jade hugging, their shadows blending into one.

How could Rainy not tell me something so important? Why had she kept this secret?

My mind raced back to a time when the family had gone

out to dinner. On our way to the restaurant, we passed two women holding hands.

"Abnormal," Mom had said.

"Disgusting," Dad had responded.

"Dykes," Stephen had muttered, chuckling. I laughed along—hadn't Rainy laughed, too?

As they faded into the dark, I could see a tear sparkle from Rainy's eye. It had to be a trick of the moonlight, I thought, or maybe just my imagination.

I would have understood, Rainy. Why did you shut me out, like you did Mom and Dad?

In his bed, Jimmy leaned into me. Touch me, I wanted to tell him. I kissed his neck, trying to be with him, but questions stormed like a wheel through my mind. Does Rainy touch Jade like this? I placed my hands on Jimmy, tracing my hands up his back, then down to his butt, legs, and ankles.

How would it feel to touch another woman? To be touched?

I remained quiet—alone in my head—while Jimmy made love to me.

"That was great," Jimmy said, when he was done. I kissed him on the shoulder.

"Yeah, great," I agreed. "Jimmy?" I asked, before he turned to the wall. He stretched, his arms out in front of me.

"Huh?"

"I was just wondering—um, well—uh." I rubbed the hair at the back of my neck. He looked at his watch.

"It's late," he said, not too impatiently. He rubbed his eyes with one hand and placed the other on the dip of my waist. "Tell me. Wondering what?"

"How do—gay people—you know, do it?" I asked. He looked at me, eyebrows raised.

"Where did *that* come from?"

"Oh, nowhere, really," I choked. "I just saw something on TV yesterday, that's all."

"How should I know?" he muttered, stretching his neck forward to bring out his football shoulders.

"You know—the asshole," he finally whispered. He watched my reaction. "Those guys should all be shot, if you ask me."

I didn't reply. I squeezed his biceps so he wouldn't worry that I thought he was queer. But I wanted to ask my question again, get it right. I didn't mean gay guys. I wanted to know about Rainy. Rainy and Jade.

How did I not know about Rainy, that she was a lesbian? I wondered, but in my gut I knew I was lying to myself. Maybe it was through the little things that Rainy had tried to tell me: the hunk calendar that she wasn't interested in, the cute guys at school she never cared about. She got asked to the prom by one of Jimmy's friends, but she still said no. Rainy had spent that night with Jade.

Jimmy turned to the wall, and in an instant, I heard sleep-breathing. For a while I stared at his back, tracing the muscles up and around his spine. I thought about the crack at the front of our house. From the crevice, threads spread outward like veins of a leaf. *Was I so horrible to come to— so unapproachable?* The sheet twisted around me. Outside the night shifted into gray. *How does Rainy make love?*

Slowly, as quietly as I could, I moved my hands over my body. Neck, breasts, stomach, legs. I tried to be still, careful not to wake Jimmy. Something in me was starving to feel every bone, every muscle, every pinch of my flesh. I had to make sure I wasn't fading into a crack on the wall.

And then I felt it. It came in waves, ripples that reached the tips of my fingers and toes. A coolness moved over me, and I drew my hands over my face and into my hair. Jimmy had never brought these tingles. Jimmy had never touched me like this.

All this time, I had thought that Jimmy and I were making love, that this was the right way to do it—pushing and shoving.

"Tramp." I imagined Mom's voice, and it was like a jellyfish stinging at the backs of my eyeballs. I had been lying next to Jimmy for months, but the part I knew most about his body was his back and the muscles that held it together.

Outside, it was dewy like a steam bath. Jimmy was wrong about so many things. I didn't want anything bad to ever happen to my Rainy.

Rainy is out there, somewhere.

Suddenly, I had to get home. I had to speak to Rainy. *Mom and Dad are wrong,* I wanted to tell her. *They are wrong about us.*

"Jimmy," I shook him. "Wake up."

"What," he muttered.

"It's time."

"It's only three. We have at least two more hours," he squinted at his watch. His head dropped to the pillow again.

I got up, naked, searching through the pile of clothes at my feet. I pulled on my undies.

"Now, Jimmy," I ordered, my voice rising. "I have to get home." I pulled my shirt on, not caring that it was inside out.

"What's wrong?" he asked. He rubbed his hand through his hair.

"Nothing."

I threw his pants and he caught them.

"Hurry."

At home, I scurried up the path, not kissing Jimmy good-bye. When I reached the back door, I realized his car lingered. He looked at me, and I waved. Maybe he thought I was breaking up with him. It hit me that I was.

Rainy was still out. She had hidden her key chain under a bush. I picked it up. RAIN was carved into the wood in big bubble letters. I had made this for her in shop class in the seventh grade.

"I'll use it forever," she had told me.

So I waited on the steps and watched the sleeping house. It had been so long since Rainy and I had just talked, but now my heart had so many questions. So many things to say.

I wasn't ready for Rainy to leave. I didn't want to be left alone here. But I wondered: *Is Rainy in love? Does she feel tingles in her fingers and toes?*

Pink filtered into the sky. I thought about Jade and how she would be a part of Rainy's new life. How Jade belonged there.

Would Rainy make a place for me?

There was a sputtering in the distance, and then the Rabbit crept to a halt in front of our drive.

"Same time, same place," Jade said to Rainy. Rainy clicked the door shut as quietly as she could, then leaned back in to finger Jade's hair. They kissed. My stomach clamped inward.

They are in love.

A heaviness fell from me. *Ha*, I thought. *Only we know.* Rainy was in love. *Rain, rain, go away...* For the first time,

I realized why it was so important for Rainy to leave home to start a new life.

Rainy stared up at the house, then at me. Alone, she seemed smaller. It brought me back to a time when we were five and she had tripped and fallen. She hadn't cried, but she had the same *ouch* in her eye. I had kissed her boo-boo the way we always did for each other. There were no boo-boos to kiss away this time.

"That's mine," Rainy said, nodding at the key chain.

"You still use it," I said, tracing the letters again with my thumb: RAIN. I placed it into her open palm. She closed her hand around mine.

We went through the back door.

New York in June
Brian Sloan

The first time I came to New York City, I was sixteen and a journalist. Well, to be honest, I was really the news editor of my high school paper, *The Whitman Gazette*, headquartered in a former janitor's changing room in the basement of Walt Whitman High School in Bethesda, Maryland. *The Gazette* was a thin monthly tabloid, usually no more than fourteen pages, that was put together with an appealing mixture of style, verve, and mischief. And it was the mischief that succeeded in bringing me to New York.

In January 1979 we were written up in *The Washington Post* because of a piece we did on three girls from our class who'd had abortions—a piece that our faculty adviser had killed in an editorial meeting but that we had slipped into the proofs at the printers. A couple months later, the story went on to win the Scholastic Journalism Golden Scribe Award. The editorial staff of the newspaper received little gold pins (that we never wore) and an all-expenses-paid trip to Columbia University for a high-minded four days of seminars, workshops, and lectures on the fine art of journalism.

On a Sunday afternoon in late June, this group of future H.L. Menckens met at the New Carrollton Amtrak station in suburban Maryland. Besides myself, there were three others who made up the editorial staff of the *Gazette*. Roger Garrett was the editor in chief, because he was a year older than I was and could spell better. Raul Rodriguez was the photo editor because he had more cameras (at the time of this trip) than anyone else at school. And finally, the layout editor was Barry Thompson because he could draw relatively straight lines without the use of a ruler.

Shortly before three o'clock, four battered suburban station wagons pulled into the parking lot of the train station. We stepped out of our family cars and greeted each other with adult handshakes. I wore a pair of khaki shorts, Docksiders, and an Izod shirt—a standard ensemble for that time. Raul wore an Aerosmith concert T-shirt with red athletic shorts, and Barry was wearing some ill-fitting jeans from Sears that made him look like a pear. Only Roger was dressed for the occasion, wearing a navy blue sport coat and long khaki pants.

Our parents expressed worries over the four of us running wild through the streets of New York City. I reminded them that Mr. Carter, the faculty adviser for the paper, would be keeping his keen eye on us as our official chaperone once we got to Penn Station. Then, feeling a bold sarcasm rise in me, I also reminded my parents that the tightly scheduled week barely gave us enough time to brush our teeth. Raul laughed when I said this. Roger didn't, but he smiled at me knowingly. Roger, though he wore the suit in this group, had already planned out a week that would have little if anything to do with the workshop schedule we'd been sent in the mail. I might add, also, that Roger had stashed two bottles of his father's vodka in his suitcase.

We hugged our parents reluctantly, and then the cars pulled away, kicking up an orange cloud of dust and scattering the loose pebbles that covered the makeshift road. We picked up our duffel bags and headed toward the station to wait for the 3:20 train. Back then, the New Carrollton station was not much of a grand send-off to the world's most infamous city. There were no marble columns, no cathedral-like waiting rooms with narrow wooden benches, no grand iron clocks. The station consisted merely of a temporary green shack with dull aluminum siding and scratched Plexiglas windows.

Inside was a row of ten plastic chairs, a cigarette machine, a pay phone, and a colorful promotional Amtrak poster that pictured a gleaming silver train rolling across the American plains, the sun melting into the west behind it.

I wondered aloud if somewhere in Montana there was a station with a poster of New Carrollton hanging on the wall. Barry snorted and told me I was weird. Roger headed to the cigarette machine and illegally purchased a pack of Marlboro Lights, despite the yellow sticker that advised against it. Raul barked with approval at Roger's purchase, and Roger tossed him a tobacco bone as a treat. Behind the ticket window, a woman with a pale face looked up disapprovingly from her romance novel. I told Raul to calm down a bit, but he only barked louder. Raul was the youngest in our group, having just turned fifteen in May, and was at that hyperteen phase where barking could be considered a respectable form of social intercourse.

Barry went up to the ticket window and politely asked how long before our train was due. Raul barked again and made some noise about the fact that Barry was talking to the ticket lady. Barry was the shyest of our group, and his pasty white face was easily brought to a crimson blush. Yelling in a room that didn't require it, Raul said that the ticket lady had the hots for Barry. Swallowing a laugh, Barry turned around to reveal his burning cheeks. Slumping away from the window, he told Raul he was acting like a dick. He came up to me and said that we should wait on the platform, since it was almost a quarter after three. I told Barry that he was blushing. He told me, very quietly, to go fuck myself.

The train arrived on time, looking a little less magnificent than the one in the poster; it was silver, yes, but the sun didn't make it glow, probably because it hadn't been washed in a couple of months. After a boisterous argument between Raul and Roger over who would get the window seat, we settled into our seats (I took the window seat myself, to resolve their argument).

Chugging through the burnt-out shells of abandoned tenements in East Philly, Roger said that it was about time we got some drinks. Raul insisted that Barry go to make the purchase, since he was tallest, standing at more than six feet, when not slouching. I killed this idea, pointing out to Raul that Barry was blushing at the mere mention of this plan. I said Roger should go up, since he was in a sports coat and looked fairly responsible.

A few minutes later, Roger returned with two Budweisers and four straws. We sucked the beers through the straws (a trick to increase the inebriation) and spent the next half hour having a burping competition. As Raul tried to say the entire alphabet in the middle a roaring release of gas, I joked that *The Washington Post* should see us now, the prize journalists of Maryland, speeding half-drunk through the Jersey flatlands, on a collision course with a city that would only encourage our wanton behavior.

We weren't heading merely for Columbia University. We were heading for trouble.

★

We arrived in New York shortly after seven in the evening, just getting over our slight beer buzzes, and Mr. Carter met us under the schedule board at Penn Station. Mr. Carter was the faculty adviser who had tried to kill the abortion story; he was not terribly fond of us. But the principal at Whitman High had been so impressed that Columbia University wanted four of her flunky newspaper geeks that she had demanded Mr. Carter chaperone us on the trip. He had arrived in New York a day early for a faculty seminar, and now retrieved us dutifully from the concourse of Penn Station, as if we were a parcel.

He greeted us with forced handshakes. Raul would not let go of his hand and just kept shaking it. Mr. Carter told him he could drop the routine now, thank you. After shaking hands, he said nothing more than a perfunctory hello and a short question on how we'd enjoyed our trip. More like a tour guide than a chaperone, he then silently led us with pointing fingers and stern, officious looks toward Broadway and 116th Street.

Columbia University was a wonder. We emerged from

the subway and were confronted by these immense, Oz-like black iron gates. Past the entrance to the campus, the stately red-brick buildings and staid ivory columns gave way to a wide-open plaza covered with an unbelievably lush lawn that glowed green in the early-evening light. On one end of the plaza was a grand domed building that we all agreed resembled the Library of Congress back home. Strolling through the quad, pointing at various buildings and coeds, I suddenly felt suave and collegiate. Even though my arms were slightly different lengths and my face was a patchwork of downy fuzz, I felt, for the first time, that I was not unfinished.

Our first stop was a twenty-five-story law school dorm where we would lodge for the week. I was set up in a room on the twenty-second floor with Roger. The most impressive thing about the room was its expansive view of Harlem and the towers of midtown in the far distance. Otherwise, it was bland and functional, with white sheet-rock walls, navy blue chairs and beds, an efficiency kitchen, and a small, pink-tiled bathroom. We had just about half an hour to get set up before the welcome dinner for all the workshop participants.

This introductory get-together was held in the main dining hall at Columbia, a vast rectangular room with massive chandeliers and narrow, high leaded-glass windows. It reminded me of something I'd seen in an episode of *Brideshead Revisited*. We ate a hearty meal and mingled with the sixty other students from various cities up and down the Eastern seaboard. Roger was the best at this social part of the evening; with his HELLO, MY NAME IS sticker plastered proudly on his breast pocket, he strolled about the room, brazenly approaching the most alluring female editors as well as the geekiest writers, introducing himself and chatting with them amiably.

I trailed closely behind Roger, nodding as I was introduced to all these "colleagues" and smiling at Roger's jokes. Barry and Raul, however, were not on the circuit. This was much less an active decision than something that just happened by chance. They were huddled over by the dessert table, eating slice after slice of apple pie. In fact, a lot of guys were gathered in that corner, crumpling up their nametags and introducing themselves to each other with mouths full of apple filling. For some reason, this group seemed more interesting to me than my rounds with Roger. I felt that Roger and I were pretending to be something we were not—adults shaking each other's hands, talking in sober voices about column inches and sans serif typestyles. All the while, I yearned to eat more pie.

The dinner broke up around ten, and Mr. Carter informed us that the first seminar started at eight the next morning, so we'd better get some rest. Good advice from a good man. Too bad he was giving it to the wrong people.

Arriving back on the twenty-second floor, Roger whipped out some index cards from his shirt pocket. On the cards were phone numbers of all the people he'd met that evening. He picked up the phone and started dialing. Within minutes, our prison cell of a room was filled with about ten girls and five guys. One industrious girl with braces and Marcia Brady hair—Sandy Bentley from Boston—brought a shopping bag filled with cartons of orange juice. Another girl had picked up some chips and dip from the student union. But Roger had the most crucial and well-planned ingredient for this impromptu cocktail hour; he opened his suitcase, took out his father's liquor, and started mixing up a party.

★

I awoke the next morning to the sound of sirens. I stumbled out of bed with my first-ever vodka hangover, and looked out the window to find the source of this wailing noise. Harlem was spread out in a brown grid just below the cliff on which Columbia was perched.

Looking to my right out the window, I noticed a police car speeding down the wrong side of a wide boulevard. Just ahead of it was a yellow Dodge Dart, moving incredibly fast. Car tires screeched to avoid this terrorizing lemon streak. Then, in my morning daze, a thought struck me that was so incredible, I had to yell it out to Roger. I was watching a car chase, and it wasn't even on TV. This was *Starsky and Hutch*—the live version!

I called Roger over to the window and we watched the chase for a good five minutes. The idiot thieves in the Dart kept turning right, eventually coming back to where they had begun. Soon, more cops showed up to cut the bandits off at the pass. Roger said he was sure the thieves would speed up when they saw the deadly barricade—just like they did on TV. I was not so sure. Roger grabbed my shoulders excitedly and squeezed them. I felt the rush of his excitement, his thrill over this real-life drama. The yellow Dart finally puttered to a stop, and two men in torn white T-shirts stumbled out of it. Little blue cops swarmed around them, and the show was over. With a disappointed sigh, Roger removed his hands from my bare shoulders and headed to the shower. The burn of his touch remained.

After he'd been showering for a few minutes, I had to go to the bathroom. I opened the door and was greeted by a burst of steam. Roger was whistling a song by Kenny Loggins as his brown form swayed and sloshed behind the blurry glass. I relieved myself and went over to the sink to wash my face. Suddenly, the shower turned off, the glass door slid open, and there was Roger. Naked Roger. This sight startled me a bit. I had worked with him side by side on the *Gazette* for hours into the night for the last year and a half. I thought I knew him well. But I did not know him naked. This was brand-new and, I have to admit, a little bit thrilling.

He shook his head and sprayed water all over the bathroom. His chest, olive-colored and hairless, was speckled with water drops that were sliding down to his crotch. And there, framed between thighs that were lean and sinewy, was a dark, thick tangle of hair, thick as the hair on his head, and a long, thin penis that was almost pink in color. Flippantly, Roger told me to move over as he stood next to me at the sink, brushing his teeth like it was no big deal.

Meanwhile, I was trying not to look down at that dark wonder just below his navel. I smiled and playfully jousted him in the ribs as we battled for a space at the small sink. In a minute he was done and, with a grin, said it was all mine. He strode out of the bathroom, and I watched him change into some O.P. shorts and a Nike T-shirt. I jumped in the shower, masturbated, and was dry and dressed in ten minutes.

We arrived twenty minutes late for the first seminar, a discussion of modern layout design with an editor from *The Boston Globe*. I kind of zoned out on the slides and graphs, layout not being my specialty. I was more interested in the image of Roger getting out of the shower that morning. It was like my own personal little porn movie; I played it again and again, rewinding, then fast-forwarding, and finally freeze-framing it, until I started to wonder if I was a little bit crazy. After all, it was only a guy getting out of the shower—it wasn't like Farrah Fawcett in a bikini or something.

✪

After dinner that night, Barry and Raul showed up in our room, excited about something. After some deft lock-picking by Raul, they'd found a way up to the roof of the dorm. Barry said the view was really neat, and you could even see the Empire State Building. Raul, smoking one of Roger's cigarettes, asked who gave a fuck about the view; he was thinking of the sexual activities one could get away with up on the roof. I listened thoughtfully, sipping some vodka and O.J., not daring to say that I thought it would be cool to see the Empire State Building. Roger pulled out his phone list and started calling.

At eleven p.m. sharp, we headed up to the roof for a party with our fellow journalists. The first to arrive was Sandra from Boston, with her supply of orange juice and a case of Michelob she'd conned a law student into buying for her. Accompanying Sandra was a new girl, Maria Juarez. She had Jaclyn Smith–style hair that was black and shiny, Aim-white teeth, and an unusually clear complexion for a sixteen-year-old. Sandra introduced her to me and we shook hands. Maria stared at me. She smiled. I asked her what paper she worked on and she smiled some more. Sandra informed me that Maria was the news editor of a Spanish-language paper out of a high school in Miami Beach.

This was a problem. The only Spanish I knew was what I'd gleaned from watching Speedy Gonzales cartoons and TV repeats of *West Side Story*. I thought I'd start with *West Side Story*, to downplay the fact that I like to watch little cartoon mice with bad Mexican accents. All I could remember from the movie was that one line Tony says when he realizes he's fallen for the girl. And that's what I said: *"Te adore Maria."* She took it the wrong way.

As the night progressed and we got more and more inebriated, Maria would not leave my side. She was staring at me like I was some sort of teen idol. I asked Barry to help me out, but he just giggled and ran off to some corner of the roof with a good view. I approached Raul, who was doing cigarette tricks for a bunch of girls from Delaware. I thought he might be able to talk some Spanish sense into Maria. Frustrated that I was interrupting his show, he spoke to her in rapid Spanish for a minute. I asked him what she said. He said that she comes from a large family and she has an aunt in Washington, D.C., who works for the Mexican Embassy. But what about me? "Oh," said Raul. "She has a crush on you and wants to make out." Then he stuck the cigarette back in his mouth, blew me a smoke ring, and returned to his adoring crowd.

Maria and I went over to where Barry had been getting a good view of the city. It was truly a spectacular sight: Manhattan lay before us, a glittering bed of colored lights and twinkling spires that seemed to go on for infinity. With the view and the vodka stirring my insides, I started to get romantic. I told Maria that *West Side Story* was my favorite movie. She told me hers was *Star Wars*. Maria reached for my hand and held it. I smiled. And then, without any verbal warning, she leaned in with her cherry red lips and kissed me. Seriously.

We made out on that ledge for about half an hour. I had kissed a couple of girls before, but nothing ever this intense, this severe. She was feeling me up, putting her hands in places that had never been touched by another person. I kept jumping every time she would grab a new area—my inner thigh, the side of my belly, my butt. She laughed when I jumped. I tried to act amused, but my humor was less than convincing. I was, frankly, a little shocked by her ease in these sexual matters. I kept wondering how someone my own age could take such things so lightly.

All this mauling ended when she realized she had to go to the bathroom. I did not wait for her to return. I headed back to my room in hopes of going to sleep. After five minutes there was a knock at the door. It was Roger, and he was high. He had smoked some dope with Sandra, and of course, he was hungry. We ordered a pizza and it arrived in minutes. Roger, stripped down to his Fruit of the Looms, talked incessantly about how cool New York was, simply because pizza was available and delivered at three in the morning. I agreed with him and tried to keep my mind off his underwear.

I told him about how I'd made out with Maria and how she grabbed me. He asked me where she grabbed me and, lying, I said she grabbed my penis. He busted out laughing, rolling onto his back and, finally, sliding onto the floor. I asked him what was so funny, and he said it was just funny to think of someone doing that to me. I asked him why, and he said I just wasn't a very sexual person.

He was right—I wasn't that much of a sexual person. That is, until that moment, just after his comment, when I jumped onto his bed and, under cover of teenage high jinks, started giving Roger the biggest, baddest wedgie of his short life. He cried in mock pain, his arms thrashing about, his legs twisting and kicking my own. Soon enough, he had found the band of my Montgomery Ward briefs and started yanking on them as well. I cried out, too, though not in pain, but something closer to ecstasy, though I didn't quite know it at the time.

We wrestled for quite a while, both of us getting erect but ignoring these "problems" by just not saying anything about them. Soon enough, they went away. And also, soon enough, we ran out of energy as we both passed out on Roger's bed, tangled in each other's limbs. Lying there, I heard Roger fall to sleep, a gentle snore rising and falling from his slack mouth. I started dreaming about what he would look like in the shower the next morning. Despite the make-out session with Maria, which was thrilling in a more scientific way, there was nothing in that half hour of heavy petting with her that had moved me as much as that morning when I'd seen Roger dripping wet.

Something was shifting inside me; the continental plates of my sexuality were grinding against each other, creating a friction, building up a heat and a tension that had to be released. An earthquake was imminent.

I missed him. I missed his shower. When I awoke the next morning, Roger was already fully clothed, combing his slick, black hair into a neat part. He told me to hurry up if I wanted any breakfast. I got out of bed, brushed my teeth, and, forgoing a shower, headed to the cafeteria with Roger.

Over a breakfast of Cap'n Crunch, powdered doughnuts, and fruit cocktail, Roger and I rehashed the details of the previous night. We joked about our wrestling match, Roger marveling at the fact that I had actually torn the band of his Fruit of the Looms halfway off. There was no nervousness on his part in talking about this—no worry. We were boys, and things like wrestling matches didn't amount to suspicion of true homosexuality. Staring at your editor in the shower? Yes. Staring, however, is something kept secret and to one's self.

The first seminar of the day was on illustrations and photos, captioning, and cropping. Raul sat on one side of me, Roger on the other. Despite this being Raul's subject, his main interest was in passing notes to the girls from Delaware, who were sitting in the row in front of us. After they had all said hi to each other on torn pieces of loose-leaf paper, Raul started playing hangman with them. Some of the more-amusing words Raul used in the game were *playboy, condom,* and *martini.*

As I sat trying to pay attention to the lecture, my stomach made some noise. After a night of cheap vodka and pepperoni pizza and a breakfast of sugar doughnuts and sugary cereal, I was starting to feel a little queasy. I put my head down on the desk in hopes of stemming the inevitable tide. Raul, noticing my head down, told me to wake up and jabbed me in the gut with his elbow. I sat upright, my eyes wide, and said quietly that I was going to throw up. Roger grabbed my elbow and practically dragged me out of the room without saying a word to the teacher.

As I raced into the bathroom, a force erupted in my gut and I unexpectedly threw up in the sink. After that initial burst, Roger hastened me into a stall, and I proceeded to lose most of the food I'd eaten in the last twelve hours. I had never thrown up from drinking before, and it was not a pleasant experience. Roger guided me through it, rubbing my back calmly and telling me just to let it all out. I sat up,

and Roger looked at me with a grimace. I said that with my
flushed face, wet eyes, and food-stained mouth I must look
like a real mess. Then I started to cry. Roger pulled some
toilet paper from the roll and handed it to me. After I
stopped crying, he squeezed my shoulder and said that I
would feel fine now. He said I looked fine; either he was
lying, or I was one of the great teen deceivers of all time. I
think he was lying.

We walked back into the classroom and half the class
turned around to stare at me. I thought I might faint.
Roger, standing behind me, saw me begin to wobble and
placed his hands discreetly against the small of my back. In
my ear, he whispered, "Steady, now, steady." The professor
asked me if I wanted to see a nurse, and I said no, I felt a
lot better now. As the professor turned back to the blackboard, I took my seat again. Raul leaned over to me and
remarked that I was a lightweight pussy who couldn't hold
liquor if it was handed to me in a shopping bag. Raul had
a way with insults.

I kept my eyes straight ahead, ignoring the comment as
best I could. Roger, however, felt the need to respond; he
leaned across my desk, pointed an accusatory finger at
Raul, and told him that he would give him an new asshole
if he didn't lay off me. I was startled by this threat. I looked
at Roger's face to see if there was a smirk that would have
dissipated the severity of his statement by tingeing it with
adolescent sarcasm. There was none. He stared straight at
Raul, fierce and steely eyed, almost ignoring my presence.
Raul melted under Roger's scrutiny and went back to doodling hangman nooses in his notebook.

In the stunned silence that followed this extraordinary
defense, a chill spread across my forehead and the rest of

my scalp. My mind was awash in the shameless chivalry of Roger's attack. No one had ever stood up for me in such a forceful, almost righteous manner. The perverse intimacy of Roger's threat thrilled me, as I tried to imagine what exactly he would do to Raul's butt to carry out his threat. As the professor droned on about the science of making perfect halftones, I sat at my desk feeling a bit dazed, even amazed. I was shocked at a discovery, a personal revelation, that occurred in the middle of a classroom filled with my journalistic peers.

I realized that I was beginning to fall in love with my editor.

A bus tour of Manhattan was scheduled for the third evening of our stay. At each stop, we were given a half hour to tour a neighborhood or historic site. We drove around to the usual spots: the U.N., Times Square, the Empire State Building, Wall Street, and Greenwich Village. At the stop for the Village, all sixty of us tramped off the bus and started strolling down Christopher Street in the hazy light of a waning summer afternoon.

There were many male and female couples—gay couples, that is—moving beside us on the sidewalks. I had never seen openly gay people before and was disappointed that they didn't all look like the Village People. I wasn't the only one who noticed the gays: Raul had a sharp eye and a bigger mouth. He yelled for us to check out the fags. In a daring retort, Roger told him it takes one to know one. We cracked up at that. Raul actually blushed a bit and started giving us all kidney punches. Raul told us all to go fuck ourselves, and said that he wasn't a fag, because he didn't even like the Village People—he was strictly an Aerosmith teen. Barry called him a macho man in a very sarcastic way. And finally, to top off all this nonsense, Roger said that Raul was more like a nacho man.

Raul stopped cold on the sidewalk. The tensions of the previous day resurfaced. I wondered if this would be the moment that Raul's rear would be physically reconstructed by Roger—or maybe vice versa. Raul glared at Roger, and, with a voice of calm authority entirely uncharacteristic of his fifteen-year-old self, he told Roger to lay off the spic jokes. It was actually okay and funny to call Raul a fag; the much more serious offense was to make a comment on his Latino heritage. Remember, this was the summer of 1979, the climax of the pre-AIDS age, before being gay was associated with a disease. The idea of homosexuality was, to us at least, a little silly and eccentric. All you have to do to understand this is look at the gay celebrities of the day: Liberace and the Village People. Not what you would call the most threatening of sorts.

After an exhausting afternoon and evening of walking around the city, we arrived back at Columbia just before eleven P.M. Mr. Carter reminded us to get some sleep, because, again, we had an early morning ahead. For once, everyone was actually tired enough to take the advice seriously. Roger and I got into our room, and he stripped down to his shorts, lay down on his bed, and was soundly asleep. I lay down on my bed, but I couldn't sleep; I was having trouble turning my mind off. Too many thoughts were crowding my head, begging for my attention: Roger in the shower, the couples in the Village, getting sick in the bathroom, and of course, the Village People. I thought that counting sheep was tacky, so I started humming "In the Navy" in the hope of lullabying myself to sleep. After going through "YMCA" and "Macho Man," I was still alert. In retrospect, I don't think disco music is useful in making a person drowsy.

I looked over at Roger sleeping. His face was very peaceful, and he had this odd little grin on his closed mouth. I wondered with horror if maybe he wasn't asleep after all and had been listening to my gay hit parade. I called out his name a few times to see if he was asleep, and he didn't move an inch. I got out of bed to see if he was dead. Really. I was getting a little worried.

I touched his arm with my finger and it was warm. He was alive, and that was good. Feeling silly, I touched his nose. No response. And then, holding my breath, I touched his lips. A gust of hot air surrounded my finger as Roger exhaled through his nose. Suddenly, his eyes blinked awake and he looked up at me with half-mast lids. My hands started shaking.

He asked me what I was doing. I told him I thought he was dead; and I was just testing to make sure. Half-asleep, he looked confused and repeated what I'd said: "Testing." I told him I was testing to see if he was breathing. With a deep sigh, he assured me that he was alive and told me to go to bed. He smiled wearily, then winked at me. Or maybe he just blinked. I wasn't sure. It was quite dark, and, being a news editor, I had a crazy tendency to exaggerate things.

I got back into bed and finally fell asleep after humming some Donna Summer and Peaches & Herb. I dreamed of Roger and me making out. In the shower.

★

The final day of classes at Columbia was unusually fun. We learned all about the upcoming trendy typestyles for the '80s (New Century Schoolbook was going to be "hot"). We wrote fake headlines for a fire that had happened on Wall Street a year before. And this crazy guy from the *New York Post*—who'd been writing headlines for the past thirty years—made up funny copy for stories that we'd suggest. By the end of the day, I actually thought being in the newspaper business could be sort of a gas.

That night, we had big plans to see a Broadway show: *A Chorus Line*. It was my first Broadway show. I put on the sport coat that my mom had packed at the last minute and a wide, red, white, and blue striped tie my dad used to wear to the office. Roger put on his train suit, and added a colorful green-and-yellow tie for variety. Barry had on a beige leisure suit that was a little snug and that, again, served to accent his unusual shape. But out of all of us, Raul was the most decked out: he actually put on a pair of green corduroy jeans. Of course, he still wore the Aerosmith T-shirt.

Arriving at the Schubert Theatre, we took our seats at the rear of the orchestra with Raul on my right and Roger on my left. Raul was in the worst mood of all time, mumbling "fucks" to himself and making wisecracks about everyone who sat near us. As you might well imagine, Raul was not a big fan of the American musical. In fact, Raul had suggested to Mr. Carter that we all go see *Oh, Calcutta!* instead, the popular all-nude review playing down the street. By this point in the trip, Mr. Carter had learned to not even bother with a response to Raul's requests.

During the show, Raul felt obliged to point out every gay reference or gay character, as if he were giving a running gay color commentary. But halfway through the show, his comments were silenced when Paul, the Puerto Rican fag, took center stage to tell his tale of growing up gay in the front rows of seedy movie houses on 42nd Street. Raul's mouth went slack and his eyes widened as Paul told the audience about being jerked off in the theater by an older man. I guess Raul had never considered the possibility that fags and Latinos were not two entirely separate states of being.

About an hour later, the lead dancer took center stage and belted out the show's big number, "What I Did for Love." I was enthralled. After sitting through most of the show as a mere spectator, just watching and applauding at the proper moments, I suddenly felt like a part of the show. The singer was reaching me, moving me, with her soaring voice and the lyrics that I still remember today as clearly as the Pledge of Allegiance:

> "Kiss today goodbye
> And point me toward tomorrow..."

Looking around, trying to feel all I could of this particular moment, I took a mental snapshot of the theater— but it was really more of a Cinerama-size home movie with Dolby Sound. I studied the faces of the strangers as they reacted to the music, some of them even crying. I glanced up and saw gold stars painted on the ceiling-sky of royal blue. I placed my left arm on the red velvet armrest, curling my hand around the front end, holding on tight. I turned to Raul and watched him sitting there, with his jaw still a little slack as he listened, mesmerized by lyrics that, for once, he could actually understand.

As the song raced to its conclusion, I felt something on my left hand, something warm. It was Roger's hand.

Roger had plunked his gorgeous hand right down on top of mine. He slipped his fingers between mine and squeezed my hand lightly. The earthquake predicted earlier in the trip had just struck, and it was a major one. Definitely an 8.1 on the Richter Scale of my life. Various sections of my brain cracked and tumbled away, while other parts shot up through the gray soggy soil, like shards of bedrock, solid and unyielding. And then, just as things began to get serious, a trembling roar rose up around me, an after-shock of applause and joyous hollering. The song had ended, the quake was subsiding, and strangely, this inti-mate world of 1,200 people was cheering my state of emergency. They approved of this disaster and screamed from the balcony, even called for an encore.

Bewildered, I turned to make sure this hand was attached to my editor's body. A brilliant white stage light, reflected off one of the stage mirrors, was making Roger's face glow and burn. The outlines were almost hard to see. I noticed one thing, however, as he watched the actress onstage receive her praise; I recognized that closed little grin. It was the grin from the night before, when he lay in bed and I touched his lips. Now, his eyes were open.

So were mine.

✪

The next morning, Roger and I awoke shortly after nine in the same bed. Naked. We made our way, bleary-eyed, to the bathroom and took a shower together. Naked. We ate some leftover pizza while sitting on the floor Indian style. Naked. We probably would have stayed naked for the rest of the day, the rest of the year if we'd had the choice. It was,

131

however, day five our stay and time to return to the clothed world of suburban Maryland.

Our trip back on the train was slightly more subdued this time, since Mr. Carter was accompanying us. We sat together in a cluster of four seats that faced one another at the end of the car. Mr. Carter sat across the aisle from us, reading the current issue of *The New Yorker*. Looking out the window at the blurry, industrial brown landscape of the Jersey meadowlands, I wondered about tomorrow—the tomorrow I had now, almost unknowingly, gotten myself into on the field trip that was supposed to have educated me about the art of journalism. I wondered how Roger and I would hold up outside of the unreality of the past week. I wondered if it was somehow possible to take him to the senior prom.

Halfway home, this pensive mood and existential questioning ceased when a glamorous couple in their late twenties boarded the train in Philadelphia and sat across from Mr. Carter. We learned that this couple had just been married and were starting their long journey to Miami Beach for their honeymoon. The man was tall and dashingly handsome, his looks verging on the ridiculousness of a Disney prince. The woman was equally attractive, but in a sassier way, her auburn hair wildly askew, resembling a funnier version of Cher.

On the seat next to Mr. Carter, they opened up a larger wicker basket and started pulling out little white bags filled with exotic cheese, baguettes, marinated vegetables, and cold cuts. They asked Mr. Carter if he would like to share their snacks. Peeking up from his magazine, he quietly demurred. Raul, however, was less polite; he said he would gladly take Mr. Carter's portion if he didn't want it. Roger piped in, too, informing the couple that the four of us were with Mr. Carter. Cher cackled a bit, charmed by our audacity, and invited us to join their movable feast.

We crossed to the other side of the train and crowded around their basket. As we munched on the gourmet snacks, we told the couple about our adventures in New York, censoring out the illegal parts in deference to Mr. Carter. Cher was duly impressed by our work at the paper, especially the abortion scandal, to which she uttered a hearty "Right on!" After seeing how much we could impress other adults, Mr. Carter lightened up a bit and started enjoying himself. He took a sort of parental pride in the four of us that would have been unthinkable five days before. He seemed to sense that something about us had changed. We had all aged, or more appropriately, we had finally caught up with the ages that we already were.

With great flourish, the Prince opened a large bottle of wine and offered Mr. Carter some. To our shock, Mr. Carter accepted and took a full Dixie cup. The Prince then offered me some. I looked over at Mr. Carter, expecting a look of disapproval, but instead he seemed pleased by the idea and said why the hell not? There was a great deal of laughter as the Prince passed three Dixie cups in our direction and filled them with a twist of his wrist. Barry declined at first, citing an uneasy stomach; but when Raul (who whispered, so as not to disturb the civility of this event) called him a lightweight pussy, Barry meekly asked Cher for another cup, his face breaking out in his trademark blush.

We all raised our Dixies in a circle, toasting their new marriage. Mr. Carter wished them a long, happy life together. The Prince said, "All righty!" with an exclamation point. Cher said, "Cheers," as she created a little tinkling noise with her bracelet to substitute for the dull sound of paper cups bumping into each other. After I took a sip, Roger turned to me, winked or blinked, smiled broadly, and made a toast to New York City. This time, I blushed.

It was official. There we were, adults sitting on a train drinking wine with other adults, who had actually *provided* the stuff. And the strange thing is that, unlike in our previous encounters with illegal liquor, none of us were barking, farting, yelling, or puking. We just sat there sipping, like regular human beings. Despite all the odds, some sort of maturity had seeped into us. For me, something else had seeped in: a growing awareness of love as an emotion and not some sort of juvenile joke. Simply put, Roger had seeped into my life, and into my heart as well. But I don't have the time or space to get into that. It's a whole different story.

It's the story of my life.

Crossing Lines
Judd Powell

FROM THE NOVELLA *CROSSING LINES*

Forrest's parents had moved to the trailer park before he was born, and it was the only neighborhood he had ever known. When he was very small, he had heard his mother refer to her "home on wheels" as if the trailer offered some advantages over other home owners. "Why, we could just up and go anytime we wanted to!" But even at that age, Forrest had come to recognize a tone in his mother's voice, a lofty, false quality she often used when she talked to those outside the family. When only Forrest and his father were within earshot, she spoke of the trailer in her real voice. "When are we going to live in a real home like respectable people?" That was the question he had heard at least once a week since birth. Sometimes muttered at the sink while she washed the dishes, sometimes shouted at the top of her lungs during one of those "discussions" she often had with his father. Yet, all the muttering and shouts had made little difference. Forrest and his family had lived in the same spot for the entire seventeen years of his life.

Forrest had had a few friends in the trailer park when he was growing up, but for whatever reasons, by the time he reached his teens, most of them had moved away. The children in the park were annoying to him, and the adults were too strange, at least the ones he knew anything about. Most of the adults had jobs of one kind or another and were gone during the day. As far as he could tell, their nights were spent like zombies, sitting beside their radios, slowly drinking themselves into stupors.

There were a few exceptions, however. Miss Upthegrove was the soloist at the Congress Avenue Church of God, and a zealot of the first order. When she wasn't slipping pamphlets under the trailer doors, she was stationed at some corner downtown, "spreading the Good Word." Hortense Hammer, on the other hand, had been a high-class hooker at the Read House in Chattanooga, Tennessee, if the trailer park gossip was to be believed. "Gospel truth!" swore Ann Durkin, the busiest body in the trailer park. "She'd probably still be there if her looks hadn't started to go. Management asked her to leave. That's what I heard. God's truth!" Why Hortense chose to relocate to a run-down trailer park in south Florida was a mystery to all— even Miss Durkin. Yet, almost nightly, Hortense could be seen slipping through the archway at the front of the park and sashaying off in the direction of downtown.

Then there was Mr. Mueller. Even with her exceptional skills, Ann Durkin was unable to come up with a single bit of gossip about Mr. Mueller. He was German—she was "pretty sure of that, just from the name"—but that was the limit of her knowledge. All of the kids in the trailer park were convinced Mr. Mueller was a Nazi. Their imaginations pumped up by the old newsreels they had seen at the Florida Theater, the kids quickly put two and two together. German subs had been spotted off the Florida coast, hadn't they? Despite warnings from their parents, they would peek in his windows at night and make up elaborate stories about what they had seen inside—Nazi uniforms, flags with swastikas in the center, maps of Florida with red pins stuck in them, and so on.

Forrest always enjoyed the children's stories, particularly the frenzied enthusiasm with which they were told, but what he did not care for was the way the kids would squeal with laughter and scatter in all directions whenever the man would emerge from his trailer. Had he been a few years younger, Forrest might have joined in the fun, but at seventeen, he was old enough to see the hurt in the old man's eyes. So he began taking the kids aside and explaining to them that what they were doing was mean-spirited. They laughed in his face at first. One of them even called him a Nazi sympathizer, a term he must have heard his father use. But in time, Forrest's remarks seemed to drain the fun from the game, and the kids turned their attention elsewhere.

Forrest could remember clearly when Mr. Mueller had moved into the park ten years ago. Although he couldn't have been more than seven at the time, Forrest had been impressed by the size of the silver trailer that was pulled into the park that day. It was several feet longer and wider than the other trailers in the park, and almost too long for the space allotted to it. He had hidden behind a nearby trailer and watched as the huge silver form was maneuvered into position. The owner, a very tall man with white hair and pale blue eyes, paid no attention to the faces that appeared in the other trailers' windows, and said very little to Mr. Durkin, who had come by to say hello.

During the first few years of his residency, neighbors would occasionally invite Mr. Mueller for coffee or to play bridge, but he always turned them down. Eventually, the invitations stopped, and Mr. Mueller was allowed to live the hermit's existence he obviously preferred. Every few years, there'd be a renewed interest, and someone, usually Miss Durkin, would attempt to spin a few stories about him, but the rumors wouldn't hold. For the most part, he was left alone. He was frequently seen—watering his plants, or picking up his mail, or on his way to the local market—but he was never spoken to. He was not open to conversation, and so he had none.

Being a loner himself, Forrest felt some kind of kinship with Mr. Mueller. Aside from reprimanding the children for their insensitivity, Forrest would sometimes criticize the adults for their prying impulses. Once, he told Miss Durkin that whatever Mr. Mueller was or might be was "none of your business, or anyone else's." Incensed by his insolence, Miss Durkin had gone directly to Forrest's mother to complain. When he refused to apologize, his mother slapped, then hugged him, then decided to forget the whole incident.

Forrest often felt that the trailer park was just one big unhappy family. There was little more than a few feet between the back of one trailer and the front of the one behind it. As a result, it was almost impossible not to know everyone else's business. Every fight his mother and father had (and fights were a nightly ritual in his trailer) could be heard by anyone in the park. The insults and accusations echoed off the sides of nearby trailers and shot across the courtyard and through the windows of the trailers on the other side. Sometimes, Forrest felt like everyone lived in one long, U-shaped trailer, each family separated from the next by paper-thin walls.

Forrest tried to spend as little time as possible in his family's trailer. It was not a place of comfort or safety for him. Never had been. In his earliest memory, which sometimes flashed in his head, he is lying up in his bed (could it have been his crib?) looking up at his parents' faces leaning into each other from opposite sides. There is no sound with the memory, but the faces are twisted up with rage. By the time he was talking, he was being asked to take sides, but he quickly learned there was a price to pay for favoring one parent over the other. Out of self-defense, he developed a kind of radar, a sixth sense, for when a fight was about to break out. He trained his ears to detect the first traces of an edge in his father's voice. The surface of his skin became like a finely tuned instrument that responded to the slightest rise in the emotional heat of the room. He eventually became adept at interpreting signals and escaping the trailer before he could be drawn into the battles. He'd slip out to the screened-in front porch and wait there for the fight to reach its peak and descend into an ominous silence. While he waited to see if the silence was a genuine conclusion or just a lull in the battle, he'd stand there staring into space through the mesh of the screen, trying to see a future beyond the chaos of his family.

After a few minutes of the silence, his mother would usually join him on the porch. She'd stand there beside him, not speaking, staring off into the same uncertain future. Sometimes that's all it would be—mother and son choosing to feel the quiet, appreciate the peace—but other times, she'd want to talk. She would begin in an even, measured tone, but as she put words to her frustration, her voice would rise, and the words would catch in her throat as the tears began to flow. Forrest would rub her back and murmur sounds of agreement, until her emotions crested and her breathing returned to normal. Once he had made the mistake of suggesting a divorce. She had turned on him with a fury that startled him, her eyes full of rage and fear.

"Now, what kind of a question is that, Forrest Powell? Divorce?! I can't believe my ears. Have I ever mentioned such a thing?"

"No, ma'am."

"No one in *my* family has *ever* been divorced. That's a fact. And I won't be the first. Do you hear me?"

"Yes, ma'am." He could not bear the naked emotion in her eyes, so he looked away.

"Divorce is a sin against God. *God* put your father and me together and that's that."

"But you don't think God wants you to be this unhappy, do you?"

"It's not my place or *yours,* young man, to imagine we know what God thinks. The vows said 'for better or for worse' and that's what they meant."

"I know that, Mom, but it just doesn't make sense. If—"

"God's will doesn't have to make sense."

Forrest knew better than to challenge that statement, so he fell silent. His mother, however, was not finished.

"And despite what you think, your father is a good man." Although the volatile discussion of divorce might have pushed this discussion off down a new path, it was now returning to familiar territory. It was time for the listing of his father's virtues.

"Your father is a good provider, Forrest. We don't have a lot, but what we do have, he is responsible for. And I'm grateful for that. I wish he didn't drink so much, but thank the Good Lord, he doesn't cheat on me. He comes home every night. Some men don't. And he never hits me. Your father has never hit me." She was running out of steam as well as virtues. She took a deep breath and then looked down at the concrete floor of the porch. Then, without lifting her eyes, she continued in a quiet, almost childlike voice. "And what would become of us, Forrest...if he wasn't around? What in the world would we do?"

She had done it again. Despite his resolve to be a rational, objective voice in these discussions, he was caving in. He turned to her. "I just want you to be happy, Mom."

She looked up at him and smiled. "Oh, don't you worry about my happiness. I'm fine. Just fine." She pushed his bangs off his forehead with her fingers and touched his cheek. "I'm a lot better off than some people I know. And so are you!"

"Right, Mom."

Like a dance routine that allowed for improvisation, Forrest would follow his mother's lead in these discussions. Although new steps were sometimes introduced, they always led back to the same old samba. If it were not for the fact that his mother drew some strange comfort from the dance, he might have abandoned it long ago.

★

One night, following one of their talks, Forrest was too restless to return inside, so he said good night and ventured out for a midnight stroll. He was walking along the lane where it stretched across the back of the park when he spotted Mr. Mueller beside his silver trailer. He was bent over in the moonlight, examining the leaves of a rosebush that climbed the latticework at the end of his trailer. Forrest stopped about ten yards away and watched the German man tenderly handle each leaf. Sensing someone nearby, Mr. Mueller looked down the lane. He showed no sign of fear when he saw Forrest standing there. Rising to his full height of over six feet, he locked eyes with the teenager. Forrest suddenly felt like a Peeping Tom. He was shifting his weight from one foot to the other and trying to concoct some explanation for standing there when the older man spoke.

"Roses—they need special care."

Forrest was surprised not only by the quality of his voice, which was warm and deep, but by the fact that he spoke English so well. There was a slight accent, but the words were quite clear.

"So I've been told, sir," Forrest replied.

"It takes more than watering, you know. You must watch them carefully...and groom them."

The words were all familiar to Forrest, but colored as they were by the accent, they sounded almost new. He thought of Tyrone Power or Claude Rains in one of those war movies set in Europe.

"I see, sir," Forrest said.

"No, you don't. You're too far away. Come over here and see what they look like more closely."

Forrest could not make his feet move. He was probably the first person in the trailer park to ever have a conversation with the man. He glanced down the lane behind him to see if anyone was watching their exchange. No witnesses. No one would believe this had happened. Finally, his feet responded, and he moved to within a few feet of the latticework.

"You're still too far away, young man. Come see what roses look like in the moonlight."

Forrest edged a little closer, once more looking down the lane behind him.

"You see how perfect these leaves are. Each one a little different, but each one perfect. Like snowflakes in that way, *ja*? And the bloom itself...is that not perfection?"

Forrest nodded. He had never looked so closely at a plant.

"Here, touch the petals." Carefully avoiding the thorns, the older man bent a branch in Forrest's direction. Forrest gingerly touched a petal.

"It won't break. Slip your finger down inside the petals. Feel the softness. Smell it. Bend over and smell it!"

Forrest did as he was instructed. It did not occur to him to resist. The petals were cool and soft between his fingers—moist. The rich, musky aroma brought a smile to his face as he inhaled it. Forrest had smelled roses before and touched them, but he had never savored the fragrance, never allowed his fingers to linger over the sensual texture that was a rose petal. He returned to a standing position to find the older man's eyes fixed on his face.

"You're different from the others, aren't you?" Mr. Mueller asked.

Forrest was a little confused by the observation. He took a moment before he responded.

"Sometimes I think I am, sir. Sometimes, I'm sure I'm not."

"*Ja*, I know what you mean."

The older man smiled at Forrest, and Forrest found himself smiling back, but a silence ensued and Forrest began to shift his weight from foot to foot again. The older man broke the silence.

"I'm Helmut, and you can call me that instead of 'sir,' if you don't mind. What's your name?"

"Forrest. I'm Forrest, sir."

"Helmut. I'm Helmut."

Forrest was confused for a moment, then felt himself begin to blush.

"Right! Right! Helmut."

"You'll get used to it," Helmut said, chuckling to himself. "Forrest. Nice name. Unusual."

"Yeah. Can't say I ever met anyone with your name either."

Helmut nodded. Another silence. Forrest broke the moment this time.

"Well, I think I'll just continue my walk. Thanks for showing me your roses."

"You're most welcome. Enjoy your walk and come back anytime, Forrest."

As he moved down the gravel lane back toward the front of the park, Forrest felt Helmut's eyes following him. He was both flattered and frightened by the attention.

★

During the next few weeks, Forrest saw Helmut once or twice but always from a distance—crossing the courtyard or heading off to the market. One afternoon, while sitting on the porch with his mother, Helmut walked up the lane past them.

"There goes weird old Mr. Mueller," his mother said.

"What's so weird about him?" Forrest asked.

"Oh, you've heard what they say about him. Cold. Unfriendly. Too private. Miss Durkin's convinced he was a spy during the war."

"And who told her that?"

"I don't know. She didn't say. You know Miss Durkin...she may have made it up."

"So why do you believe that stuff?"

"Who said I believed it?"

"Then why repeat it?"

"I don't think I like your tone, young man! Are you calling me a gossip?"

"No. I just don't know why people say the things they do. Nobody knows anything about the man, so they just make things up. It isn't fair."

"Well, I stand corrected, Saint Forrest!"

"I didn't mean it like that, Mom."

"And what do you mean? You know something the rest of us don't?"

"No. Not really. I just think he's probably okay. Not so weird. Just different."

"And how would you know?"

"We've talked."

"Well, you'd be the first, then. About what?"

"Roses."

"Roses? Well, howdy do. Roses, Forrest?" His mother was genuinely surprised.

"Yes. He knows a lot about plants and things. He was all right. Not weird. Not really."

His mother shifted into her parent tone.

"Well, I think that's sweet, Forrest. He's probably very

lonely, living in that trailer by himself all these years. It's good to spend a little time with older people. It means the world to them, and you might learn a thing or two."

Forrest turned away from his mother. Focusing on the courtyard through the screen door on the porch, he pretended to be interested in the shadows the palm trees were casting on the concrete. He made a mental note: Do not discuss Helmut with your mother.

✪

A row of Australian pine trees defined the back edge of the trailer park property. When he was much younger, Forrest would start at one end, climb to the top of the first pine, allow his weight to lean the treetop into the second tree, leap to the second tree, which would lean into the third, and so forth, until he had ridden the row of pines from end to the other. His mother would have "tanned his hide" had she ever seen this, but he was careful to keep this his secret. His mother would never have understood that the danger of it, the risk of injury, was part of the thrill.

But as Forrest grew older, the trees, of course, grew as well, becoming thicker and more flexible. By the time he was a teenager, they were completely unsuitable for riding, but the now-sturdier top branches were perfect as perches. From his favorite perch, Forrest was high enough to see over the low buildings that made up downtown, past the rippling water of the inlet, and beyond the estates of Palm Beach—all the way to the horizon,. where the ocean met the sky. Watching the world from up there helped him let go of things. He was high enough to not hear the radios blaring or the kids squealing or the parents fighting.

He would sometimes haul a sketch pad up the tree with him and draw whatever caught his eye. The Florida sky was a favorite, if difficult, subject. The most he could ever hope to capture was a quick impression, because the clouds would change faster than his hand could sketch. The clouds were always forming and dissolving, grouping and regrouping, billowing up to crowd out the sun or flattening out to disappear. When a storm was gathering over the ocean, the show was even more dramatic—great fluffs of whiteness folding in on themselves, growing dark, and reexpanding into ominous black masses. In fact, he was madly trying to sketch out an approaching storm when his second encounter with Helmut occurred.

Helmut had placed all of houseplants on the tiny patch of grass in front of his trailer to soak up some direct sunlight. When he saw the sky rapidly growing black, he began to rush about the yard, rapidly scooping up his plants to spare them the damage of a heavy storm. From his perch, Forrest could see the rain coming up fast. Realizing Helmut could never retrieve his plants without getting soaked himself, Forrest decided to help. He descended the pine and raced over to Helmut's trailer.

Without saying anything, Forrest picked up two plants and headed toward the trailer door. He almost ran head-on into Helmut, who was emerging. Helmut's eyes widened in surprise, and they both froze for a split second, then brushed past each other to continue their rescue mission. To get all the plants to safety required several more trips for both of them. Soon, however, they found themselves facing each other across the small expanse of Helmut's living room, smiling and waiting for their breathing to return to normal. Forrest's gaze dropped to the floor at his feet; then to his left and right, then he turned in a complete circle and began to laugh. Every available inch of floor space was, at the moment, occupied by some kind of plant, and the air was thick with the smell of damp earth.

"I feel like I just stepped into a greenhouse," he remarked.

"*Ja,* sometimes I think I *live* in a greenhouse," Helmut replied.

"Why so many?"

"Why *not* so many?"

"Where do they all go?" Forrest asked.

"Well, if you have the time, I'll show you. Here, give me a hand."

He handed Forrest a huge fern and pointed to a hook above the kitchen window. They continued in this assembly-line fashion until all the plants were in the proper places—the larger ones in corners, smaller ones in rows on counters and shelves; some hung from hooks on the ceiling, others had places on ornate metal stands. When they were finished, Forrest stood in the middle of the room, smiling at the effect. The room felt warm and lush, nothing like the starkness of his own home.

"You're soaking wet, aren't you?" Helmut asked. "Take off that shirt, I'll be right back."

"No! No…" Forrest began, but Helmut had already disappeared into the bedroom. In a moment, he returned. He had replaced his own wet shirt with a gray bathrobe, tied at the waist. Over one arm was a white towel; a wine-colored silk robe was draped over the other."

"No, really, I…" Forrest protested. "I'll be all right. I'll change at home."

"Nonsense!" Helmut replied with an edge to his voice that stilled any further protests. Helmut's directness, coupled with his age, made Forrest feel passive and child-like in his presence. Helmut continued, "Take off that shirt, dry yourself with the towel, then put the robe on to keep yourself warm. You were very kind to help me. This is the least I can do."

Forrest did as he was told. He pulled the wet cotton shirt over his head and dropped it on the floor, but quickly retrieved it when he saw the look of reproach in Helmut's eyes. Helmut then took the shirt and handed him the towel. As Forrest dried his hair and upper torso he was aware that Helmut was watching him very intently. Forrest was not ashamed of his body. In fact, he had spent a good deal of time in front of the mirror lately, feeling both surprise and delight with the changes in his body. The pudginess he had carried with him as a boy had become a lean muscularity during the last few years. The dark hair that now fanned out over his upper chest was a particular point of pride. Even so, he was not used to this kind of scrutiny. He glanced up at Helmut and gave a self-conscious smile. Helmut returned the smile and spoke.

"You're a shy one, aren't you?" Forrest did not reply. "You mustn't be. Your body is beautiful. Here, put the robe on."

Helmut turned sharply and headed for the kitchen. Forrest was grateful for his departure; the compliment had caused his face to flush. As he slipped his arms into the cool silk sleeves of the bathrobe, gooseflesh rose on his back and upper torso. He thought of his mother's nightgown and her hugs at the doorway on school mornings.

Helmut's voice came from the kitchen. "It's a little old,

that bathrobe, but it will keep you warm. Have a seat. I'll make us some tea."

Forrest chose the wide leather chair in the corner of the living room and eased himself into it. It creaked with his weight, and he heard a whoosh of air escaping from somewhere. He ran his hands along the smooth surface of the chair's wooden arms and gazed around the room. Aside from the plants, there was a tall bookcase filled with leather-bound books at one side of the door that led outside, and a very old phonograph (the kind with the horn) sat on top of an ornately carved cabinet to the right of the door. A big floor radio (like in the Montgomery Ward catalog, Forrest thought) was next to the phonograph, and another cabinet, which extended from floor to ceiling and reflected light in its black lacquered surface, was angled to serve as a partition from the kitchen and living room. To Forrest's right as he sat in the leather chair was a high-backed sofa covered in a dark blue fabric that seemed to absorb the light. Its cushions were deep and plush and three small pillows, made from the same fabric as the sofa, were arranged at each end. On three sides of the room, the trailer windows were covered with red velvet curtains, which, when drawn, would undoubtedly close the place off from the rest of the world. There wasn't a lot of room to move around, but, to Forrest, the room definitely felt elegant in an old-world European way. Like a painting, he thought. His mother would love this room.

By this time the tea was steeping, and Helmut had returned to the room. Standing by the phonograph, he addressed Forrest.

"Would you like some music?"

"If you would," Forrest answered.

"I think I might enjoy it."

Helmut switched on the phonograph and knelt in front of the cabinet. Opening the doors in front, he began to thumb through the stack of records.

"Since it's still pouring outside, let's see if I can find some rain music. Hmm." One record seemed to meet his requirements. He picked it up. "Ah, yes. Perhaps a little of the *Ring* cycle would do it."

Helmut placed the record on the turntable, carefully positioned the needle, and the dramatic sound of Wagner filled the narrow space of the trailer. He then returned to the tiny kitchen and poured two cups of tea.

"Cream and sugar?"

"Yes, please."

In a moment, Helmut emerged from the kitchen carrying silver tray with two cups of tea. He placed the tray on the coffee table in front of the sofa and handed Forrest's cup and saucer to him. Forrest fumbled with the cup and saucer, the clatter of the china giving away his discomfort. He couldn't decide whether to hold the cup and saucer in his lap or take a sip and return it to the table. He lowered the china toward his lap, but finding no flat surface, he moved the cup toward his right knee. Realizes that was a poor choice, he considered the arm of the chair. No, the cup and saucer would slide back toward his lap. He had decided to return the china to the coffee table when he realized he had forgotten to take a sip. Abruptly pulling the china back toward his mouth, he watched the tea slosh over the lip of the cup. He suddenly felt Helmut's eyes on him, and a flash of shame moved through his chest and colored his face. He had given himself away; he was completely out of place in these elegant surroundings. His hands began to tremble, and once again the china clattered, adding to his embarrassment.

"You're trembling. Are you still cold?" Helmut asked.

"A little," Forrest lied.

"Well, I can help with that," Helmut responded. "Here, give me your tea."

Forrest was relieved to surrender the noisy china but quite surprised by the next development. After Helmut had returned the cup and saucer to the tray, he knelt in front of Forrest. Placing Forrest's left hand between the palms of his hands, Helmut began to rub gently back and forth. Forrest was startled by this sudden intimacy and pulled his hand away.

"Don't be frightened, Forrest. I won't hurt you. If I rub your hands, it will warm your whole body. I learned this as a little boy in Germany. Let me show you."

Without waiting for permission, Helmut pulled Forrest's hand back between his palms and resumed the massage. This time Forrest did not resist. Helmut became very focused on the activity and continued for several minutes in silence, alternating between Forrest's left and right hands. Forrest's discomfort began to slowly ebb away. Although he had not been cold, the gentle massage of his hands was having its effect. He closed his eyes and gave in to the pleasant sensations that moved up his arms from his hands and spread across his torso. In a few minutes, the sensations began to gather in his crotch. In a matter of seconds, his penis began to swell, stretching up against his lower belly and pushing against the fabric of his jeans. When he looked up he could see that Helmut had noticed this change as well. He knew he should pull his hand free and make some excuse to escape the trailer, but he did not move. When Helmut released Forrest's hand and began to slide his own hand along Forrest's inner thigh, there was an even stronger impulse to escape; but once again, Forrest ignored it. When Helmut's hand reached his lower belly, and the warmth of the palm radiated right through the denim to the underside of his penis, Forrest dropped his head against the back of the chair and sucked air into his expanding chest. He held his breath for several long seconds, and with its release, he could feel the last traces of resistance dissolving.

★

Following school the next day, Forrest dropped his books on the porch and headed directly for his perch. Once he was comfortably situated, he gazed out toward the ocean and let his mind drift back through his sexual history, such as it was. Before his boyhood friends moved away, Forrest had engaged in what he thought of as sexual play. He and his friends would show their "things" to each other, comparing sizes and shapes; sometimes, they'd even masturbate together. Although none of them was old enough to actually climax, they had a great time pretending to. They called it their "sex club" and their only rule was that you could not tell anyone, especially your parents, about it.

This continued for a few years, but then most of those friends moved away, and the club disbanded. In the years that followed, although it never happened in any organized club-like fashion, Forrest and Eddie Palm (the one who was still around) would occasionally get together. Eddie would invite Forrest for a sleepover, and they'd wind up showering together, and that usually led to masturbation. But now that they were older and puberty had set in, the routine had changed. It would always begin as a competition (who had the most pubic hair? whose hard-on was bigger?) then quickly escalate into verbal fantasies about specific girls— Paula Weiss, the girl in English class with the big tits, or Ellen "Red Snapper" Korn, the redheaded majorette with the long, long legs.

As Forrest reflected on this from his pine tree perch, it all seemed fairly normal to him. He figured most boys had done the same stuff growing up. Sure, the sex club members were fascinated with each other's private parts, and yes, sometimes they touched each other, but all that stopped when the club disbanded. And, yes, he and Eddie watched each other closely as they competed to see who could ejaculate first, but they never touched each other. They were teenagers, after all, and there were unspoken rules. Even though Forrest had often been naked with other boys, it was never about that. It was about girls. And it was just playing around. So why had this happened...this thing with Helmut?

Forrest was a virgin, as far as girls were concerned, but he never really worried about that. He knew he'd get around to that sooner or later. He suspected that some of his classmates had "done the deed," as they liked to say, but he wasn't sure. He knew most of them were lying about their sexual prowess, and he considered it a point of pride that he never tried to bullshit anybody during those gym class bragfests. When asked, his reply was always "Not yet." He'd have to ignore the snickers that would always follow his reply, but it seemed a small price to pay. If he lied like the others, he'd be forced to provide details, adding more lies to the first one. He never wanted to get in that deep. Besides, he wasn't worried. All in good time, he told himself.

He had *never* had a sexual fantasy about a man; he was sure of that. Cheerleaders in short skirts, teachers with open blouses, movie stars in bikinis, the model with the torn slip on the cover of a crime magazine—those were the images that filled his head when he masturbated. So why had this happened?

He could have stopped Helmut at any point. That's what bothered him. Once Helmut's hand had started moving up his thigh, he knew what the old guy was after. He really couldn't have been forced into it; he was younger and stronger. No, there was no force. He *chose* to let it happen. What did that mean? Was it normal to get an erection when your hands were being massaged? Would any guy respond that way? He kind of liked Helmut, but he wasn't attracted to the guy. He *knew* that. So, how had this happened? Why had Helmut chosen him?

✪

Forrest avoided Helmut for weeks following their encounter. He couldn't imagine what he would say to him; his thoughts and feelings were a hopeless jumble. One minute he'd be trying to shake off the edgy discomfort he felt when he thought about what had happened; the next minute he'd be considering whether he'd like it to happen again. Disturbing images from that afternoon often floated across his mind: Helmut's red, sweaty smiling face; his own fumbling with his pants in his rush to cover himself and get out of the trailer; Helmut struggling to his feet, pulling his robe together, and pleading with Forrest to "stay for just one more cup of tea." Yet, following those troubling images would come a flood of sensual memories—the wet warmth that had surrounded his penis, the tingling that had spread out across his chest and danced down his legs, the explosive flash of energy at the last moment. Would it feel that way with a girl, too?

Forrest knew that he would not be able to avoid Helmut forever, but he put their eventual meeting far into the future. Helmut was certainly not on his mind when Forrest stopped by the trailer park mail room. And when he saw Helmut struggling to lift what was obviously a very heavy package, he could have backed out the door unseen. But he did not leave. He stood still and waited for Helmut to see him. When Helmut finally gave up his efforts to lift the box and rose from his kneeling position, his face was flushed and beads of sweat stood out on his forehead. A startled expression swept across his face when his eyes locked with Forrest's. They stared at each other for a long moment before Helmut spoke.

"Well..." he began, but he had to stop to catch his breath. Pulling a handkerchief from his back pocket, he wiped his face and then took three deep breaths before continuing. "How are *you*?"

Forrest did not answer at first, focusing instead on the beads of sweat as they rolled down Helmut's now-scarlet cheeks. He chose to ignore the feeling of pity that welled up inside of him. "Okay," he finally said, shifting his attention to the tops of his sneakers and shoving his hands into the pockets of his jeans.

"I asked my sister to send over some books," Helmut continued. "They're rather rare, actually. From the family library. And here they are. Never dreamed they'd be so heavy, though!"

Forrest heard the unspoken request behind Helmut's words but chose not to respond.

"I was thinking of dragging the box back to my trailer, but that would certainly damage the books, and I don't want that. They've come all the way from Germany, after all, to this little trailer park. It would be a shame to have them ruined now. Don't you think?"

Forrest refused to take the bait. "Dragging might work," he replied, shifting his gaze from his feet to the sunlit lane outside the door. After a moment, he heard Helmut's exasperated sigh.

"Would you mind helping me, Forrest?"

Forrest noted the rush of pleasure he felt when he heard the pleading tone in Helmut's voice. It was a small victory, but he relished it.

"No, I don't mind. I'll help you." Forrest crossed the small room, knelt, and slipped his hands under one end of the box. "Let's go."

It was about a hundred yards to the far corner of the trailer park where Helmut's trailer was situated. The box was, indeed, heavy, and they had to stop every fifty feet or so to give Helmut a rest. By the time they had reached Helmut's trailer and gotten the box inside, they both needed to sit down and catch their breath. Forrest flopped into the leather chair, then immediately felt uneasy with his choice. Helmut smiled at him from his place on the sofa.

"Thanks for your help. I don't know what I would have done."

"You're welcome," Forrest replied, as he stood and crossed to the door.

"Wait!" Helmut said, rising quickly to his feet. "You can't leave without seeing the books."

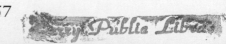

"Thank you very much," Forrest answered, "but I can't stay. I've got lots of things to do."

"Oh, but you must see them. They are truly beautiful books with exquisite illustrations. Like nothing you have ever seen. I promise you."

"No, I really—"

"Come!" Helmut interrupted. "At least help me open the box. It'll only take a minute."

Forrest's brief moment of being in control had slipped away from him. He knelt on the floor with Helmut and began to pull at the cardboard flaps on the top of the box. The staples holding the flaps together gave way, and Helmut began digging inside. Shortly, he pulled out a large leather-bound book.

"Is this not beautiful, Forrest?" Helmut asked, sliding his hand across the embossed leather front of an edition of *Grimm's Fairy Tales*. "Please touch it."

Forrest ran his fingertips along the bottom edge of the cover where the images of vines and flowers had been pressed into the leather.

"Have you ever seen such a book?" Helmut asked. "This is a very famous edition. And look inside...the illustrations are beyond compare!"

As Helmut flipped through the pages, Forrest watched over his shoulder. The vibrant colors and startling images of the illustrations grabbed his eye.

"Wait! You're going too fast!" Forrest was surprised by the urgency in his own voice.

"Well, here," Helmut said, placing the book in Forrest's hands. "Sit down and go through it at your own speed. I want to see what else is in the box."

Forrest slid into the leather chair once again and slowly

began to thumb through the heavy text. He thought of his own fifth-grade trip to the Norton Art Gallery downtown. He had wanted to linger then, to study all of the colors and faces in the paintings, but the other children were bored and already thinking about the ice cream that was waiting in the courtyard. They whined and sighed and jostled each other, until the teacher lost patience and ushered them all outside. Although he wanted to return to the library, somehow he had never gotten around to it. Now, here he sat, feeling the weight of the book against his thighs, smelling the musty pages as they passed under his nose, and drinking in all the color and detail of the images. He dwelled on the illustrations of grotesque ogres hiding behind gnarled tree trunks and of pale, innocent children walking along stony paths.

"Tea?" Helmut's voice broke the spell.

"Huh?" Forrest mumbled.

"I've made us some tea," Helmut said, placing the tray on the table next to the sofa. Forrest glanced at the tea, then brought his gaze back to an illustration. Was the former scene going to replay itself? He began to trace the image of a gnarled root with his fingertip. Helmut watched his finger move along the page for several moments before he spoke again. "I used to get lost in those pictures myself...when I was a small boy. That's why I wanted to have the books. Took a long time to track them down. My sister had to sort through the family tree to locate them. It seems some cousin had claimed them for himself."

Helmut took a deep breath, as if he planned to continue what would be a long story, then released the breath and grew quiet instead. He studied Forrest's face.

"You've been avoiding me, haven't you?" he finally asked.

Forrest closed the book and met Helmut's eyes with his own for the first time since they had entered the trailer.

"Yes," he replied.

"Because of what happened before?"

Forrest broke the contact once again, returning his attention to the book in his lap. He began to pick with his fingernail at one of the vines embossed in the book's cover. Finally, he spoke.

"Yes."

"That doesn't ever have to happen again, you know." Helmut watched Forrest's face for a response. He wanted to look into the boy's eyes, but Forest would not give him that, so he settled for his profile, waiting to interpret the smallest change—a tightening of the mouth, a furrowing of the brow. Seeing nothing, he continued. "I would be happy just to have your company."

"Thank you," Forrest said after the briefest glance in Helmut's direction. "I'll think about that."

There was no sex that day or even the suggestion of it. They sipped tea and talked about art for the remainder of the afternoon. At one point, Forrest admitted that he sometimes liked to sketch a little, and Helmut confessed that he often watched Forrest climb to his place in the tree and labor over his sketch pad. The conversation flowed easily after that, but in spite of the earlier promise, Forrest kept expecting Helmut to make some kind of advance. He never did. Later, when Forrest reflected on this, he couldn't decide if he was relieved or disappointed.

Two Left Feet
Jane Summer

Red was Miss Sydney's color. Red knit dresses with a flamenco ruffle, a short of shiver, at the hem. Shawls the color of cherries. Lipstick like sweet red peppers. Pumps as dark as the dried blood my dad buys to keep the garden rabbit free.

The moment she appeared at the head of the classroom, we knew Spanish 101 was going to be a different sort of high school class. I don't think it's wrong of me to say that all of us were eager for the third-period bell to sound. What we had been used to was teachers who only took a good look at you if they were about to throw an eraser at your head.

Our English teacher wore ridiculous baby-doll dresses and a spun-sugar beauty-parlor hairdo. She reminded me of the nouns *tuffet, toadstool, cupboard, lavatory*. Out-of-use words, pitiful words. Mrs. Prudhorn.

For history, we had Mrs. (though everyone knew she was a divorcée) Catherine di Matteo, who hastened through the hall in Chanel suits and shoes never worn more

161

than once. She was in love with the Virgin Mary, who still hadn't helped her to quit smoking, and gabbled on and on about the Virgin's influence on European cathedrals, which none of us, being from this Ohio farm town, had ever seen.

Mrs. Ethelane Mustee, our gym teacher, formerly of the U.S. Olympic gymnastics team, never let us play ball. Just gymnastics—somersaults, vaulting over the horse, the parallel bars, the balance beam. Most of thought it was no fun and somewhat hazardous. Fearing the snap of my neck, spending my last living moment on a mat rank with the sweat of feet, I tried every excuse to get out of class.

Then there was the gym teacher's husband, our science teacher, in his dreary tweeds. Morton Mustee. Mr. Mustee had a limp from the war, so our gym teacher drove the Mustee car. We thought it the strangest thing, seeing her—the woman, the wife—maneuver their Chevrolet out of the parking lot and then drive on home, wherever that was, with Mr. Mustee looking like a shrunken head in the passenger seat. Every time I'd see him, I'd remember the egg experiment, where he took this big glass jug in which he'd create a vacuum by heating it over a Bunsen burner. Then he'd place a hardboiled egg, peeled, at the mouth of the jug and whap! Without warning the vacuum sucked the egg right through the jug's skinny neck. Mr. Mustee seemed surprised by the class's sudden good humor. I wonder how he got the egg out every year.

Add to the menagerie Vodachek, assistant principal and math teacher. None of us understood her English, few understood her math, but the symphonic feeling of the class was one of sympathy. It just works that way, the liking a class takes to a teacher for no good reason. For me, I suppose things turned in her favor when I noticed

Mrs. Vodachek's slip showed every time she plotted a parabola on the blackboard, and I realized she must have her own sorrows. But feeling pity for a teacher isn't the same as liking her.

We were twelve in Miss Sydney's class. A year before her arrival we had signed a petition to have the school add Spanish to its language program. Our mothers initiated the petition. More and more of our migrant help was coming up from Mexico and someone had to be able to communicate with them. But to tell you the truth, many of us had heard that trying to learn German and Latin, which the school had offered since our parents' time, would kill us.

All of us grew up in the central plains, leveled by glaciers I had seen in my daydreams. Nothing takes Ohioans by surprise, though we remain an optimistic people. Our state motto is, "With God, All Things Are Possible." The absurd thing is, even those of us who don't believe in God still believe in possibility. Doesn't mean we're broad-minded. In fact, it's best to be ordinary round here. Shotguns have mutilated many of God's children in this town, including the retard who used to hug strangers and the Negro, Mr. Jamison, who came back from Columbus with a college degree. Mr. Jamison got shot in the eye the day after he opened us a library. These are the conditions under which Miss Sydney walked into our classroom, her smile as generous as our imagination of the Mediterranean. We knew she was doomed.

None of us spoke of it. Not in the beginning. We were too captivated to face the truth. You have to understand that all our other teachers had been in the school for so long—some had even taught our grandparents—that they were practically inanimate, unchanging, like the sports trophies in the display case outside the principal's office. Miss Sydney, however, was flesh and blood. The minute she stepped into our classroom, the temperature rose, as if we *were* in Guadalajara or Madrid.

She probably wasn't even much older than we were, though it seemed she had lived many fascinating lives, which she kept inside her like quintuplets. She came from gypsies, we surmised from the gold hoop earrings she wore, her wavy hair that brushed past her shoulder blades, that huge smile in which a student might lose her way. She even had a guitar she sometimes brought to class on Fridays. Someone said she came all the way from Los Angeles. Or at least that had been her most recent address. In those days, traveling east was a bad omen. Sensible folks went west, west to catch the surf, west to retirement, west to flower power. Or to the west side of town, to the state capitol, with political aspirations. But all that went east was the freight train and the bad wind that would chew up all the crops.

My ma warned me about eastward travel. "You can't fight destiny," she'd say. She thought New York was a myth, Boston for eggheads, Washington full of charlatans. If I were ever to leave the land, she counseled me, "There's Chicago— we have kin there." Kin? Only immigrants journey toward kin! And then she'd warn, "Remember Walter Schmidt," and my father would utter some snide grunt-like thing. "He's taking charity from the church, that Walter Schmidt, while his wife works her nails to the bone at the Agway."

Schmidt was my best friend's father. When we were in seventh grade, he deserted his family for New York. He was going to make it big in the sausage business, but he never sent his address and someone said he took soup, bread, and blessings from a church, though he'd always cursed at God as long as I'd known him, and that was since kindergarten. There I'd be, in the top bunk of my best friend's bunk bed, giggling my head off at her father who was downstairs at the kitchen table, drunk as a slug in a beer barrel, screaming the nastiest things about Christ, throwing the salt and pepper shakers at the cat who wanted only to love his trouser leg. And then, the snotty weeping. "Ma, Ma, I'm so sorry," he'd say, and my best friend would pretend to sleep through it all while I'd end up hoping he'd fumble his way up the stairs and start a fight with us so I could throw the fire ladder out the window and escape in the moonlight.

Because our town was populated with families who'd trekked west from Europe—Germany, Norway, and Russia—eastward travel was a sign of a downfall, the final journey. "Man was made to follow the sun," father said, his full sentence for the day. "What Father means..." my mother began.

But that was just talk. Old-fashioned stuff. By 1968 people were traveling every which way. Hell, you could even buy a ticket on TWA in the morning and by the after-noon be cracking coconuts on a beach somewhere.

I couldn't imagine her on the Los Angeles freeway. Most anyone can learn to drive, even nose-in-books poets (I think they make the best drivers, seeing everything all at once), but Miss Sydney was too easily enchanted to be able to downshift, pass on the left, and keep her eyes on the asphalt. Miss Sydney was distractible, like a fuzzy-headed newborn. Driving a car seemed totally out of her element. Clearly, she'd materialized in our class from another world, from the royal court of Aragon, from an Andalusian bullring, from a pod of cacao in the Mexican plateau. With God, anything is possible.

By the time we'd gotten far enough in our textbooks to learn the past tense, we were all under her spell. We confided in her, laughing at the other teachers, and in jest and perfect Spanish I taught the class how to roast a pig. In return, she brought us records of Peruvian mountain music, slides from her dusty travels, enchiladas and flan (not homemade, she said—she was not to be trusted in the kitchen, which we found strangest of all). We scrutinized her slide shows for a peek at her boyfriend or maybe even her mother, but there was no one, just mariachi men and kids in costumes. Maybe she was a Miss, but she was certainly not a spinster. Unattached, she became for a short while an object of our affections.

She must have seen in our faces the gift she was offering, the alternate language, the words with which to say secret things. I know some classmates struggled with it, but for me, Spanish was a treasure chest of jewels, avocados, paella, black mantillas, Salvador Dalí, Bunuel movies. A world of privacy.

Ohio wasn't for her, and we knew she wouldn't be with us for long. Maybe she was hiding from a jealous lover, maybe from the law. One thing about which we were certain was that unlike any other teacher we ever had, Miss Sydney enjoyed teaching us. How do I know? For one, she smiled, she came into the classroom like sun breaking through clouds. What we had known of teachers was that they suck on bitter pills and buy sensible shoes, Hush Puppies, while she wore espadrilles and fashionable high heels.

✪

But things began to change when she infringed on my dreams and I found myself sitting in class in my ratty old nightgown or even naked, having completely forgotten to dress myself for school. And when I *did* get to school after a dream like that, I took it out on Miss Sydney. I became untouchable. After a while I no longer raised my hand. I despised her flowing honey hair, the sweet smell of coffee on her breath, the tender bones of her ankle, her kindness.

And then she made the terrible mistake of teaching us about idioms.

Miss Sydney sat on her desk in that red knit dress of hers, her long legs accented by her high-heeled shoes the color of cayenne, and explained the concept of vernacular speech. She was wearing her hair loose, like a flamenco dancer at the end of the night. She told us, in Spanish of course, that while living in Mexico she attended a party, *una fiesta,* in the town square. There was music, *música,* and candy, *dulces,* and beer, *cerveza,* and lots of great good cheer. Someone asked her to dance but she, sitting under a pink paper light, had to refuse, explaining, "*Tengo dos pies izquierdas.*" All of a sudden the man, startled, stepped back. There was a murmur among the crowd as the word spread. Everyone crushed near her, staring down at her feet, horrified. The music stopped. Children began wailing. Women covered their eyes with their shawls. Men shuddered. Cats screamed. Bats flew off. The church bell tumbled out of its tower. The trolley ran off its track. "I have two left feet," she'd said.

When she explained that that was just an American expression denoting awkwardness, the party resumed, though at a lower key, and the children in the crowd still pushed their way through the legs of the adults to look at the American woman's feet.

The class was silent. Horrified. She shouldn't have told

us that story. We were repelled by the intimacy of it. But by
the next day, my classmates were back to the easy way they
had been with Miss Sydney. Not me. I was changed irrevo-
cably. Had I fallen in love? Or had I fallen in hate?

I wasn't the only one. Ask any one of my former classmates. They'll remember her. I know. At our high school
reunion, where all the perfect girls had turned into hags and
all the boys who had been called "Faggot!" were stunningly
attractive, I asked. Everyone remembered Miss Sydney.

"Do you still have that scar?" the kid she called Esteban
wanted to know. As did Diana, Pablo, Juana, Miguel,
Bernardo, and Elena. Our sweet Spanish names, our code
names.

Miss Sydney had brought a piñata to celebrate spring
and, blindfolded, we all took swipes. I, who was not accus-
tomed to hitting things, needed a little direction. Miss
Sydney put her hand on my shoulder as she steered me
toward the frilly swaying horse, and the next thing I knew,
Elena, always an overachiever, was throwing lemonade at
me trying to put the fire out.

Bernardo had been the traitor, Bernardo, who couldn't
roll his R's. He told the principal Miss Sydney was a witch,
that it was her hand that caused the fire. Everyone else—
Esteban, Diana, Pablo, Juana, Miguel, Elena—told the
truth, said I got burned when the piñata came down,
pulling the overhead light with it, starting the conflagra-
tion. But Bernardo insisted, offered to take a lie detector
test, and one thing led to another, and parents raised their
voices at the school board meeting, and we protested in
front of the school in our bell-bottoms and fringed leather
vests but it was to no avail. The accusations went from
witch to lesbian to child molester, and then my own father

sided with Bernardo's dad (who happened to be our sheriff) and the school board because he thought he'd get some money out of it.

And so the pyre was lit.

Vodachek of all people stood up for Miss Sydney. But she wasn't effective, maybe because few people could understand her point through her accent. I complained of the injustice of it. I wrote a letter to the school board. I played hooky and moped about. Then I threw away my barrettes and grew my hair like Miss Sydney's and lost my language. "Snap out of it," my dad said, disgusted. "And while you're at it, pass the potatoes." But I wouldn't snap out of it, and I wouldn't pass the potatoes. I went deeper into my loss, mirroring my father's betrayal, trying to get him to throw his boots at me. "*¿Quiere Usted las papas?*" I asked him. "*No comprendo íngles.*" "Please, honey," my mother pleaded. "You know we don't understand any of that Spanish." But I continued. "*Las papas, el agua, su postre, mis padres.*"

One day I found the switch, the on-off to my father's temper, and he cracked his dinner plate over my head. It wasn't as noble as I had anticipated, egg noodles in my hair, but it was good enough, and there was plenty of blood from the minor head wound. There I was, the Martyr of Miss Sydney, telling every doctor and nurse and candy striper in St. Joseph's Hospital how the "accident" happened and why. And that was worst of all for my dad, because it was the truth I told them, that my parents had ripped out my heart because it belonged to the woman in red. And they all listened to my whole story.

Mostly, I told the details in case anyone knew something of Miss Sydney's whereabouts. No one ever did.

My dad ran out of the emergency room and took off in our old heap, leaving me and my mom in the hospital. We had to take the bus home. We were having one of our enormous Ohio thunderstorms. "Shall we forget all about this now?" she said, moving ever so slightly away in her seat as the lightning tore open the night, and my dad's efforts at sowing dried blood from the slaughterhouse got washed away in the downpour.

The scar on my shoulder and the three stitches at my hairline tell me who am I and for whom I am looking.

Happy Birthday
Nan Prener

I met Willie on my birthday. I consider it the best present I ever got.

It was at the Fieldcrest picnic, only last year, but it feels like five years ago. I was a baby then, though I didn't know it. I was sixteen. I thought I was fully grown, because I felt above everyone and everything around me.

All of my friends were vying for titles—Best Dressed, Most Witty—that kind of thing. To me it was childish to put on a show for others. I had drawn the curtains around my act when I was ten.

I was a private person. I spent a lot of time in my room, devoting myself to high-quality art and mathematics. I was very grown-up.

I sat apart from others whenever I could. I liked a perch, a spot from which I could watch the goings-on.

That sunny Saturday, I sat cross-legged on a stone wall a few feet away from a blanketful of kids.

I knew most of them. We all went to the same school, and it wasn't that big, but I didn't know the person they seemed to be gathered around. Sitting on one corner of the blanket, his arms wrapped around his knees, was someone I'd never seen before.

His dark hair, parted in the middle, swung down on both sides of his face. He kept pushing it back as he talked. He spoke quickly, as if he had a lot to say and not enough time to say it. He was talking about mushrooms.

"The destroying angel is beautiful," he said. "Pure white. A temptress. The deadly amanita."

As he said this, he looked up at me, seated at the edge of his audience, and winked. It was a big wink. Everyone saw it.

I pulled back into myself. I'd been caught acting interested. I was never interested in anything anyone my age said. I was interested in learning—what could other kids teach me?

I suppose I was something of a prig. I spent my time with books and computers and didn't do much socializing. I was there at the picnic only because it was practically in my backyard, and I liked to observe people.

That's what I told myself. Now I wonder if I wasn't a little afraid of them.

From the other end of the field, there was a call for volleyball. Enough people abandoned the blanket to break up the crowd, and Willie was left with three girls.

Stretched out on their bellies, I could tell from the angle of their necks that their eyes were concentrating on his. They probably didn't know, or care, what he was talking about. After a five-minute mini-lecture on snakes, they picked themselves up and, as a trio, marched off to watch the volleyball game.

Willie stood and sauntered over my way. I was surprised to see him coming in my direction.

As he came close, he stuck out his hand. He was only slightly older than me, yet he acted as if he'd never been a kid. We shook.

"Willie Oliver," he said. "And you're?"

"Grant Mosley," I answered. My voice sounded like it belonged in someone else. The adult handshake had done something to my vocal chords.

"Pleased to meet you," he said. "Are these people friends of yours?" He waved his arm to take in the entire picnic.

"Sort of," I said. "I live over there."

I pointed vaguely in the direction of my house.

"Oh, an invited guest."

"Not exactly. I came over the fence," I admitted.

He laughed. "I came over the mountain," he confessed.

"You did?" It was an hour's hike up and down the mountain. He nodded, and we both looked toward the bulk.

"What happened? Did your car break down?" I asked. There was a highway on the other side. The mountain was in a park, so there were no houses there.

"No. Chanterelles grow under the oak trees about halfway up. I thought I'd check them out, and somehow I just kept going."

"Did you find them?" I asked.

"A few. They were small and dried up. Take a whiff."

He unhooked a cloth bag that was suspended from his belt, and held it under my nose.

"Dried apricots," I said.

"Very good," he answered. "The fruity aroma of chanterelles."

"Can I see them?"

He opened the bag wider. Inside was a collection of leathery, orange, ruffle-edged inverted cones.

"So those are chanterelles," I said.

"Not to be confused with the poisonous jack-o'-lanterns, which are shiny and gelatinous," he informed me.

I thought about that for a minute. I was hungry for facts and the kind of conversation that revolves around them. I asked him how many varieties of mushrooms he had eaten.

"About fifty," he informed me.

"Fifty!"

"Well, not all of them here. We travel a lot, my family. I've tasted mushrooms all over the country."

We were walking now, heading toward the mountain, away from the festivities.

"What's the best-tasting one you ever had?" I asked.

"The best-tasting one was the ugliest. I found it about a hundred miles north of here. The old man of the woods, it's called. Black and bumpy outside. The inside is white. When you touch it, it turns red, then black. It was growing alone in the middle of a path through a hemlock forest."

We were definitely going up the mountain now. Our talk had become a game: a question-and-answer session.

"What's the biggest find you ever had?" I asked.

"That's a hard one." He stopped and kicked at a stone. "There was a huge chicken mushroom—orange-and-yellow-striped shelves—growing in the crotch of an oak tree. But I think what you mean was the eighty pounds of oysters I happened upon in an area that had been lumbered three years before. It was down in a gully, and at the very bottom, they'd left some trunks lying. They were covered…" He paused. "Positively covered, with big white fans. What a sight!"

"Eighty pounds!" I was trying to imagine it.

His eyes twinkled. "I lugged them up the mountain in big plastic garbage bags. Like Santa on the Fourth of July."

We had started up the winding path that led past the pool where people went skinny-dipping. There were two girls and a boy splashing water on each other. We ignored them, and kept on walking.

We got off the topic of mushrooms, and talked about snakes, cars, computers, goats, electricity, and music. I couldn't believe that he hadn't lived twenty years longer than I had. I had read, but he had *done.* He'd put together cars, built his own computer, raised goats and made mozzarella cheese, unofficially electrified the houses of friends, and played in a rock band.

He acted as if all these things took place in other lifetimes; as if they were as remote to him now as they were to me. There was something unsettling and exhilarating about his talk. His hands flew, his eyes bulged. He recited his history in terms of the objects he'd encountered and conquered.

For the first time since I'd been a little kid, I found myself anxiously hanging on each word. When we reached the top of the mountain, a pang passed through me at the thought of parting.

He seemed oblivious to the momentous goodbye. "Well," he said. "I guess this is it." Once more, he stuck out his hand.

I grasped it—too eagerly, perhaps. His eyes peered quickly and deeply into mine.

"Till we meet again," he said.

I couldn't leave it at that. My tongue stumbled all over itself and finally got out, "I've never met anyone like you."

He chuckled. "There isn't anyone like me," he said. "Thank God."

Then he grabbed my shoulder, squeezed it, and threw his other arm around me in a hug.

It was quickly over. He stepped back, gave me a long, questioning look, punched my shoulder, and started down the other side.

Love can make a fool of anyone, no matter how many books he's read, or how many computer programs he's personal friends with. I turned back down that mountain feeling like I could do anything.

And I did. I did the first dumb thing that presented itself. We hadn't seen any mushrooms on the way up— Willie had been disappointed. He wanted to show me some rudiments of identification, but it was a dry time. Even the chanterelles he'd found on the other side had dried while still rooted.

Now, as I came back down through the pines, my glance fell upon a solitary chestnut brown mushroom growing on a dead log. It was a perfect shape. I knelt and touched its velvety cap.

I have no excuse for being a jerk, but I can tell you how it happened. I saw that mushroom, and Willie and I were connected again. The mushroom was the verification of a bond between us. I had met a flesh-and-blood person who was interesting and varied as the ones on my bookshelves and disks.

I was moved to confirm the event, to symbolize our union. I was a first-class idiot. I plucked the mushroom and bit off half of it.

It tasted good. I stuck the rest in my pocket and continued down the hill.

Back at the picnic, the world had changed. I was no longer the same person. Or perhaps I just knew who I was.

I had told myself I didn't need a special relationship. But I had lied—I could see that now. It was true that I didn't want to join the social whirl, to woo a girl, to get caught up in the squabbles and strategies I saw my classmates involved in. But I had met someone whose company excited me, whose conversation gave me pleasure tinged with joy.

As I went back down to the throng, a feeling of empathy overwhelmed me. I thought I could feel the wants and desires of humanity floating toward me up on the hill. I waded into the sea of revelers.

I had forbidden my parents to put together anything resembling a birthday party for me. Now I felt like celebrating.

I went over to one of the tables, around which everyone had clustered earlier, and helped myself to a plate of shrimp salad, which I'd spotted before being shunned. Eating would have made me one of them. Suddenly, that's exactly what I wanted to be.

I felt a strange sensation in my face. When I got home and looked in the mirror, I saw what it was—I was smiling.

The house was quiet. I went gently up the stairs.

In my room, I surveyed my belongings through other eyes. I ran my hand along the spines of my books. I didn't turn on my computer. I wanted no competition for my thoughts. I lay down on my bed and closed my eyes, ready to sink into a semi-sleep filled with dreams of the future.

Instead, there was a disturbing pattern behind my eyelids. A field of broken color. A sheet of smashed glass. It moved downward, falling forever. A queasy sensation in my stomach seemed related to it.

I tried to change my position, but my shoulders and arms ached. I had walked up and down the mountain, but

I hadn't done anything with my arms, not even played volleyball. Eyes open, I turned my head, and the room spun. I closed them again. Colored globules swam sickeningly toward the center of my inner vision. *Poisoned,* I thought. *I've been poisoned.*

I remembered the mushroom. I was a moron! IQ meant nothing—I couldn't survive in the world. I was a stupid baby who couldn't be left alone in the woods.

What should I do now? I could lie there and die, or I could call for help. My parents would probably notice an ambulance coming to the house. I had to tell them.

I raised my upper body, preparing to stand. Nothing doing. My stomach and eyes combined in one nauseating wave that sent me crashing back down to the pillow.

I tried once more. My belly hurt. I couldn't sit up. This time fear grabbed me, and I bawled for my mother.

I hadn't called her like that in years. At last she came, and I felt a soothing hand on my forehead. I was a little boy again. Mommy would make me better.

But not unless I'd told her what I'd done.

"I ate a mushroom, Mom."

"You *what*?" I heard the shock in her voice, and saw the horror in her face. It increased my fear.

"I ate a mushroom, at the picnic."

She looked relieved. "Well, it's all right then. It was in someone's dish."

"No. No, it wasn't. It was in the woods."

"Stan!" she yelled. "Stan! He's been poisoned!"

"In my pocket, the rest of it," I said, a hero on his deathbed.

"Call Poison Control!" my mother shouted.

I heard my father's normal subdued tones from the

phone in the hall, but I couldn't hear what he was saying. I only knew it was being taken care of.

I didn't open my eyes when he came in. I heard his voice through the clamor of the shifting patterns in my mind, and the surge of sickness in my stomach.

"They've got a mushroom expert on call. They're trying to get in touch with him now. They'll meet us at the hospital."

My parents bundled me up in my blanket, and my father carried me out to the car. I thought about walking myself, but it got no further than a feeble wish.

The ride to the hospital was a blend of tension and calm.

I could be dying. Needlessly, for being stupid. It was a disgusting way to die, not being able to sit up straight, or look the world in the eye. There were flashing lights outside the emergency-room entrance. We pulled up alongside an ambulance. My father left the engine running, came around to the backseat, and hauled me out. A wheelchair was waiting at the curb. He dumped me into it. My mother slid into the driver's seat and drove the car away, while my father wheeled me in.

At the desk, he explained our situation. Poison Control had called to alert them. I was going to be taken to a room to have my stomach pumped.

I heard this through a veil. I was far from the outside world, my attention absorbed by the malfunctioning.

The door opened, and we all turned expectantly. It was only my mother.

A gurney rolled down the hall toward us. *The wagon to hell,* I thought.

I heard the door open behind me.

"Mr. Oliver," the receptionist said. "Just in time." I looked to see if my savior had come.

My eyes were playing tricks on me. What I saw was
Willie. He was carrying a satchel, like a doctor's bag.

He came to the desk. "Where?" he asked urgently.

"Right here," she said.

He turned his head and saw me.

"You!"

It was embarrassing. He had told me several times on our
walk not to eat any mushroom without checking it in the
books, and performing whatever tests were appropriate. I'd
been enthralled by his voice and had not heeded his warning.

"Where is the specimen?"

My mother opened her purse and took out a Baggie with
the evidence.

Willie examined it.

"What color was the underside when you picked it?"

"Yellow." It was burgundy now.

"Are you sure it wasn't red?"

I was sure.

He consulted two books, then set up shop on the corner
of the desk, taking two vials of liquid from his bag. He
broke off two pieces of the mushroom. Drops from one of
the vials turned the cap surface bluish green. "Iron sulfate,"
he announced. Drops from the other, which smelled like
ammonia, turned it green.

"Ammonia," he said. "It's a young bay bolete. I suspected as much, but I had to be sure. *Boletus badius*. Edible,
delicious," he pronounced. "You don't have mushroom
poisoning."

Our small gathering was shocked. I was obviously sick
from something. Was he sure? He'd bet his bolete on it, he said.

It was Willie who led the inquisition and uncovered the
hours-old, left-in-the-heat shrimp salad.

"But why didn't anyone else get sick?" I asked.

"They ate it when it was fresh," he said. "You waited till the end of the day."

Adding to my misery was the knowledge that I was not a fit companion to someone with so much sense. I'd felt scorn for everyone, and now I was the one who most deserved it.

"It was a dumb thing to do," he said, and I saw my mother nodding vigorously. "But at least you remembered what I told you about saving a piece."

He finished packing up his bag, "I think you need mushrooming lessons. When you're feeling better, we'll go out." My mother was still nodding.

The gurney had been parked. I was going to be allowed to recover naturally.

Willie shock hands with my father. My mother hugged him and kissed him on the check, as though he'd saved my life.

In a way, he had. My body was still sick as dog when it left the hospital, but my soul, for the first time, was healthy.

Just Like a Woman
Lesléa Newman

The screen door slammed behind Cassie, who winced before she realized with a jolt of relief that no one was home to yell at her. Her mother had taken the train into the city to go to a museum—she had signed up for some lecture series or something—and her father, the original Mr. Type-A Personality, had gone into the office even though it was Saturday. Cassie rummaged through what her mother had dubbed the "flotsam and jetsam" that lay on the kitchen counter—piles of mail, old newspapers and magazines, potholders, coupons, and other assorted junk—looking for the wallet she'd forgotten, while her best friend, Tammy, and her mother waited in the car. Mrs. Ryan was driving them to the mall, and they'd gotten almost halfway there before Cassie realized she'd left her wallet at home. Mrs. Ryan had been pretty nice about it, saying everyone makes mistakes, no big deal, that she didn't do it on purpose and blah, blah, blah, but Tammy had turned around to roll her eyes at Cassie in the back-seat and proclaim, "Parker, you are so pathetic."

"Oh, shut up, Ryan."

"Girls, this isn't the army." Mrs. Ryan glanced sideways at her daughter and then met Cassie's eyes for a split second in the rearview mirror. "Must you call each other by your last names?"

"Sorry, Mom," Tammy mumbled. Then she swiveled around again. "Cassie, you are so pathetic."

"Oh, shut up, Tammy."

Mrs. Ryan laughed. "That's much better."

Cassie ran upstairs, taking the steps two at a time, almost tripping on the laces of her high-tops, which were forever untying themselves. Maybe her wallet was in the "shipwreck" of her room, as her mother called it. Cassie's mom had seen *Titanic* at least a dozen times. "Don't you just love that Leonardo DiCaprio?" she asked Cassie whenever they were in Stop & Shop and saw his face on the cover of *People* or some other magazine.

"Mom," Cassie would groan and shake her head like her mother was the teenager and she was the...the what? Parent? Yeah, right. That was the last thing Cassie ever wanted to be, someone who spent all her time yelling at someone to do her homework, clean up her room, get off the phone...

If your room wasn't such a disaster area, you'd know where your wallet was. Even though Cassie's mother was a good thirty miles away, her voice was right here, yammering inside her head. She threw aside dirty jeans, inside-out sweaters, mismatched socks, candy wrappers, and comic books, all to no avail. Just when she was about to give up, she spotted her purple backpack sprawled sideways in the corner with all its contents spilling out like it had just been in a terrible accident. Cassie plucked her wallet from the debris along with an old orange baseball cap her mother had forbidden her to wear out of the house. She stuffed the wallet into the back pocket of her baggy jeans and pulled the cap down low over her short, slicked-back hair. One quick glance in the mirror and she was ready. But just as she was about to run down the stairs, she heard something. Music. Coming from her parents' bedroom. *Did Mom forget to turn off the CD player again?* Cassie wondered. They were both getting so forgetful lately. Mrs. Parker blamed it all on hormones.

"Our bodies are changing, sweetheart," she said to Cassie one night when her father was working late and it was just the two of them. "Girls' night out," her mother called it, even though they didn't go anywhere—just ordered a pizza and ate it off paper plates at the kitchen table. "I used to bleed for five, six days at a time, sometimes even a whole week, but now it's drip, drip, drip for half a day and then I'm through. Oh, well." Mrs. Parker shrugged her shoulders at Cassie, who didn't know what to say to this information about her mother, which was way more than she wanted to know. "I'm like the last rose of summer," Mrs. Parker went on, then paused to sigh dramatically, "while you, my dear, are just beginning to bloom." Cassie's mother studied her wolfing down a slice of pizza. "After we eat, I'm going to give myself a facial. Would you like to join me?" Her voice was almost wistful. "I've got some ripe avocados we could mash up. They're supposed to be very good for the skin. Or we could give each other manicures. Or—"

"When's Dad getting home?" Cassie asked, eager to change the subject.

"Don't talk with your mouth full, honey." If Mrs. Parker

couldn't get Cassie to stop being a tomboy, the least she could do was teach her to mind her manners. "Your father," she curled her lower lip inward, shook her head, and sighed again. "He's so afraid to leave that office if there's one thing left undone, if there's one last task he hasn't crossed off that never-ending list. He has to do, do, do like he's playing beat the clock with his own mortality." Mrs. Parker dropped her voice slightly, about to confide something else Cassie was sure she didn't want to hear. "There's definitely such a thing as male menopause, sweetie. It's not so obvious, since men don't have a period, of course. But they get cranky and moody, too, believe me. Your father's been acting very strange lately...I don't know what to do with him. The other night I—"

"May I please be excused?" Cassie was still a little hungry, but her need to end this heart-to-heart conversation she never wanted to have in the first place was stronger than her desire for another piece of pizza.

Mrs. Ryan gave the horn two swift toots, and Cassie hurried down the hallway. The door to her parents' bedroom was closed tightly, and Cassie hesitated. She didn't especially like going in there—that's where they did it, after all—but she knew she had to or she'd be the one to catch hell for leaving the CD player on, even though she hadn't been listening to it in the first place. "You were the last one to leave the house," her mother would be sure to say. Cassie turned the knob and opened the door gently, but before she could step into the room she saw something that froze her to the spot. Her father. At least she thought it was her father. Someone who looked an awful lot like him was sitting at her mother's dressing table, wearing one of her mother's long pink nightgowns with some sort of matching sheer pink jacket with lace at the collar and sleeves. Cassie blinked once, twice, as her mind reeled. *Mom's going to kill him for stretching out her clothes like that.* Then Cassie switched into logic mode. *Wait a minute. Those can't be her clothes. She's like a size two and he's almost six feet tall, not to mention a 180 pounds, besides.*

Then whose nightgown is that? Cassie wondered, though she guessed that didn't really matter. What mattered was that was definitely her dad, all pretty in pink with his face pressed up against the mirror like he couldn't get close enough to his own reflection. Cassie wanted to run, but instead she stayed put and watched her father outline his lips in a ridiculous shade of red, touch up his eyelashes with jet-black mascara, and brush his cheeks with a rosy blush until he totally transformed himself into...into what? A monster, a weirdo, a fucking freak.

"Hey, Parker, you coming or what?" Tammy called through the screen door.

Cassie started, like she'd been shaken out of a dream— or a nightmare—and then ran downstairs and out the door before Tammy could run up. Had her father heard them? She doubted it. The music was pretty loud, and her father was singing along. "I Feel Pretty" from *West Side Story*— both her parents were completely into Broadway musicals. My God, how corny could you get?

"C'mon, girls." Mrs. Ryan's patience was finally beginning to wear thin. "I haven't got all day."

"Sorry," Cassie mumbled as she slid into the backseat.

"I don't know why you girls can't just ride your bikes to the Fairview Mall like everyone else. It's a lot closer than Riverdale, and then I wouldn't have to drive you."

"Mom, I've told you a million times, the stores are better at Riverdale."

"You'd get some exercise while you were at it and—Cassie, are you buckled up?" Tammy's mother paused her hand on the ignition key, waiting to hear a reassuring click from behind before she started the engine. Mrs. Ryan had been in an accident last year, nothing serious, just a little fender bender, but ever since she wouldn't even back out of the driveway until everyone's seat belt was on.

"Sorry," Cassie said again, fumbling for her strap.

"I don't know why you care so much about the shops anyway, Tammy." Mrs. Ryan turned back to her daughter. "It's not like you ever come home with a pretty sweater or a skirt, God forbid. You too, Cassie. I know it would make your mother very happy if you bought yourself a nice outfit."

"Sorry," Cassie muttered for the third time. She knew Mrs. Ryan thought she was a bad influence on Tammy, who, until she started hanging out with Cassie, had kept her hair long and even worn a dress once in a while.

"What's with you?" Tammy flung herself sideways in the front seat so she could glare at Cassie, who usually bailed her out when her mother started in like this. They couldn't tell Mrs. Ryan the real reason they wanted her to take them to Riverdale—they could barely admit it to themselves—but Cassie was usually a lot more talkative and good at distracting Tammy's mother. Today she was no help whatsoever.

"You sick or something?" Tammy asked, narrowing her eyes at her friend.

"No," Cassie said, but her voice was caught somewhere down in her throat and came out in a little squeak.

"You okay, honey?" Mrs. Ryan stopped the car at a red light and turned to look at Cassie.

"Yeah," she said softly, then repeated it louder, "Yeah, I'm fine," in order to convince them.

Or to convince herself, because the truth was, Cassie wasn't fine at all. She felt sick to her stomach and a little dizzy, like she had just stepped off the Drop of Fear, a ride Tammy had dared her to go on at Six Flags a couple of months ago. The man running the ride had motioned to Cassie to take her place on a bench-like contraption, and once she was seated he lowered a metal safety bar around her that clicked into place with a loud, final clank. Then the man started the ride, and Cassie, along with eleven other brave souls, was raised up, up, up into the air before she could change her mind. The bench rose so high that Cassie had a great view of the entire amusement park, including Tammy, who looked no bigger than the microscopic whitehead she had popped on her chin that morning. The bench finally came to a standstill at the top of the ride, and just as Cassie relaxed, thinking, *This won't be so bad,* the bench plunged to the ground like a crazy elevator let loose from its shaft. Cassie's arms and legs flew straight up in the air as her body raced toward the ground. After the ride landed, she managed to climb down from her seat, but her legs were wobbly and her stomach was queasy the rest of the afternoon. Of course she hadn't told Tammy that; then she'd know she was nothing but a big baby. "It was great," she said to her, thinking that the Drop of Fear was exactly like life: Just when you think everything's going to be okey dokey—wham! The bottom gets dropped right out from under you.

Like today. What was up with her father? Was he sneaking out to a costume party? Was he some kind of pervert like those freaks who were always on *Jerry Springer*? But how could that be? Her father was normal. Her mother was normal. They were the most normal people around, so normal they were downright boring. Cassie was the weirdo, the freakazoid, the one who marched to the beat of a different drummer. But that was another story.

Mrs. Ryan pulled into the mall parking lot and stopped the car at the east entrance. "I'll pick you up right here at four o'clock. Does that give you enough time?"

"Yeah, Mom. Great. See you."

"You're welcome." Mrs. Ryan tilted her head and waited. Tammy leaned across the front seat and reluctantly kissed her cheek.

"Thanks, Mrs. Ryan." Cassie lumbered out of the car and walked with Tammy toward the polished glass doors of the mall.

"So what do you want to do?" Tammy asked once they were inside.

"I don't know."

"Want to get something to eat?"

"I don't care." A fresh wave of nausea swept through Cassie's stomach. The lights, the music, the stores, the people—it was all too much for her. "Can we just sit down for a minute?" She pointed to a bench next to a planter filled with artificial trees.

"What gives, Parker?" Tammy flopped down next to her and slung an arm around her shoulder.

"Hey, quit it!" Cassie jumped up as quickly as she'd sat down.

"What's with you?" Tammy frowned at Cassie, more puzzled than angry. "Nobody knows us here."

"I don't know. I'm just jumpy, I guess."

"Teenagers." Tammy shook her head in a perfect imitation

of her mother, which made Cassie laugh and relax a little. These mall excursions, while they excited her, also made her somewhat nervous. But she could never tell Tammy that.

They headed toward the escalators and rode down to the food court. Cassie wished she could tell Tammy why she wasn't herself today—*And if I'm not myself, who am I?* Cassie wondered—but this was a secret she wasn't ready to share yet, not even with Tammy.

They got two vanilla milk shakes and a large order of fries and sat down at a table to watch the shoppers stroll by. "Don't look over there." Tammy shifted her eyes to the left, and Cassie's head immediately snapped in that direction. "Hey!" Tammy grabbed Cassie's arm and Cassie yanked it away. "I said 'Don't look,' you dork. What's with you anyway?"

"I…" Could she say it? Tell Tammy what she'd seen? Or what she thought she'd seen? Maybe it had been a mirage, a vision, a figment of her warped imagination. But then again maybe it wasn't. "I have my period," Cassie finally said, taking the easy way out. "You know how weird I get."

"I'll say." Tammy picked up a French fry and traced a "W" for weird in the puddle of ketchup on the plate between them. "All right. They're gone anyway. Let's see." She swept the area with her eyes. "Ooh, over there. Three o'clock. The two with the pizza and the gigantic Sears box."

Cassie turned her head slowly to the left. "Where? I don't see them."

"You busy signal, that's because you're looking at nine o'clock. How many times do I have to tell you, twelve o'clock is straight ahead, six o'clock is behind you, three o'clock is to your right, nine o'clock is to your left."

"Okay, okay, I see them." Cassie studied the two women. "You think?"

"First of all, they both have short hair, and they're both wearing leather jackets, jeans, and work boots. Second of all, what do they have there? Some kind of appliance, right? An air filter, a toaster oven? I'd say they're members of the Pink Triangle Club. Definitely."

"I don't know. I guess so." Usually, Cassie was more into this game, and she knew she wasn't being fair to Tammy. It wasn't Tammy's fault that Cassie's father was losing his mind, and it wasn't fair to let that spoil her day. "Hey, look over there. Ten-thirty."

"Ten-thirty?" Tammy laughed, raised her eyebrows, and glanced to her right. "Where?"

"The babes with the Diet Cokes." Cassie didn't need X-ray vision to know what was in the giant plastic cups the two girls were sipping from. Girls like that always drank Diet Cokes.

"Are you out of your freakin' mind?" Tammy scowled at the girls, who looked maybe a year or two older than her and Cassie. The blond one wore an orange fuzzy sweater, low-slung faded jeans, and three-inch platform shoes; her dark-haired friend was all in black: an off-the-shoulder leotard tucked into a pair of skintight pants. Both of them had perfectly manicured nails and perfectly made-up faces and wore a ton of jewelry.

"You wish," Tammy said, popping a last French fry into her mouth.

"Yeah, maybe I do." Cassie stared at the girls—girls she knew wouldn't give her the time of day, with her short hair, oversize sweater, and ratty jacket and jeans.

"Hey, what's that supposed to mean?" Tammy asked in a voice full of hurt.

191

"Nothing. Hey, I have to go to the bathroom. Come with me?" Cassie softened her voice, giving Tammy the words she knew she'd been waiting to hear. Somehow it had been decided, even though they'd never discussed it, that Cassie would always be the one to give the signal. And so she did.

They stood up quietly, both of them in a hurry now, but nevertheless, each taking her time. Tammy put their milk shake cups one inside the other and wiped a smear of ketchup off the table with a paper napkin. Cassie made sure her wallet was secure in her back pocket and her orange cap was tilted at just the right angle while Tammy tossed the remains of their snack into a trash can marked "Please." Then without a word they rode the escalator up two floors and walked past a row of stores—The Gap, Victoria's Secret, Fashion Bug, The Disney Store, Waldenbooks, The Body Shop—until they came to their destination.

Cassie pushed open the door of the women's room, strode inside, and then stopped short at the sight of a woman leaning toward the mirror over the sinks.

"Oof." Tammy collided with Cassie, who stumbled forward.

Just our luck, on today of all days, Cassie thought. There was never anyone in this bathroom; it was so out of the way. *Never say never:* Cassie's mother's voice chanted in her head. And for once in her life she was right, because this woman was big as life, frowning at her reflection as she pulled at a clump of mascara on her eyelashes with her forefinger and thumb.

"Hey, this is the ladies' room." The woman turned to face them, a wand of mascara paused in midair. "You can't bring your boyfriend in here." Though the woman was staring at Cassie, it was Tammy she addressed.

"My boyfriend?" Tammy spat out the word. "What are you, blind?"

"Don't get fresh with me, young lady. Do you want me to call security?"

"Oh, for chrissake," Cassie mumbled. She reached up with one hand to whip her cap off her head like she usually did in these situations. But then she got a better idea. With both hands, Cassie ripped open her jacket, the snaps popping like tiny firecrackers, and flung her sweater up over her head, leaving her bare chest exposed for a good ten seconds before covering herself up again. "There. Satisfied?" she asked the woman, whose face was as red as the small stain of ketchup on the sleeve of Tammy's white sweater.

"Oh, dear, I'm so sorry. It's just with your short hair and your baggy clothes and that cap and all—"

"Yeah, yeah, yeah. Tell it to the Marines." Cassie motioned with her head, indicating for Tammy to follow her into the handicapped stall. No need to wait—the woman surely wouldn't bother them now.

Tammy bolted the door behind them, then fell back against it, laughing. "What's with you today, Parker? I can't believe you did that."

"I can't believe it either." A burst of laughter flew out of Cassie's mouth. It wasn't the first time she'd been mistaken for a boy—far from it—but it was definitely the first time she'd ever done anything like that before.

"Did you see her face? Oh, man." Tammy cracked up again. "Why didn't you just take off your cap? Or let her hear your voice?"

"I don't know." Cassie felt so weird today, she might do anything. "C'mere now." She shrugged off her jacket and laid it on the floor as she heard the door to the bathroom close. Alone at last. Tammy plopped down on Cassie's jacket and Cassie did the same. Both girls curled their legs under them so they wouldn't be automatically seen by anyone waiting to use the stall.

Suddenly, the bathroom got very, very quiet. Cassie looked at Tammy and felt the same ache in her chest she always did when they were finally together. It was this strange physical sensation, like her heart was getting bigger and smaller at the same time. Or like there was a hole in her heart that could only be plugged up by being as close to Tammy as possible. Cassie slowly took off her cap, then wrapped both arms around Tammy and hugged her as tightly as she dared.

"Hey." Tammy smiled and shut her eyes, waiting for Cassie to kiss her. Cassie let her wait a few seconds, then blew on her eyelids. Tammy's smile widened. Cassie always teased her like this.

"I missed you," Cassie said, tracing the softness of Tammy's cheek with the pads of her fingers.

"I missed you too," Tammy murmured, her eyes still closed. Cassie loved to look at Tammy, to study her, to drink her in. Tammy was so breathtaking, with her smooth skin, high cheekbones, and full movie-star lips. She wasn't a misfit like Cassie, not by a long shot. Even with her short hair and sloppy clothes, she would never be mistaken for a guy in a million years. No, if anything, Tammy could have any guy she wanted, but for some mysterious reason Cassie couldn't even begin to figure out, Tammy didn't want a guy. Tammy wanted her.

Cassie leaned toward Tammy and gave her tickling butter-fly kisses with her eyelashes. Then she rubbed Tammy's nose with her own and then, finally, placed her lips on Tammy's. A sweet little groan began at the back of Tammy's throat.

"Shh," Cassie whispered. "We don't want company, do we?"

Tammy looked up at Cassie with wide eyes and shook her head. Then she squeezed her eyelids tightly together, and in one second Cassie was all over her, kissing her and touching her with an urgency that was new and exciting. Almost dangerous.

"Cassie," Tammy breathed out her name, letting her know she was willing, more than willing, for Cassie to touch her everywhere. She let her unbutton her sweater and unhook her bra, and now Cassie did feel like the teenage boy she was always being mistaken for. With the soft lushness of Tammy's breasts under her hands, Cassie knew her life could end right now and she'd die perfectly happy. Tammy was running her fingers through Cassie's buzz cut and breathing quickly, and Cassie didn't care who heard them now. Anyone could walk in this very second and still Cassie wouldn't stop what she was doing. That bitch who was in here before, a security officer, the kids from school, Tammy's mother, Cassie's mother, Cassie's father...

At the thought of her father, Cassie felt something well up in her throat, and she pulled away from Tammy. She lay her head on Tammy's chest and felt her cool, smooth breast against her cheek.

"What's wrong, babe?" Tammy stroked Cassie's face with the flat of her hand.

Cassie let out a long, deep sigh. She didn't know what

was wrong exactly. So her father liked to wear makeup and lacy nightgowns. Big deal. Who was she to judge? If anything, Cassie should sympathize. After all, she knew only too well what it was like to look different, to act different, to want different things. *But that's different,* Cassie thought. *He's my father.*

"I just wish we could hold hands and walk around like everyone else, you know?" Even though this wasn't what was on Cassie's mind, it was true. "I mean, we have to sneak around in a bathroom stall, for chrissake. It's pathetic."

"I know, babe, but I don't care. And anyway, it's only till we're in college next year." Cassie and Tammy had applied to the same schools, and even if they both didn't get into their first choice—Antioch—they'd promised each other they'd go to schools that were, at the most, only an hour apart. "And besides, you can hold my hand if you want. Everyone thinks you're a boy anyway."

"I know, but it's not like I can relax or anything. I mean, I'm always afraid someone's going to catch on and then beat me up."

"My poor baby." Tammy continued to caress Cassie's cheek.

"Let's get out of here." Cassie sat up and buttoned Tammy's sweater gently, like her body was a sleepy child that needed to be tucked in.

"I have to pee." Tammy shooed Cassie out of the stall, and Cassie used the next one over. When they went to the sinks to wash their hands, the automatic faucet Cassie stood in front of didn't work. She moved to the next sink, but nothing came out of that one either.

"What the…?" Cassie thrust her hands into every sink but couldn't get a drop out of any of the faucets.

"What's the matter now?" Tammy came up beside Cassie and rubbed her hands together under a faucet. Instantly water rushed out.

"Hey, I thought that one didn't work." Cassie put her hands into the sink and immediately the water stopped.

"What are you, an alien?" Tammy asked, laughing.

"I guess so." Cassie frowned, and her chin quivered like she was about to cry.

"Hey, it's no big deal." Tammy put her hands back in the sink so the water would run for Cassie, but she turned away. "Hey," Tammy said again. "You are acting really weird today. Are you sure you're all right?"

Cassie nodded, not trusting herself to speak, afraid she'd voice the thoughts running through her mind. Was she an alien? Was her whole family from Planet of the Wackos? Cassie wondered if her father was gay, if that's where she got it from. But what would that make her mother? A fag hag? A lesbian? And did all this mean she could now tell her parents that she liked girls? She doubted it. They still asked her insane questions like "Any boys call lately?" and "Who's taking you to the prom?" It was so ridiculous. Look at me, she wanted to shout at them. Open your eyes! Your daughter's a dyke!

"You ready?" Tammy asked.

Cassie nodded again, reached for Tammy's hand, and just for kicks held onto it as they left the bathroom. This is what it feels like to be normal, she thought as they started walking through the mall. But as soon as she saw some kids their age walking toward them, she squeezed Tammy's hand once and then dropped it.

"What do you want to do?" Tammy asked, looking at her watch. "We still have about an hour."

"I don't know." Cassie said. "Don't you have to buy anything?"

"Like what?"

"I don't know," Cassie said again. It seemed that was all she ever said these days: *I don't know...I don't care...*

"Let's get a cookie," Tammy said, steering Cassie in the direction of the Cookie Shack on the other side of the mall.

"Okay." Cassie wasn't really hungry, but at least it was something to do.

They rode the escalator down one flight and fell in step with the rest of the shoppers: young mothers pushing babies in strollers, pairs of middle-aged women lugging enormous shopping bags, packs of teenagers teasing each other. As they passed Lord & Taylor, a woman in a white lab coat with a wicker basket slung over her arm accosted them. "Free makeovers today," she said in a singsong voice, handing Tammy a card.

"Get real," Tammy singsonged back, tossing the card over her shoulder.

"Tammy, I'm surprised at you," Cassie said, shaking her head. "Every woman can stand a little improvement." It was something Cassie's mother had said to her many times.

"Right this way." The woman extended her arm toward the store as if she were inviting them to enter the land of their dreams.

"C'mon, Tammy," Cassie said, heading inside.

"What are you doing, Parker?" Tammy couldn't figure out if Cassie was kidding or not.

"I'm getting a makeover, Ryan." Cassie slid onto a stool in front of a counter piled high with lipsticks and eye shadows.

"This I've got to see," Tammy said, taking a seat next to Cassie.

"Can I help you?" A woman with eyebrows that looked drawn with a black magic marker and bright fuchsia lips smiled at Tammy. She had a nametag that said CRYSTAL pinned to her white lab coat.

"My girlfriend," Tammy exaggerated the word as she gestured toward Cassie, "wants a makeover."

"Great." Crystal looked over at Cassie and paused. Cassie could just imagine what she was thinking: *Oh, shit, this'll be a challenge!* Or, *Christ, as if my day hasn't been hard enough.* But Crystal merely shook her head slightly as if to compose herself, smiled, and asked, "What's your name, honey?"

"Tiffany," Cassie said, removing her cap as Tammy burst out laughing. "Don't mind her," Cassie glared at Tammy. "She doesn't get out much."

"I see," Crystal said, two worry lines creasing her heavily powdered forehead. "So, Tiffany, do you want an everyday look, or is this for a special occasion?"

"She's getting married." Tammy folded her arms.

"Really? How exciting. Congratulations."

"Yep. Soon she'll be Mrs. Michael Williams," Tammy said, nodding. "Tiffany Williams. Tiffany Cassandra Williams." Tammy paused between each word and moved her hand through the air as if she were tracing the name on a marquee.

"That's lovely," Crystal said. "Can I see your ring?"

"Uh..."

"She left it at home. It's huge, and you just can't be too careful these days."

"Of course."

"Bite me," Cassie whispered to Tammy as Crystal turned her back and started rummaging through a drawer full of compacts and brushes. Michael Williams was the biggest dickbrain in their class. He was always busting Cassie's chops by making up little chants like "Parker eats pussy" and "Cassie is a lezzie" and singing them out whenever he passed her in the hall.

"I'd love to," Tammy said, clicking her teeth together and leaning toward Cassie.

"Now then…" Crystal turned back around and pushed up her sleeves like a woman who knew she had her work cut out for her. "You don't really need foundation, you have lovely skin. So, let's start with the eyes. They are the mirror to the soul, you know." She narrowed her own eyes at Cassie as though she were an artist appraising a blank canvas. "Let's try Spring Rain and Autumn Dew. That's usually a good combination for hazel eyes." She leaned toward Cassie and applied the eye shadow with a tiny foam applicator. "What do you think?" Crystal took Cassie by the shoulders and turned her toward Tammy.

"Just darling," Tammy said.

"Now, I think a dark eyeliner and mascara, don't you?" Crystal directed the question to Tammy as if she were some kind of expert. Somehow—and Cassie couldn't quite figure out how this had happened—Crystal and Tammy had become conspirators, and she, the one getting the damn makeover, was still the outsider. She remained silent as Crystal wiped, brushed, smoothed, and smeared gooey-feeling products all over her: cover-up, blush, pressed powder, and God only knows what else.

"And now for the finishing touch." Crystal uncapped a lipstick tube with a flourish. "This is the cherry on the sundae, the icing on the cake. It's called 'Just Like a Woman' and I haven't found anyone it doesn't look good on yet."

There's always a first time, Cassie thought and would have said out loud if Crystal hadn't been messing with her mouth.

"There." Crystal dabbed Cassie's nose one last time with a small foam sponge and stepped back. "Ta-da!" She whipped a big round mirror out from under the counter and held it up in front of Cassie. "What do you think?"

"Whoa." Cassie recoiled from her reflection, all the makeup in the world unable to hide the startled look in her eyes. *Christ,* she thought. *Even with all this stuff on my face, I still don't look like a girl.* No, in fact, Cassie looked more like a boy than ever—only now she looked like a boy who'd been caught red-handed playing with his mother's makeup. Jesus. Cassie shut her eyes for a few seconds, then opened them again, but her reflection remained the same. *Well, what did you expect?* she asked herself silently. *I'm damned if I do and damned if I don't.*

"It is kind of a shock, isn't it?" Crystal put the mirror back under the counter. "Makeup can do amazing things to a face."

"I'll say," Tammy chuckled.

Cassie remained mute as Crystal started putting her supplies away and launching into her sales pitch. "Now, Tiffany, if you don't want such a heavily made-up look for every day, you can just use lipstick, blush, and mascara. That's what I'd recommend for someone your age." Clearly, Crystal hadn't bought the wedding ruse for one second. "The mascara is $12, the blush is $15, and the lipstick is $10, so that would only come to $37."

"She'll think about it," Tammy said, hopping off her stool. "C'mon, Parker, wipe that shit off your face and let's go."

"Tammy." Cassie's voice was full of reproach. "I told you," she turned to Crystal, "she has no social skills whatsoever. Especially when she doesn't take her medicine." Tammy hung her head loosely from her neck, stuck her tongue out of one side of her mouth, and blew a spit bubble. "I'd better get her out of here before she starts to drool. Thank you very much." Cassie slid off her stool, took Tammy by the arm, and led her out of the store.

"What the hell was that about?" Tammy looked at her girlfriend, her head cocked at a questioning angle. "Oh, my God, Cassie, you look just like a woman...*not!* C'mon, let's go wash your face. We have to meet my mother."

"Why would I want to wash my face? Don't I look pretty? I feel pretty." Cassie started singing. "I feel pretty, oh, so pretty. I feel pretty and witty and gay." As Cassie sang out the word "gay," she flung her arms wide and raised her voice. People turned to look at her.

"Cassie, I think you're the one who needs medication." Tammy kept her head down as they walked to the east entrance of the mall. "Seriously, you're making me kind of nervous."

"Not as nervous as some people are going to be," Cassie muttered, opening the door for Tammy.

"What did you say?" Tammy raised one hand over her eyes and skimmed the parking lot for her mother's car. "She's late. Figures."

"There she is." Cassie nodded toward the green station wagon rounding the corner. She put on her cap, pulling the visor down over her face as low as it would go. "Don't want to give the poor woman a heart attack."

"Hi, girls." Mrs. Ryan barely glanced at Cassie as she

slid into the backseat, focusing instead on her daughter. "Where are all your packages?"

"They didn't have anything good."

"In the entire mall?" Mrs. Ryan frowned as she pulled away from the curb. "Tammy, you need some new clothes. You can't go around in the same pair of filthy jeans all spring."

"Okay, okay." Tammy turned away from her mother and stared out the window without saying another word until they pulled up to Cassie's house. "See you, Parker. Call me later?"

"Yeah, sure." If it weren't for the makeup, Cassie would have tipped her hat to Tammy, but she wasn't in the mood to deal with Mrs. Ryan, who would definitely say something if she saw what Cassie looked like. "Thanks for picking us up, Mrs. Ryan."

"You're welcome. Say hi to your mom for me."

"I will." Cassie shut the car door and they were gone.

Time to face the music. Cassie yanked off her cap and put it in her back pocket—no use having her mother yell at her for wearing it—and put her key in the door. She knew by the white Dodge in the driveway that her mother was home; she wasn't sure about her father since he kept his car locked up tightly in the garage.

"Hello-o-o," Cassie sang out as she stepped into the house.

"Is that you?" yelled her father.

"We're in here," her mother called from the kitchen. "Come help me make a salad."

Cassie walked toward her parents' voices and stopped in the doorway. Her mother stood at the sink washing a handful of tomatoes and her father was sitting at the table, his head buried behind *The New York Times*. Cassie knew without even looking that he was reading the business section.

"How was the mall?" Cassie's mother asked, as she moved from sink to cutting board, wet tomatoes in hand.

"Fine."

"Here, slice these up for—oh, my God, what happened to you?" Mrs. Parker froze, the knife she had just taken out of a drawer clenched in her fist like she was just about to stab someone. "Cassie, what in the world did you do to yourself?"

"What happened?" Mr. Parker put down his paper and looked up. At the sight of his daughter leaning against the doorjamb, his mouth dropped open. Cassie watched a sea of emotions wash over his face: disgust, anger, guilt, shame…or were those the emotions she was feeling?

"Cassie," he barked, his hand flying up to his own face. "How could you?"

How could I what? Cassie wanted to ask, but before she could get the words out her mother sprang back to life.

"You look just like your father," Mrs. Parker whispered, before turning to address her husband. "Are you happy now, Tootsie?" she shrieked.

"As happy as you are, Mrs. Robinson," Mr. Parker replied.

"What's that supposed to mean?"

"You know exactly what it means." Cassie's father slapped both his hands down flat against the newspaper. "Museum trip—yeah, right. You wouldn't know a piece of art if it bit you in the ass. Which is probably exactly what a certain young man is doing while I'm—"

"While you're what? Working?" Mrs. Parker laughed

bitterly. "Maybe I wouldn't have to go into the city every weekend if I wasn't married to a—"

"To a what?"

"To a…" Whatever Cassie's mother was going to say was swallowed up by a great big sob that burst out of her throat. Without another word, she brushed past Cassie and ran up the stairs.

"Honey, wait." Cassie's father dashed out after her without even a backward glance at his daughter.

Cassie heard her parents' bedroom door slam, and then the house was silent except for the loud humming of the refrigerator and the steady ticking of the kettle-shaped clock on the wall. *Shit,* she thought, letting her body sink into a kitchen chair. She put her arms on the table, rested her head on top of them, and shut her gunky eyes. What was going to happen now? Cassie had no idea. Was she going to get in trouble? She didn't know that either. She stood up slowly, and with a deep sigh stepped over to the cutting board to pick up the knife her mother had dropped. She sliced a tomato in half and then halved the halves and then halved them again. The rich redness of the fruit swam before her eyes as she realized with a start that she knew much less about her parents' lives than they knew about her own.

The Honorary Shepherds

Gregory Maguire

To satisfy that particular curiosity first: Yes, this is a story about two boys who sleep together. Eventually. Not genitally, or anyway not at the time of this writing. But focus, liberally as you like, on the picture of it. Two teenage boys on a single-size futon, under a fraying tangerine-colored afghan reeking of mothballs. Two boys. Naked, warm, scared. Unbelieving. Alive. Cautious. Too alert, too new to each other to giggle or wisecrack. They are both beautiful, at least to each other. The casting department of a film company might not agree.

Sex sells everything, even sex you disapprove of. That's why the image of the boys abed starts this story. It used to be stories could work up to such a development. But in the current day there's no time for the slow buildup. Notice how movie musicals are passé? Now we make do with three-minute music videos. Notice how the trailers they show at Cineplex 1-12 often are more interesting than the eighty-nine-minute feature film you've paid good money to see? In the future there will be no movies, only coming attractions. No symphonies, only advertising jingles. No novels, only short stories. Maybe only postcards. Vignettes.

The camera is about to leave this opening vignette, and not return, so take it all in while you can. The afghan slips off in a manner suspiciously gratifying of our natural voyeurism. The strictest moralists need not be alarmed— both boys are lying on their stomachs. Their naked legs and behinds, the hollows of their backs look like honey in the strengthening dawn light. Both of their necks are turned so their faces can look at each other, at close range. Three inches apart. Two inches. One.

Cut.

★

The younger of the two boys is Lee Rosario Kincaid. Not to get overly schematic, but he is the thinker of the two. The older, Pete Blake, is the gutted, trembling one. Between them they represent the gene pools of four continents. Lee's family is Puerto Rican, Polish, and Irish. Pete's mom is Chinese and his dad is, was, an American black from western Africa, Gambia probably, all those troubled generations ago. It's the melting pot thing carried to absurdity, but it's true. Full-blooded American boys. These things happen.

Lee Rosario Kincaid has thrown a scarf around his neck and drawn the afghan up to his armpits. His shoulders are white, like the porcelain on old faucet fixtures. He tells Pete Blake about his background:

It's pure U. S. of A. It's like *West Side Story II*. That's how I imagine it. The story of my life. Start in 1959. Remember Tony and Maria in the movie? After the rumble, after Tony the Polack kills Maria the Spic's brother, she runs to Tony anyway—in true love? But Tony gets shot. Maria catches the falling hero. Love should be stronger than hate. Across their ethnic differences, true love. It's great.

When they showed that movie at Dunster Institute, at an assembly, everyone laughed, except the girls. (Some of the girls did laugh, harder than the guys.) Next day a black kid from the housing project got knifed in the locker room. So much for tolerance.

Here's what happened next, though. As I imagine it. Maria is pregnant from her one ecstatic wedding night with Tony. What do you think "One Hand, One Heart" was all about anyway? This was pre-AIDS, and people didn't have condoms in their pockets and pocketbooks all the time. They made love. Tony and Maria. I hope it was wonderful because it was Tony's only time.

Maria's family sends her back to Puerto Rico to have the baby. Rita Moreno has to go, too, to chaperone her. She is bored the whole time. Doing hot tamale dances with big white teeth clicking like castanets for an eight-months-pregnant steamboat— that's not how she cares to spend her time. The baby is born, though: they name her Antonetta. That's my mom, who really is half Polish and half Puerto Rican. A little bit of Hispanic-Polish bacon. Maria sings "There's a Place for Us" to get the baby to go to sleep at three in the morning.

Momma and baby go back to Manhattan's West Side. They're tearing down the slums to build Lincoln Center. Antonetta grows up hated for being part Polack. She can make galumpkes like the best of them, though.

At a bar in Queens in 1975, when she's sixteen, Antonetta meets up with Brendan Kincaid, an illegal immigrant from County Cork, Ireland. A couple of beers too many, and not having learned the family lesson, Antonetta conceives me. Brendan, however, being Catholic, marries her on the spot. Grandma Maria, by 1975, has gotten dumpy and is still trailing around Lincoln Center in that same virginal white dress. (She's had to have her seamstress friends take it out at the sides three times.) She misses Tony still, but she curses her daughter Antonetta for having made the same mistake she did.

But contrary to all cautionary tales, Antonetta and Brendan are happily married. They get a better deal of it than Maria and Tony did. Nobody shoots Brendan. He turns into a good father, moves the little family to Poughkeepsie, starts his own roofing concern. He's pretty happy.

Until the day he learns that his only son, Lee Rosario Kincaid, is gay. Then he begins to wish he'd used a condom sixteen years ago.

Pete Blake laughs at this story—the kind of laugh that has a knowing wince knitted all through it. He's not sure what parts of this are true, but there sits Lee Rosario Kincaid across from him in his bed, a face as grim as Churchill's. Lee has the turnip-like forehead of the Irish, a complexion of scalded milk like the Polish, and dark hair, rigid in its iron curls, like the Puerto Ricans. Lee thinks he is hideous. He isn't good-looking, it's true, except in love: but he is striking.

✪

Pete Blake is gorgeous, but doesn't know it.

He can't tell Lee his story in so dramatic a fashion. It comes out in sentence fragments, reservations, ellipses, breathy hesitations. Lee finally pieces it together as such:

Pete Blake's mom is from Boston's Chinatown. His dad is from Mattapan, a ghetto-grim place to be from and hard to get out of. Religion never entered into their story, at least not to hear Pete tell it. They got married. Pete's dad was a professional soldier, not a draftee, and he didn't get killed in Vietnam, but died in a jeep crash in the Philippines in 1976. His mom went back to live with her Chinese-speaking family above—you guessed it—a dim sum restaurant.

Pete is part black, part Chinese. His mom's family hates him for looking so black.

His dad's family had loved him, but that was before. They were a small family and they died off. An uncle got shot in a gunfight. A grandma died of grief, or obesity, or both. A cousin got a scholarship to Princeton and left and never came back. Pete would go wandering around the littered sidewalks of Mattapan where his black grandma had lived, missing her. His mom, whom he loved, had little time for him.

South Boston High was full of racial trouble. Pete, taking a clue from his cousin's escape, got the guidance counselor to do some work for a change. Pete Blake applied to Dunster Institute, a fancy private high school in upstate New York. A boarding school. He got in. Full scholarship.

His mom was pissed. His Chinese relatives were relieved and gave him money on the sly to ensure his departure. Pete had never stopped being a mighty shame to them, those sensual Negroid lips, that very un-Asian fanny that stuck out like a bumper on a car.

The color. The browned oak-leaf color. Unacceptable. Shaming.

Pete Blake didn't have so much of a problem being gay because he'd hardly had time to realize it yet. It was being neither Chinese nor black that bothered him. He was so twisted up inside about it, too, that he had no idea how tormentingly handsome he was.

He would probably learn, and in the sad—or maybe lucky—irony of it, he would figure it out only after his beauty had begun to fade.

★

This story has a plot, and here it goes.

Lee and Pete are just meeting each other for the first time. It's a film seminar, senior elective. The class consists of fourteen kids. Some brainy girls who dress in black and never smile. The usual three or four girls who take any course Pete Blake takes, because he smites them so with true lust. A couple of jocks who mistakenly think a film class will be easy sailing and boost their grade-point average (it won't and it doesn't). Pete, of course, always looking for images of himself to relate to. And Lee, who is a junior but his good grades permit a few allowances, like entry into this class.

The plot is not about how Lee and Pete meet and fall in love, or only tangentially so. They're both still a bit in the dark about sex, and while they've heard all about sexual preference liberty they haven't thought it applied to them. But they do notice each other in the classroom. They also both notice the teacher, a Ms. Cabbage. Sounds like the name has been changed to protect the innocent or amuse the readers, but it's real: Violet Cabbage. She's in her mid forties, thick-waisted, sharp as a tack, wears a wig because of chemotherapy treatments, and has a husband named Dennis who has pecs like watermelons and adores her.

Ms. Cabbage starts the class on thinking about myths. "Myths are the understructure of culture," she says.

"Everything we have an opinion about is supported in one of our cultural myths." Nobody knows what she means. She adjusts her wig, about which she makes no pretense. Then she takes it off. It sits in her hand like the pelt of a raccoon. Her baldish head startles, even scares students.

"The myth of beauty," she says, "says that beauty is the outward sign of inner moral goodness. As, weekly, I become less beautiful, I fear the loss of my moral value. What are the myths that teach me this equation? That beauty and goodness are related?"

Lee, who is quick off the mark, shoots his hand up. "Sleeping Beauty."

"She wasn't good," says Violet Cabbage. "She was neutral."

"She wasn't bad," says Lee, "which is almost the same thing as being good. In the United States of Amnesia. Where apathy is king."

"Point taken. Don't be a smart-ass. Anyone else?"

Everyone stares and looks stupid. "Christian art," says Ms. Cabbage. "You ever see a homely Madonna? Mary is innocent and pure, so she can only be perfectly made. Ravishing. Naturally, being good, she's not aware of her beauty and so has no sin of pride in her magnificent features."

"Snow White," says Pete, the only black (or blackish) kid there.

"Better than Sleeping Beauty," agrees Ms. Cabbage, "because it's her selfless beauty that inflames her stepmother the Queen."

"Beauty and the Beast," says someone, and Violet Cabbage does a creditable imitation of crackly-voiced Angela Lansbury as Jessica Fletcher, solving the mystery of virtue and appearance. "Tale as old as time…" she sings.

She stops. "Tale as old as time," she repeats sternly. "That's myth. Now the modern versions. Move from the beauty of Mary and the female saints, in Western European culture, to the beauty of Venus, and the Three Fates, to Guinevere, the beauty of Britannia, the romantic statues of blind Justice governing the courthouses of the land, the film stars of the '20s, and so on. A direct link."

"Guinevere was a hussy," says Lee, bravely, because really he's not supposed to be in this class and shouldn't be rocking the boat so early, but he's afraid of being thought slow because he's a junior, so he's overcompensating. "Gorgeous Natalie Wood as Maria in *West Side Story* probably slept with Tony. Premaritally. Which as Catholics means they'd both go to hell."

"But they suffer for it, don't they?" says Ms. Cabbage. "Tony dies and Maria is left all alone. They're redeemed by their suffering, so Maria is still beautiful during the closing credits." She is getting a bit off course and takes them back on target. "Ten minutes. Pair off. Discuss the myths that created your sense of yourself. Count off, one-two." They count off. Lee and Pete (oh, the cleverness of the beautiful Fates!) are a pair. They don't look at each other and mumble out of mutual glum shyness.

★

Here the scene changes gratuitously. Because these days you can't be expected to have an attention span of longer than two pages. No offense intended. It's all a result of too much TV, just like they say.

A flash-forward. It's a Saturday. Lee takes the bus from

his house in Hyde Park and meets Pete at the school gate. Pete has a video camera recorder. They have gotten teamed up for a semester project, and want to familiarize themselves with the school's equipment. Dunster Institute, despite its sobriquet as Dumpster Institute, is well-endowed in the audiovisual department.

If this story ever gets bought for an after-school TV special, please note: The soundtrack of this montage should be more staccato than legato. No strings. High hats, cymbals, maybe a mysterious Indonesian gamelan chant-melody, but quick. Jumpy. This isn't the bit about puppy love. The boys are devilish.

They are coming to know each other, not by unimpeded observation, but by looking at each other through the camera. And by being looked at. Pete walks on the back of a park bench as if it's a balance beam. Lee holds the camera at shoulder height, which exaggerates the bulge of both crotch and bum. Pete does a gymnastic thing and slips. The film still rolls as Lee drops the camera, and the film will show only fallen leaves and the underside of a van parked at the curb, as Lee puts his hands on Pete for the first time, scared that Pete has hurt himself badly. He hasn't, actually, but Pete lies there not even knowing he's pretending to be winded. Not knowing the reason why: because Lee leaves his hands, lightly but tellingly, on the frayed lapels of Pete's denim jacket.

Remember: no strings.

No strings attached.

Not yet.

Pete grumpily gets up at last and hobbles to reclaim the camcorder. It's Lee's turn in front of the lens. Lee, who is less athletic than Pete, becomes verbal, spouting lines of poetry, doing imitations of the teachers, including Ms. Cabbage, then Bette Midler (being campy without knowing what camp is, or why), then, devastatingly, an imitation of Pete. Lowering his eyelashes in that unconscious denial of beauty that makes Pete the more enticing. Sucking in his gut and moving with a dancer's airy gracefulness. Pete is awed at Lee's ruinous talent at mimicry and ashamed of how he is seen. Lee, of course, can't feed Pete's beauty back to him, because Lee doesn't have it; so what Pete reads is narcissism and self-love, exactly the opposite of what he feels, and just as ugly, though in a different way, as self-hatred.

"Let's stop," says Pete, still filming.

"Don't stop," says Lee, in a voice still imitating Pete's. "Don't stop, Lee! Film me! Let me reveal to the world my immense love for you! I can't help myself! Hee hee hee!" The laughs are in Lee's real voice, not in the one copying Pete, for Pete has set the camera down and he has run to tackle Lee into the rustling blanket of maple leaves. They both yell and squeal and wrestle, and if you must read this as foreshadowing sex despite my instructions, I can't stop you. But Pete is mostly angry, and his punches and jabs really hurt Lee, who is confused and doesn't know what he's done wrong.

✪

What should come next is a dialogue, a painful one. It's several weeks later. November is cupping its cold hands around our boys. Key colors: slate, pumpkin, brown. Aromas: the cold dull stink of soil turned over for the planting of spring bulbs, coffee, burning leaves (though illegal, people still do it). For background music cue in the Adagio of Shostakovich's Second Piano Concerto. Neither

Lee nor Pete is especially interested in classical music, but struggling to identify their growing friendship with something outside themselves, they notice a poster announcing a famous pianist coming to Vassar College. They attend, the youngest members of the audience. Lee is beginning to notice how Pete attracts the glances of women and men alike. This makes Lee think for the first time the dynamite question: *Am I attracted to him? And does that mean?...* *Yikes.*

The dialogue follows in a Greek diner downtown. The coffee comes in paper cups with the Acropolis printed in Aegean blue between borders of the Greek key design. Editorial advice about this story, however, suggests fifteen typed pages max. So I'll skip the dialogue.

It's the ugly one, the lying one. How many girls they've come on to, and how successfully. Neither Pete nor Lee is usually given to lying, but fear prompts them. It's not a very different conversation for girls than for boys, or for straight kids than for gay and lesbian kids. You can fill in the blanks yourself. If you're lucky, you outgrow this kind of sneakiness. If you're strong, you don't need it.

Well, that's my myth anyway: Lying is weak. But I guess there are situational complexities. And an ideal, after all, is something to aim for.

Each one is acutely aware of his own lies, of course. As Pete leans past Lee to pay the cashier on the way out, brushing into his side from hip to shoulder, it's as if their clothes have heat-melted away and they've touched private skin for those twenty inches. Each knows that the other has been lying, and rather than drawing them together this divides them. They pretend a boredom, a nonchalance, as they part. And this pretense gives them both the creeps.

★

Now, quixotically, the focus of this story changes. You'll see why I started it with naked boys in bed when I tell you it now veers into religion. If I'd started with religion whoever would have bothered to read this far?

Lee and Pete have fallen in love. But let's leave them their pet names, their explorations, their little alibis, and especially their fears of AIDS. They will get through things okay; they're smart, and the school distributes pamphlets, much to the loud chagrin of some parents. Each is the other's world, for a while. Terrified, they're also inspired. It doesn't escape the notice of Ms. Cabbage, but frankly she has other things on her mind, namely her health, which is deteriorating.

Also, she's secretly pleased for both of them, but of course, if she let it be known, she'd probably be sacked, and she needs her health insurance now more than ever.

The end-of-semester assignment is a big one. Students can work independently or in pairs. They are to rewrite a myth and film it.

Naturally, Pete and Lee are working on it together. They meet in Pete's room in the dorm and sit in each other's laps and stroke each other's hair and kiss each other, gently, and jump up from time to time to check the lock on the door, which is always still locked, of course. Eventually they get down to work. At first Lee wants to remake *West Side Story*, showing a very pregnant Maria coming back into the ghetto with an Uzi or something. But Pete correctly points out that *West Side Story* is the reworking of older myths and stories, and they should get to the root of something.

They are becoming bolder through their love of each

other. (Lee has bought in a bookstore, with blushing courage, two postcards of David Hockney's painting *We Two Boys Together Clinging,* and they each use one of the postcards to mark their place in whatever book they're reading at the moment.) Pete suggests they redo a myth that has rendered the world only in heterosexual images, to create a place for themselves there. "There's a place for us," he sings, to tease Lee and tempt him to say yes.

Of course this is a bold move, but they both know that Ms. Cabbage is dying, and in an unspoken way they want to show her she is helping them change their lives. So maybe they'll be shunned by their classmates or laughed at. So what. They'll deal with that when it comes, they say to each other, and because of their innocence they're blissfully unaware of how much it'll hurt.

But what myth to rewrite? First they think of stereotypes of gay guys. Chisel-jawed, lean and rich and white and strong, coolly aloof from society, from family, from the past, from attachments of any sort except sex. Both Pete, with his aching and unanswerable need of Chinese and black American families, and Lee, whose dad is going to throw up when he learns Lee is gay, hate this modern myth, this stereotype. "I don't want to be alone," says Pete. "I want to be with you, first"—(time out for some disgusting nuzzling and coyness)—"and I want to belong to my families and cultures still. Why should I allow myself to be kicked out?"

Lee feels the same and only now realizes it. He's proud of the Puerto Rican in his blood and of the Polish and the Irish. And what binds them all together, he realizes with a gulp, is Catholicism. The only thing he is on all sides, besides American, is Catholic. All his genes have been Catholic for a thousand years or more.

"Can't be Catholic and gay," says Pete, who doesn't actually know. "Pope says so, I think."

"Why should I allow myself to be kicked out?" Lee feeds Pete's words right back to him. "Besides, you can't be kicked out of a faith. Faith starts inside your heart and ends up in eternity. All you can be kicked out of is a building, which is the bus stop of faith, sort of, and what's a building?"

And that's how they make their final project, called *The Honorary Shepherds*. Since all the fellow students are helping each other, Pete and Lee talk one of the jocks into being Joseph, and one of the girls in a permanent black turtleneck to be Mary. They use a tool shed out by the football field for the manger, and a clamp light hidden in some weeds to be the light of the baby Jesus in the crib. The music is maybe a little too avant-garde a choice: snitches of the Adagio of Shostakovich's Second Piano Concerto. But they've come to think of it as their song. An indulgence.

And what the six-minute video shows is this:

Night sky. Stars. Sheep. (Real sheep: There's a sheep farm about twelve miles out of Poughkeepsie, and since it's been an unseasonably warm fall, the sheep aren't penned in for the night yet—a lucky stroke.) No music. Lee and Pete, in bathrobes and towels just like kindergartners in a pageant, are crouched around a dying campfire. They break a French baguette and share it. Nobody speaks in the whole film, since no one knows what Aramaic sounds like and it's already weird enough to have a half-Chinese-half-black shepherd in the hills in the suburbs of Bethlehem.

The camera lingers on the touch of hands, one shepherd to another. It is a warming touch, a touch of friendship. There are other shepherds on the hills, farther away. (Some are played by girls in the class, and this is important to Lee and Pete but it doesn't come out very clearly in the finished project.) A round of waves and glances as the various shepherds settle down for the night. Lee and Pete sit close, shivering, and then closer, to keep warm, apparently. Pete's arm encircles Lee and Lee's head goes onto Pete's shoulder. (They've discussed renting fake beards but discarded that idea early.) It's not a sex film. It's a film about love.

The music starts. The boys sit up, first apart from each other in fear, then their arms encircling each other, as they look all around. Some fancy camera work (Pete has read up on creating the effect) having to do with photographing the reflection of light on water, using mirrors. It looks stagey and amateur, but you get the idea. It's like a comet. It's like the end of the world. It's like the beginning of the world.

The boys begin to run. In the final version there isn't any denying that Pete is stunningly photogenic.

Cut to the inside of the stable.

The camera doesn't linger here, just enough to give you the traditional idea. Traditional and radical, too—radical meaning "root" or "at the root": This is Christianity at the root, where it all began. The child who would be the Christ and grow up to preach the Gospel of love is ably portrayed by the 150-watt bulb. No matter what else would happen to Christianity, the story could certainly tolerate this: that along with the grizzled, careworn shepherds there might have been two young men, who brought their love for each other with them when they came to adore at the manger. And the proud mother didn't care who loved her wonderful child—how could she care? That's why all children are born: to be loved.

The film ends with a slow, scrutinizing pan over a fifteenth-century Nativity printed on page 553 of Jansen's

The History of Art, 1985 edition. A Nativity in ochres, attributed to Geertgen tot Sint Jans. The Virgin is, of course, graceful and pure as an egg. The cow is placid. The angels look like elves, disproportionately small to Mary's looming loveliness. Seen through the door of the stable, in the background, is a white blur in the sky, and this is the messenger angel. The distant shepherds are silhouetted, dark forms against the lighted hillside. One is on his knees in fear. Two are standing near each other, shadowy, shoulder to shoulder, one pair. Maybe those are female shepherds further on, and mixed-race shepherds just on the other side of the hill, and handicapped shepherds in wheelchairs just out of sight. And Buddhist and atheist and vegetarian and every kind of shepherd you can think of.

"Ah," writes Ms. Cabbage, "my only criticism is that of course the Holy Birth was always meant to bring people together, not tear them apart. Very fine work, boys. Live out the old myth, pour new life into it. You belong there."

Truth be told, not many of the parents or kids of Dunster Institute actually even get the point of *The Honorary Shepherds* when they see it on Student Display Night. They clap politely. But Lee and Pete have both learned something. Ms. Cabbage has taught them well.

A myth is yours only if you choose to own it.

Myths, like faith, are wide and capacious and of their nature generous.

There is more that Ms. Cabbage teaches them, but it can't all be put in words. They put it on their lips and give it to each other from time to time, and in this way they remember her after she dies.

God Lies in the Details
Donna Allegra

Christmas Day and my shorts cling like Gran's girdle. I wish some wind would whisper my way. Last night the heat crawled all over me like my mother about homework. I tried to shake some breeze from the fan, but it just rattled out noise.

I look up and see green leaves that overdress papaya and banana trees so plump I could milk them for nectar. The sky isn't clear, isn't fogged. A film of gray keeps the blue from showing full face.

The *thwap* of the djimbe drum inhabits my head. The drum talk makes more sense than human language. The *thwomp* call and *bwoomp* replies pose surreal questions and supply answers I don't yet understand about my life.

Voices carry on the frail wind—not English or even French. The Guinea boys on the porch below speak Susu, and New York City is two days and a universe behind. I'm in la République de Guinée-Conakry on the coast of the Atlantic Ocean.

In three weeks I'll be able to tell the kids at school how

I went back to the roots in Africa and all that happy horse shit. But my time here hasn't been like the fairy tales told by blacks who've never been here.

★

On the plane ride over I sensed an excitement shaped by different kinds of apprehension on the faces of the American blacks, Europeans, and white Americans.

I saw a handful of sisters in their thirties with dreadlocks who looked like the kind of people my mother would talk to in African dance class. I felt sure these women were going with me on the same dance and drum study tour. But I didn't want to identify myself to them yet. I saw no one my age, and it figures Ibrahim would lie about other teens coming on this trip with him to Guinea.

When we got off the plane in Conakry, the capital, it was night. Ibrahim was waiting and introduced me to the women: Daria, Sauda, Khadija, Nubia, Fatima, and Lacina, Fatima's eleven-year-old.

As the group of us waited to go through customs, the African checking passports frowned when Nubia didn't hurry handing over her passport, then scowled when he finished looking it over. He tossed Daria's and Fatima's passports to the table the way I'd flick a paper cup in the garbage. I don't know if he was all seditty because we were African-Americans or because we didn't have male companions, but his attitude sure walked the border between duty and disrespect.

While we waited on yet another line, I saw white Americans and Europeans shown patience, given courtesy and all-around respect that we didn't get. A Guinean woman, her skin like old bronze, inspected our vaccination cards. She looked me up and down the way the white girls at school measure each other's body size and the skinniest wins.

I don't know why this woman cut her eyes over me, but I sure got the message.

Welcome to the motherland.

✪

Sauda has two large bags but didn't want anyone handling them. You'd think she'd want the help, being so pint-sized. She has big eyes, and her gold-brown hair has short ringlets like a plate of macaroni, probably from her hair being let loose after being in braids a long time. It'll be at least a few months before her good hair—that's what Gran would call it—will lock for dreads.

We've been held up in customs because Ibrahim is arguing with one of the officials about going through Sauda's luggage. When we finally get to the baggage claim area, several men rush over, saying "*ça va?*" to start conversation.

I hear Sauda say to Khadija, "Phew, that was close. I sure wouldn't have wanted to starve in Africa if they'd confiscated my vittles."

"You wouldn't have starved. You'd just have to eat like everyone else for a change." Khadija looks like one of the regal African women pictured on the Kwanzaa cards. I like how she's styled her dreads into a French braid.

The African men hover to make their claim to carry our luggage and get tipped. Sauda and Khadija drag Sauda's gear outside. I wait with the other women from Detroit, and when

Sauda returns, she says, "Looks like African brothers see us black Americans as people to hustle for fun and profit." No one says anything, but the emotional temperature of the muggy airport descends several chilly degrees.

Outside the airport, Guinea women rove with platters on their heads. Their plates are piled with white balls perfect for playing tennis, and I wonder what dough or confection they carry with more grace than I tote the knapsack across my shoulders.

In the car that will take us to the villa, I look out the windows seeking stars and see white petals reach from a black sky. The road is lit with candles from wooden stands where people sell liters of gasoline, loaves of bread, and paper funnels of peanuts late into the night.

✪

I awaken my first morning in Guinea to the sound of a baby's endless wail. Outside my window a baobab, its trunk thick, twisted, and gnarled, looks like an old soul. Beyond that tree, goats roam the yard, leaving trails of black turds. A single neighing kid makes a sound like a baby's cry.

The cock crows every fifteen minutes and does so throughout the day. At eight A.M. my room fan shuts off. Will Ibrahim get me another when I tell him it is broken?

"Those mosquitoes was having breakfast, lunch, and dinner off of me," I hear Khadija say as I step onto the porch. She pores over the table set with breakfast fixings, disappointment creasing her forehead. Her eyebrows look like slivers of lemon; her skin, the color of a new penny. White flour rolls with packets of butter and jelly are laid out for us.

Sauda, her face waxed from sleep, wears shokotos. In

New York, the people in the African dance and drum scene call them "djimbe pants." They're a traditional costume for African men. What makes them different from pants any other people in the world wear is the billowing crotch that has enough cloth to look like a droopy diaper. Sauda's shokotos are a patchwork of African fabrics.

Her light-brown eyes don't even glance at the food table. She munches an apple I'd like a bite from.

★

By noon Ibrahim has our first dance class going. Khadija's long lapa trips her into an awkward-looking fall. She untangles it like African women have for centuries, wrapping a length of fabric around the waist to make a temporary skirt.

Sauda makes everybody move back so Khadija can have space. Sauda then helps her up, asking, "Will somebody please get an ice pack from Ibrahim?"

"Sauda," Khadija tries to restrain her friend, then, more quietly as if to block out everyone from hearing, says, "We're okay." She tries to laugh it off, bunching up the lapa fabric to cradle her belly as if she has a stomachache.

"You know that's her wife," Nubia nudges Daria.

"Um-hm. And don't even try to hide it," Daria hisses to keep me from hearing. "I used to know Khadija from way back, and she wasn't always funny like that."

"Well, we don't really know that," Nubia says gently.

Sauda snatches the ice pack from Ibrahim. "I want to make sure this is done right."

Khadija seems almost amused. "Sauda, I am not hurt. I don't think the ankle is sprained. I'll walk on it in a minute to get out the crink."

"I don't think you should walk anywhere for a while. Just rest," Sauda warns.

"Girl, stop. I love all this attention you good people are giving me, but I'm fine. It barely hurts now. I had a bad landing and twisted my ankle for a scary minute. Warning pain, no damaged goods. Go back to class so I can enjoy myself watching you learn the choreography," Khadija says lightly, waving us all away. I see a look of pleading that Khadija telegraphs to Sauda.

Sauda takes a last critical look at Khadija's ankle, as if trying to see through the flesh for injured tendons, bone, ligament. Khadija's ankle, her legs, all her body, are like Shona wood carvings—all limb and elegance.

Sauda is made of sturdier stuff—you almost don't realize that she's more pretty than handsome because her usual expression looks stern. Her profile makes me think of the man on an American nickel. Her amber eyes and sienna hair make me wonder which of her parents is white or if they're both mixed black.

My gran would call Sauda "colored," approving of her skin like a roasted cashew. My mother would frown about Gran's unspoken attitudes and say, "We're all black, Mama." Me? I notice shades of skin. Color still matters on people.

Reluctantly, Sauda leaves Khadija to return to learn steps. For the rest of class, Sauda dances indifferently, when just moments ago she was so keen to sculpt movement to the song of the drums.

✪

I'm glad I brought books to fill the hours when I can't dance. I didn't think we'd have much free time, but

Ibrahim hasn't organized any other activities. He raved to my mother about the culture and history I would experience to convince her how educational this tour would be.

It's not so much that I study. I look up words in my *Larousse,* and one lovely word leads to another I want to know. I go over my French lessons to better speak with the Guinea drummers. Pico, a djimbe player, teaches me phrases in Sousou. I remember the phrases by associating the Sousou sounds with names. "Donna Marie" for the good morning greeting, which translates to "How was your journey in sleep?"

I scrunch my face over a frustrating verb conjugation when I hear, "Studying at seventeen. Karimoko."

I look up and see Sauda shouldering a drum shell. Who told her my age? She places an apple in the crotch of my book, chuckles, and leaves me to my pages.

"What does it mean?" I ask Khadija.

"Studious. They called Sauda 'Karimoko' in Mali. It also means one who studies the Koran deeply, high priestess, or people who were warriors."

This exchange is picked up by the others. Karimoko becomes my name to the group.

✪

Of the five women from Detroit, Sauda says the least but means the most to me. Her skin is glossed golden by the sun. Her smiles are also a delicacy. During a pause in dance class, she remarks, "Dancing is acting, too, you know. You're an entertainer."

She's my partner on line today. I get lessons in how to perform from the pictures she uses to describe things. "In some movements you're the animal about to pounce on food," she says. "In others, you're the one preyed upon, and then there's a moment of surrender when they both agree to their roles." The way she talks makes me feel like I'm special to her, too.

★

On our second day, Ibrahim drives our group into Conakry to check in at the American embassy. The car ride lets me stare the way I want at the people of Guinea. Houses along the road, simple shacks, have their doors and windows open wide. African fabrics hang on clotheslines or dry on the ground, a jubilation of color. I see people engaged in acts of life: A woman combs a child's hair, an adolescent carries a bucket of water, a woman in her twenties plays with a toddler who tries eagerly to walk then stumbles into waiting arms. I want to spend my time gazing and know I look like a smiling idiot. I wonder if I could live in Guinea.

I say to Khadija, "These faces are just like the kids I grew up with." Indeed, the dark brown skin and facial features remind me of people I know from my neighborhood and African dance classes.

Khadija's smile shows the gap between her two front teeth. "I was thinking the same thing!"

Like a kid enjoying the freedom of the backseat, I hope this ride lasts forever, even as I begin to feel nauseous from the smells of engine exhaust. The cars—Toyota, Nissan, Suzuki—look like models from a time before I was born.

"Why do the cars look so old-fashioned?" Lacina tugs on her mother's arm. She looks startled, and her breath is laced with peppermint. More sedate and watchful, Fatima turns her head to the side window.

They looked like an Ultra Sheen mother-and-daughter ad. Except their hair is in dreads. Lacina is glossy-skinned, the color of saffron. Her mother's skin has a more muted cinnamon sheen.

"I don't know, lamb, but these drivers race like they're out of their minds." Fatima strokes her daughter's head and looks calm but ready to pounce over her cub. The girl's face is all eyes as she looks up at her mother.

"Khadija, don't lean so hard against the door," Sauda says.

"I'm not."

"That car was going so fast it'd take a week to stop if it smashed into us. Don't put yourself in harm's way."

"Sauda?" Khadija turns in her seat to give the rest of us a look of hopelessness over Sauda's illogic. Then she moves closer, waving her finger around a spot at her forehead, pointing to her friend's lunacy.

"People don't even move out of the way," I say, wanting to connect with Sauda. She gives me a half-smile and rolls her shoulders back and forth. Khadija turns Sauda's back toward her and massages behind Sauda's neck to further relax her. Sauda sighs and settles into Khadija's hands.

Along the roads, billboards advertise Harley-Davidson cigarettes and Budweiser, "*la vraie Américaine.*" I translate for the others because this shocks me: "*Prudence—notre préservatif contre le SIDA*"—"Our protection against AIDS"—an ad for condoms.

Many posters urge people to elect Lansana Conté. Ibrahim tells us that this Friday Guinea is having its first elections since Sékou Touré ruled.

"Lansana Conté took over in 1984, and now in 1992 he

wants to be elected?" Daria scowls as if Ibrahim is to blame for his country's political system.

Ibrahim shrugs. "There may be trouble."

We see carcasses of streetlights on the highway. "Those lights don't work because when the French pulled out of Guinea in 1958, they took the technical know-how with them," Daria says.

"It figures," Sauda snorts.

✪

I wonder why the Guinea women still wear only traditional lapa outfits in African fabrics while a lot of Guinea men sport up-to-date Western styles. African brothers prefer *GQ* leisure wear more than a *Vibe* '90s B-boy American look. I haven't seen any sisters in pants or even Western dresses. It bothers me that most African women straighten their hair. I've seen only the men smoke. "My Winstons are as advertised as Marlboro here," Daria crows. I don't want anybody to smoke and don't think it's fair that my country imports cancer to Africans.

After our check-in at the embassy, we head for the market in Madina. Our two cars stop at a roadside checkpoint for some kind of military inspection. Guinea soldiers look into the car and ask for identification. As one soldier peers at our passports, three others stare, more with arrogance than curiosity. I'd never expected Africans wouldn't want American blacks in the motherland.

"If you're gonna look at me like that," Daria says irritatedly, sure the men don't understand English, "y'all should at least say something or pay admission."

Looking past the soldiers, I notice a girl my age wearing

just a lapa and no bouba as a blouse. The fabric tied at her waist sings of birds in flight across a rainbow-checkered sky. Her head is also tied with this fabric. She doesn't wear a shirt. Many women on Guinean roads do not. Or else they wear tops that reveal their breasts through the sides. I'd be embarrassed to dress like that, but I'm glad Guinea women aren't shamed into hiding all that pretty brown skin.

This girl's bare chest emerges innocently as she sits by a bucket of greenish oranges. With a knife she peels off slivers of skin until its rim of white underwear is exposed. She places each orange on a platter piled with other shaven heads, and I realize that what had looked like platters of eggs in the airport were oranges like these.

A soldier shifts the rifle at his shoulder and saunters toward the girl. Men with guns are a common sight, but they don't act like the bullies police are back home. I wonder this aloud and Nubia says, "That's because they're people's brothers, fathers, and cousins, little sister." Nubia sounds peaceful and approving.

"Still, they're men with guns," Sauda says, and Nubia's face wrinkles.

Our car is parked close enough that I can see the man with a gun hand the girl 200 Guinea francs for five oranges—that's 20 cents American. He sucks out the juice and tosses the pulpy inner flesh to the ground.

Khadija, whose skin glows like silver honey in the tropical heat, gets out of the car to buy some oranges. She sections one, swallowing the pieces, leaving no remains. A woman passing by sees this and turns around to point at her eating an entire orange. Khadija frowns in discomfort as the woman laughs behind her hand. Do other Africans laugh at us in our American ways?

When we arrive at the Madina market and explore, people stare. We're all dreadlocked black Americans: Nubia, Khadija, Sauda, Fatima, Daria, Fatima's daughter, Lacina, and me. Guinea men approach us curiously. They try first French, then English. Africans, like other people who speak more than one language, are more patient than Americans would be at piecing together language and facial expressions for fragments of communication.

The women of Conakry seem to glower—if they let on at all that we cause any interest. It pains me to sense women turn away yet scrutinize us from the corners of their eyes. In their behavior, I see the way American sisters scowl when white women enter a black scene and the brothers welcome them with sexually appraising friendliness.

In the fabric area, market women wearing an extravaganza of African prints flock to us like birds. Their faces are as smooth as buffed leather, and they want to sell fabric. They know we're not Africans because, while the Detroit women wrap themselves with fairly convincing lapas, each one's hair is in some manner of dreadlocks.

✪

By the third day at the villa, a pattern is set: We have breakfast, dance class, lunch, dance class. When lunch is set out, the rickety wooden table holds a large bowl containing rice cooked with uncertain vegetables and fish.

Even though I'm sick of Mama Ibrahim's one-trick pony meals, I say to Sauda, "Aren't you eating?" I feel connected to her and like this feeling of warmth.

She raises her eyebrows to make a skeptical face at the meal, which will reappear at dinner and all the days to come. "I carried a good twenty pounds of raw vegetables in my luggage. I know better than to trust in Ibrahim's notions of vegetarianism. Fried chicken and small vegetable portions drowned in cream sauce don't do it for me."

Lacina, Fatima's eleven-year-old, bunches her forehead and questions, "But we're vegetarian, and we eat chicken and fish."

It pains me to feel the group energy chill toward Sauda again.

✪

On the days that follow, our master dance teacher is Sekouba. He's the artistic director of Ballet Coyah, a national dance company. Each day he works us long and hard to learn the folkloric dances. He teaches steps from kookoo, sosolay, yankadee, macoo, dundunba, and mandgiani. He is building an expanding opera from the folklore, and still we haven't scratched the surface of Guinea's dances for occasions of harvest, initiation, marriage, and other life passages.

My body feasts on this folklore I've been dancing from the time my mother could take me along with her to classes in New York studios. My favorite has always been mandgiani. Sekouba tells us mandgiani is a dance made up of girls who are twelve or thirteen. They wear necklaces and bonnets with pompons. Mandgiani is the name of the bonnet in the Konkon in Upper Haute, Guinea.

The costumes have raffia—the material that's probably the reason why white moviemakers forever show Africans wearing straw skirts.

Sekouba says, "The dance has to do with teenage years when girls' breasts are firm." I frown a questioning look

234

toward my little titties, but that's because I'd been looking at Khadija's bosom and felt caught. He grins at me, "After three babies, breasts start to hang."

"If we were doing it traditionally, you guys would dance it topless," Ibrahim breaks in to say.

I wish I were grown and could punch both the men. Why don't the women say anything back?

Sekouba cuts Ibrahim off and continues. "The next day, the girls go off for their initiation in the forest. They spend a year out in the bush learning how to do everything, to make tools and do women's work. When they return, everyone gives the girls gifts."

The drummers have settled into place, and Sekouba begins teaching. During the past week of classes, I've had the stamina to push my physical intelligence to keep learning new steps. Even though I've liked Sekouba's urging me to give more, my mind can't take in any new information, and my body won't follow directions. I just want some time alone and wish the boys who drum for us would go home.

Maybe I'm the one who should leave Africa. I don't like living with five older sisters and twenty flirty boy cousins.

We take a rest break from dance, and Fatima says to Sauda, "I need an apple from you for Lacina."

I frown behind Fatima for her manner of "asking," but Sauda goes to her room and returns with two apples from what I know is a dwindling supply of food.

✪

In the later afternoon, the drummers relax in their circle. I guess them to be between thirteen and nineteen years old because they're still lovely. Foeday, Malay, Abdolaye,

Nabi, Pico, and Mohammed are flirty with me in a way that feels sweet and doesn't make me mad like I get with boys back home.

The men in Guinea aren't so aggressive with their sexual interest or so hard-core in their ways of being men. I even think African men have a love for the nature of women that I don't find in brothers around my way in the States or at school.

On our trips to Conakry, several times I saw two men walk holding hands or with arms linked in friendship, kissing each other on the cheek. That freedom of affection stirs a longing in me for someone who's all my own and the hope that someday I'll have a mate.

★

Except for Khadija, the women from Detroit don't seem to care for Sauda. Khadija is the link between two poles of womanliness. Khadija can be with Sauda and still have a lot in common with Daria, Fatima, and Nubia.

But I like Sauda. I sit with her while we lunch. She eats from her store of foods: cucumber, cabbage, red pepper, carrot, and bean sprouts. Behind her back, Daria makes faces about Sauda eating it raw. I try some cabbage, and the sweet crunch surprises me.

After lunch when we have a break, I go to my room to jerk off. After dance and drum class, there's nothing here to do. It's boring with no one my age to talk to, so I give myself sex every chance I get. I take a nap intending to skip the afternoon dance class, but I hear a drum rhythm that sounds so good I leave my room.

I see Sauda playing with the rhythm she's just learned.

From the hallway, I hear Daria talking to Fatima. "Well, she's all hincty and wants to be in her own little world."

I wonder if she means me or Sauda?

✪

The Guinea folks call the drum "tam tam." Ibrahim's drum lessons are really for the Guinea boys, but they're supposed to be for us in the workshop. I tried to play sometimes back home, but my mother said, "That's for the men. What kind of woman are you trying to be?" She wasn't really asking, just talking mad. I didn't know how to answer. I put down the drum but thought someday I'd show her.

Sauda plays as well as the Guinea boys, and she gets veiled admiration from the women of Detroit.

As I try my hand alongside her, I feel a scary freedom, like swimming without any clothes on. I don't hit the djimbe properly, and she shows me how to strike the drum with just the length of my fingers, not the palm of my hand. I didn't know the drum was such a painful instrument. I now see Sauda has a ridge of calluses where her fingers meet the palms. Playing is hard on my hands, but I like being in this energy field. Sometimes I watch the dancers working a step, and I want to be on the floor with them. But there's a joy conjured by the drums that calls me to sit next to Sauda and play.

Later she shows me the djimbe she is making with Ibrahim's instruction.

The wooden drum shells laid across the grass look like large goblets ready to receive wine. Skin will cover them. Sauda goes to a line of pelts that have been drying in the sun for several days. It took that much time for the skins to be cured enough to be shaved clean. She takes a razor blade and shows me how to scrape the fur that once lived on a goat.

"Pretend you're taking off a man's beard," she says.

I frown at the smell of what I know is the flesh of a once-live creature. She sees me cringe and says, "I know, but this is the path to a drum."

She flaps the pelt the way she would a shirt from a clothesline, with a snapping motion to take out wrinkles from fabric. But Sauda is straightening dried flesh, and part of me is horrified. She directs me to work on the skin with the razor and leaves.

It seems a long time before she returns. "That's good." Sauda picks up the layer of flesh I've worked on; I'm still distressed by the smell that remains from the goat's life. "Use this skin for your own djimbe, Karimoko. I was going to make a djun-djun drum, but don't have enough skin for the size I want, so I'll just do a djimbe."

I hesitate. "Sauda, I feel like this goat's spirit will haunt me with that smell every time I play it."

"Keep the drum, Karimoko. Let the scent of the dead goat be a friendly reminder of the give-and-take in life."

★

I wish I could be invisible when they talk together. I want to know what they say when they're alone.

"James Brown was hot in his time," Khadija says.

"Well, I still think he's roasting it," Sauda tells her. "You know what 'old' I like? The blues, but it's got to be the funny blues."

"How you mean?" Khadija presses a damp cloth against the back of Sauda's neck.

"Oh, stuff like 'If you leave me, Mister, take your stupid dog and ugly cat, too.'"

✪

My room is next to theirs. At night the fan snores as it stirs the heat. I can hear only fragments through the plaster wall.

"You've got to be careful. You shouldn't be taking any chances. We shouldn't have come this year. We can barely afford this trip right now. You should be taking it easy, Khadija."

"I am careful. Don't treat me like a child. I know what it took to get this far. I'm not up for another two years of trying to inseminate."

I think of a flower in Mr. Fink's biology class, able to reproduce by itself. But then it hits me. *Oh, I get it: a donor. How'd they'd do it? How'd they find someone? Isn't that expensive? Why not just use a man? I guess it's not all that easy. You'd want to be choosy, wouldn't you?*

I push my sleeping bag next to the adjoining wall to hear better and feel closer to them.

"Sauda, I'm only three months along. My sister spent Carnival dancing samba in Trinidad in her third trimester, and you know Bahia was an easy birth."

They stop speaking, but I hear murmurs, sighs. Somehow I'm sure it's mostly Khadija. "Umm, oh, yes. There. Don't stop. Please."

Their sounds of pleasure spread warm rivers between my legs to my center better than the sex books I read at home. I feel my pussy lips swell, and the small marble nestled in my labia stretches out toward my pussy petals.

I hug my pillow and pretend I'm Sauda. My hand under the pillow case is caressing Khadija's chest. I kiss my arm and suck at the skin, smell the tang from my underarm, and from the stew of feeling, wafts of my scent rise.

I'm flushed with sensation. Soon I become stirred enough that my breath becomes short, steady gasps. A gush erupts from the kneading base of my palm and stretches me like a plank from my hip to my chest. When I am plumped enough with emotion, I release in a whoosh like a balloon squirting water.

There's quiet on the other side of the wall. I pretend I am their child and they want to love and take care of me.

★

As the days go by, I don't feel so eager to dance the Guinea folklore. I want to cry behind feeling this way because I love dance and this trip is my birthday and graduation present.

The glimpses reflected in the window glass show that I have a strong back. Still, I crave time and space alone. The drummers bother me, always trying to get my attention. I wish they weren't at the villa all the time or that I could just take a bus into town. But this is Africa and life isn't so easy.

★

It's around 8:20 P.M., and the half-light is so faded that I can't read anymore. The weather has been cooler at night, and I turn off my fan. That lets me enjoy the night sounds—crickets, the cock crowing, lone bird's call, a dog barking. I also hear gunfire this night before Guinea holds her first national elections in eighteen years.

I awake around three A.M. to queasy bowels and stumble my way to the bathroom. In the main room of the villa, I see the Guinea boys asleep on mats, curled in fetal positions, some snuggled into one another. Back home in the States, boys would never take such comfort. Jeers of "faggot," "punk," and "homo" would douse that affection between friends. Maybe that's why men bully the tenderness they need from women.

The bathroom is a torment of toilet odors. I lurch back to my room and lift the fabric spread across my window to drink in fresher air. The Guinea moon is a gleaming coin that, in a little while, will buy dreams from the store at the edge of the sky.

In my slumber, I hear several small angry violins tuning up. I open my eyes again, this time feeling the touch of virus has a handhold on me. I still hear the humming fiddles in my head as clearly as the goat's neigh, the cock's crow, and the morning bird-twitters.

A swarm of mosquitoes has entered in the predawn when I'd pulled aside the curtain of fabric. They now circle my mosquito netting, as hungry and frustrated as I've felt wanting time and space alone.

I coax myself back to sleep with a fantasy. I am one of the Guinea boys in love with another. We get hard at the sight of each other and plan to make a life together.

★

I'm glad when morning dance class is over. I was a cranky baby today. During the drum lesson that Ibrahim gives the boys, I look for some place to be by myself. I felt so angry-tired in class, I couldn't get my body to do the steps.

My mind drifts somewhere in the shimmering air, and I feel my blood come down. I go to my room for Kotex. The heat of Guinea has turned the walls of my room into an oven. I think how high heat transforms dough to cake, how in cold temperatures water becomes ice that with enough heat could become vapor. What started the change from ape to man? How long before we become God? Seeds lead to trees, leaves go to compost, grass enters a cow and leaves as milk. The cow to hamburger that Sauda says leads to cancer, taking the body back to the earth. From tree to drum, from a neighing goat under a tree to a drum singing for dancers. I hope there's a happy ending for Sauda and Khadija.

When I return to the porch, I see Daria and Khadija talking with Ibrahim. "She's real protective with her energy," Khadija says. "She won't open up to you unless she feels you. But once she does, she's can be nice."

"You're the nice one," Ibrahim says and puts his arm across her shoulder.

Khadija laughs, "Oh, you're so sweet."

She's flirting with him, and I feel as if I've bitten into a section of a rotted apple. I want to spit furiously in surprise. You'd think I was falsely accused, I feel so ashamed of the invitation in Khadija's laughter.

I pour a cup from the morning's tea, taste the charcoal from the water boiled in a burned pot. As I start to leave, Pico asks me in French if I am married. Before I can answer, he says, "You marry me and take me to America, Karimoko."

The simplest grammar would be to say I have a boyfriend. I toss the hot water off the porch and say, "I don't want a husband."

I think of how Sauda has given me a name—
Karimoko—and of a dream: I want to be a husband. The
feeling is so strong, I want to go to my room and hump the
heel of my hand till I crest with pleasure. But it's too hot in
there now. I head for the roof to get away from everyone.

★

I'm stung with frustration because the others are loung-
ing on the roof. I half-listen to their conversation to escape
my angry swirl of feelings.

There's something soothing in the Southern sound in the
Detroit women's voices. They lean the weight of a tone on
selected sounds, drawing out the flavor and wading in
meaning.

"I understand the whole lapa thing," Nubia says to
Fatima, "but with a unitard, you can see what a person is
doing. With some women in their big old baggy lapas and
T-shirts twelve sizes too big, you can't tell what's going on.
There could be two or three people up in there."

Lacina slurps a mango as she huddles between her
mother's legs to get her hair fashioned in a new style. Her
skin looks ripe and tender, and her toes look like caterpil-
lars. She squirms and Fatima says, "Sit still, puddin'."

"She's almost as tall as you are," Daria says.

"Yeah, she's getting bigger than the Empire State
Building." Fatima palms her daughter's forehead. Her
comb creates a row along Lacina's scalp that she oils with
coconut lotion. As she strokes Lacina's head, Fatima
neither smiles nor frowns, but she looks like peace.

"My mama's a beautician—a nap-buster," Fatima
says to Daria. "When she first saw my dreads, she'd say,

'Come here, baby, and let me look at that hair. You still work, baby?'"

Daria laughs softly. "Yeah, my father was like, 'You ain't gonna get no job with that hair.'"

"The only people that give us any trouble about it is our own. White people don't know if its braids or extensions or what so they don't trip on it. It's our women saying, 'You need to press that hair. Let me put a hot comb on your head.'"

Nubia "uh-hms" as Fatima massages her daughter's scalp, and I wish I were sitting in Lacina's place—safe between her mother's thighs.

✪

In the evening the others decide to hire cabs to take them to town for dinner. I'm staying. It's too dark to read, and I can't sleep. My menstrual hormones are having a party.

After midnight I feel nauseous and close to tears. The others haven't returned yet and I'm worried. I imagine my companions dead, the country in a civil war. Guinea's first national elections in eighteen years are today. How am I to get home? Will I be raped?

Ah: the sound of an engine, the women's voices; doors slam. They've returned, they're safe, I'm safe.

There's loud conversation in the hallway. Daria argues with Ibrahim, "But we didn't even get our food until ten o' clock!" I piece together their evening: The electricity went out in the restaurant. On the ride back, military police stopped them. Fatima and Daria didn't have their passports. The military guys were looking for a bribe. Ibrahim paid some money, and the women are now trying to sort it out.

"But the corruption here isn't like it is in the United States." Nubia means she didn't feel afraid. "It's like you don't know what they want."

I still can't sleep, so I get up to turn off the fan, which is loud and useless. I listen for Khadija and Sauda next door. I hope they're going to have sex—that would give me some relief. I move my sleeping bag nearer to the wall. Their controlled voices are loud enough that I hear everything.

"I'm not one of these newfangled queers who sleeps with both boys and girls. I'm an old-fashioned bull dagger. I go with women only. And how come you call yourself a lesbian if you're making out to be so willing to sleep with him? Isn't *bisexual* a good word for you? Your friends would like that better than *lesbian*."

"Why don't you just stop it?"

"How come you ask questions I have to answer, but turnabout is not fair play? You're making like you're not really a lesbian in a lot of these conversations with Daria and them."

"Oh, God forbid any man or bisexual or hetero woman contaminate your lesbian-pure body, Sauda."

"That's not it, Khadija, and you know it. If you want to sleep with a man, I'm out. Have the kid with him. You think I'm supposed to be glad and welcome some guy into my bed? Or is sleeping with a native a part of your back-to-Africa experience? Something you can share with the sisters. What's the deal, Khadija?"

"I haven't slept with anyone besides you."

"Well, you're sure as shit acting for all the world to see like you'd sleep with Ibrahim if you had half a chance."

"I'm being friendly, I like him. What's the harm?"

"Khadija, I don't play flirty sex games with men. I don't

even do that with women in front of you. When I'm committed to a relationship, I respect it. I don't put it out that I'm up for grabs."

"I don't either."

"Oh, come on. Ibrahim is chasing after you, and you're riding right along. That's not harmless and playful."

"You just refuse to understand anything other than lesbian this, lesbian that."

"Not true, but I don't pretend that the world is hunkydory and that men and women are equally free and that there's no such thing as rape or might makes right or that women don't have to worry about what some man might do if he's drunk/mad/in love/feels wronged/just feels like taking some. You think the traditional African way is so great? The women here have to get married if they want to survive. They can't just go out and get a job and live single."

"So what's wrong with getting married?"

"Jesus. Have you become really stupid or are you just pretending?"

"Don't you call me names. If you want to call names, I can come up with some, too."

"You're deliberately missing the point and changing the subject, Khadija."

"You take that back right now."

"Okay. I'm sorry I implied you were severely retarded, Mama Africa, keeper of the traditions. And as far as I'm concerned, sleep with anyone you want to fit in with your friends and show how bisexual you are for their approval. I'm not your girlfriend anymore."

✪

I awaken early the next morning. I feel touchy, easily hurt. It takes me ten minutes to find my Kotex. The others are sleeping late, and I have the front porch all to myself. By the steps I notice a spiderweb wrapped around the leaves of a bush like a skirt hugging a sturdy woman's hips. It would take so little energy to destroy such fragile work. I have to consciously restrain myself from tearing it apart. I wonder if others are so tempted.

I don't want Sauda and Khadija to break up.

✪

I'm bored. Sekouba isn't teaching today, and my books are all read.

Sauda steps out of the villa first. Her face full of thought is so handsome, I wish I could have her problems and be so good-looking. She carries her djimbe. She looks from me to the breakfast table and shudders. She bites into one of her apples and chews thoughtfully.

"Here, come have a drum lesson, Karimoko. First straighten your back like you're yawning from your spine. Practice slapping the skin with this part of your hand."

"Ouch."

"Yes, it hurts, but your skin gets tougher. Keep your fingers together. Tight, like this. It's a small adjustment, but God lies in the details." During the seconds it takes me to understand she means God is to be found, not God deceives, Sauda positions my hand. She then plays the drum call that signals me to play a response.

Gradually, the others file out. Daria slathers a roll with jelly. When Lacina pushes open the door, her mother says, "What's the thing with your dress?"

247

"Huh?"

"It's all tied up in the back," Fatima says.

"It's just a knot, Mommy."

"It looks corny. Fix it."

Nubia, walking behind Lacina, reties the sash. I'm glad I'm not a kid anymore.

A moment later, Khadija arrives with a vague "good morning" to everyone. She and Sauda don't exchange any of their usual looks.

For once it seems none of the boys are around, and I don't know if Ibrahim has arranged any plans for us on this election day.

Daria goes back in the villa for cards, and the Detroit women start up a game of bid whist. I look over my French grammar book so I won't appear lonely. Sauda picks at rhythms on her djimbe, then joins the card game.

Nubia fans out her spread of cards. "I guess I just stubbed you out, Miss Cigarette."

Daria lifts an eyebrow and sights down her nose, "Don't start with me."

"Honey," Nubia says, "I am glad Sekouba and them aren't around today. I'm feeling so tired, it would take me two hours to watch *60 Minutes*."

"Amen," Daria says, then nudges Sauda. "You haven't bought much fabric here, Sauda. Even if the people here are hosing us for dollars, the fabric is a lot cheaper than back home."

Daria throws down a card and cackles at Nubia. "If you snooze, you lose."

"She's choicy," Khadija answers Daria. "Sauda always says, 'I don't buy everything. I like what I like.'"

"Well, sometimes you got to like what you get. Ha!" Daria crows. "How you like them cards?"

"Not me," Sauda says forcefully. "I can wait until it's time. Nobody's pushing me and God." Her eyes are gauze covering a wound, and she frowns into her cards.

Khadija lets loose several short sneezes like *thwaps* of a drum.

"My gran would say you have dusty brains," I say.

"I do need to clear my head, pumpkin." Khadija throws cards out to the table as she grins, "See? My partner's got me covered."

"You trying to sell wolf tickets nobody's buying," Sauda gestures with her forehead as if a tusk were there that could tap Khadija with its ivory.

"You want in on this next round, Fatima? I need to work on my drum." Sauda gets up from the table and doesn't linger for Khadija's eyes that try to reach out to her.

"Don't go too far from us," Nubia calls after her.

I get up. "Can I come with you and work on my drum too?" As I stand, I look to see if I've leaked blood onto my djimbe pants.

We don't go far from the others. A gazebo-like hut stands to the side of the villa. We sit under the grass roof on the benching inside where I can see the card game in progress, with Lacina leaning on her mother's shoulder. The pelt I shaved is ready to be tied to the body of the drum. It's tedious work to secure the skin to my instrument.

Sauda's thoughts are somewhere else. I watch the bend of her back as she cradles the wooden bowl of her drum. Her arm carves into the work, like a woman rocking an adolescent too large for the nursery, too young to relish sleeping alone. Sauda doesn't pay attention to me for a while. She bastes her drum with palm oil, smoothing its wooden frame like a mother powdering her child after a bath. Taking care to fill in the notches of the parts carved into the wood, she makes filigree-like designs on the palm of a leaf. Then she directs my work to make sure it's correct.

"Pull the rope tight, Karimoko. This is the foundation that will let your drum have its own strong sound." She squats before the skeleton of my djimbe like a supplicant at worship. "It's all hard work, really. Bit by bit you build a drum, a home, a life." She laces the cord that will hold the skin tightly in place. "They seem like petty details when you're doing them, but later on you look back and you have something." She grunts to tug the rope.

"Or not," she sighs and rests a moment.

"What if something you put a lot of energy into doesn't work out?" I ask as I help pull the cord to a tightness that meets her approval.

"You live with it. I don't mean you're stuck. You can always walk away. But sometimes you look at what you have and think about its worth. It's never easy to walk away from time, energy, love, and hope you put into something."

I think how hurt I would feel if I had a girlfriend who left me for a boy. The smooth planes of Sauda's face glisten in the heat.

"A lot of times something looks good and draws you in. Up close, you see it's not all it's cracked up to be. But maybe it has other virtues that make it worth keeping. It's not easy to know when to go and when to stay. Life costs time and energy, Karimoko. It's easier to manage when you're on your own, but then being alone is a different kind of hard."

I think maybe it's better to be alone.

"Pull tighter on your cord, Karimoko. You have to stretch and sweat to make this skin and wood fit. More. Good. I think God tricks us into wanting things that seem so good and right, and then when we've got them, we see it's not what we meant, and soon we want something else. I don't think that's bad." Sauda looks at me, and her eyes are soft as a lullaby. "The Creator seduces you with a vision and then shows you that the reality doesn't feel like the picture you had in mind. Maybe that's how God makes sure that life goes on, because if I'd thought some things through, I would have made a lot of different choices. But you'll see for yourself and come to your own conclusions. I barely have my own answers." She smiles from the tip of a sadness I wish I could soothe. What will become of me if this woman who looks like my future isn't happy?

Her hands test my instrument by rattling off a djimbe call. "You've got a good drum, Karimoko. The skin is tight enough. It'll sing with your voice."

Khadija walks over to the gazebo. She sits beside Sauda, dribbles her fingers on the drum head. Questions pass between their eyes. I want to watch but feel embarrassed, as if looking will show my greed for someone else's plate. I'm bleeding thick as ketchup and have to get up and change my Kotex.

When I return, they're talking quietly, and I'm not sure if I should go over to continue work on my drum. I hear Khadija say, "We have a lot ahead of us, so we should take our time and make good decisions." She offers her water bottle to Sauda, then takes a sip, placing her lips on the spot Sauda's mouth had been.

They look up and see me. Sauda smiles, and I feel entitled to go to them. I pray for them to have a happy ending and feel safe again. Gladness throbs as my hands test my drum and feel a response arousing me. In excitement I look up to Sauda who's shown me this other way to sing. I straighten my back as she taught me and meet eyes that are the windows of a haunted house, but Sauda smiles as quietly as sunlight. She remains silent as a shadow, but her eyes tell me there are no guarantees.

Taking to the language of the drum, my hands and heart talk back to her. I know people we love aren't always honest, brave, and true. We do get tricked into following a different path along the road, but I'm keeping to the name she's given me.

I may never know the end of Sauda's story, but I'm throbbing to begin my own. I have a dream strong enough to draw blood. I want this rhythm to take me onward, and I don't care if God lies in the details.

Throwing Rocks at Cats
Brent Hartinger

I couldn't figure out why Trey was so eager to go out that night. I mean, we'd pretty much spent the whole summer just hanging out, drinking Big Gulps and fooling around in the front seat of his pickup truck. But now here he was, standing just outside my open bedroom window, wide-eyed and trembling, demanding that I follow him out into the darkness. Something told me this wasn't about sex. So why the sudden urgency?

"Just because!" Trey said. "There's somewhere we gotta go."

It was well after midnight, but I'd slept enough that summer to go without shut-eye until October. So I shrugged and crawled out my bedroom window, joining him in the expectant stillness of that sultry August night.

"Where?" I said.

"This way," he whispered, and led me off into the shadows of the woods behind my house.

I hadn't even known Trey three months yet. I'd met him that June, my first week in a new town. That same June day, three states away, my dad was getting married. Soon he

253

would have a new wife and, not long after that, a new kid. But his old wife and kid hadn't been able to afford the big house in the big city, even with the contested child support. So we'd had to move, not that my dad had been real broken up about that. Now it was June in the summer of my seventeenth year, but my closest friend was 900 miles away, and I was in a pissy mood, sitting on a stump in a vacant lot near my new house and throwing rocks at cats.

"Don't do that," a voice had said. It was my first look at Trey, ankle deep in the mounds of rotten grass clippings. He was already brown from the summer sun, but long-haired and twitchy—shifty-eyed, my dad would say—a natural loner. Nothing like me, with my laser-whitened teeth and throng of 900-miles-away friends.

"Why not?" I'd said. "They're just feral."

Trey shrugged. "That just makes 'em mean. And what the hell good is a mean cat?"

I stopped throwing rocks, and the two of us had been inseparable ever since. The sex had come fast. It wasn't my first gay fling, but it was Trey's, and he'd taken to it like a puppy to a rubber ball. I knew Trey and I would never end up as "life - partners," spending summers in a shared house on Fire Island, but for the time being, he was a comfort food, a guilty pleasure, an aimless distraction in the Summer of My Big Resentment. So wherever he was leading me that sticky night in August, I was plenty happy to follow.

"This way," Trey said, angling me left at a fork in the darkened forest path. But there was only one place this trail led—or so I thought.

"We're going to the dump," I said suddenly.

Trey thought for a second, then said, "Yeah."

He and I had been to the city landfill many times before, to scavenge for junk and to watch the great clouds of gray seagulls that swirled above the garbage pit like water down a giant toilet. Once we'd found a whole box of perfectly good CDs and sold them to a pawnshop for almost a hundred bucks. The dump was off-limits, of course, but the fat security guard never chased you on foot, and even if he did, it'd be way too easy to lose him in the woods that surrounded the landfill.

"You sure you want to go there?" I said to Trey. Yeah, we'd been there before, but never at night. "Come on, let's go back to my room and fool around."

"No," he said, his voice as steady as the light of the unwavering moon. "I need to do this."

I wanted to ask why—what was at the dump, especially at night? But our relationship was about doing, not talking, and somehow I knew Trey couldn't tell me what he had in mind. Whatever it was, it had to be shown.

We needed to cross the freeway to get to the dump, eight lanes of cars that swerved out from around a nasty curve. Trey and I waited for a lull in the late-night traffic, then darted across the pavement; the heat of the day rose up from the grooved concrete as if from the smolder of burning coals. That's when I noticed Trey was limping, and at first I thought he was somehow being burned by the heat of the freeway through the soles of his tennis shoes. But then we reached the concrete divider that separated the two directions of traffic, and Trey was barely able to make the leap. He winced when he touched down on the other side.

"Hey," I said. "You okay?"

"Yeah," he said. "Don't stop." From around the curve, I saw the glow of headlights rising up like the eruption of some nearby volcano.

When we reached the woods on the other side of the freeway, Trey didn't stop, even though his limp was more pronounced now. He never told me how he got the bruises that were always appearing on his legs and back. He didn't need to. Another beating from his dad. Yeah, Trey could cop an attitude, could project tidal waves of disgust with his eyes. But I knew these beatings weren't about anything Trey did, not really. They were about the fact that Trey was young and strong with his whole life ahead of him, and his dad was old and tired, with nothing to look forward to except a receding hairline and a lawn filled with dandelions. Growing old was the only reason why dads ever hit their teenage sons. It was the same reason why dads got their twenty-six-year-old legal assistants pregnant and then divorced their fifty-one-year-old wives. Trey and I didn't have a whole lot in common—he was Peechees and Dairy Queen, I was Palm Pilots and bubble teas (or at least I had been, before the move, before my parents' divorce). But we had the exact same asshole of a dad, and for one summer at least, that was enough to bind us together like a sundial to its shadow (for once in my life, I was the shadow).

A few minutes later, the trees fell away and we came to an unnaturally flat expanse of grass, already seared to a crisp by the harsh August sun. The landfill. Once this had all been a great excavation, but little by little, over the years, it had been filled with garbage and covered with dirt. Then they'd buried pipes in the ground to release the methane created by all the decomposing garbage. Since the methane had to be burned off, the ends of the pipes had been lit. Now they flared up into great silent flames—flickering tikis in some perverse Hawaiian luau of the damned. The closest of the torches was a good thirty feet from the woods, but I could feel its heat where we stood, could smell its stench of sulfur and smoke. But even as pungent as it was, it couldn't cover the sweet underodor from all the garbage lying exposed and festering in the nearby pit.

We'd hiked halfway across that field when I noticed something lurking in the shadows of those flickering torches, something else smoldering in the night.

"Trey?" I said.

"Dogs," he whispered, more to himself than to me. "I forgot about the dogs."

It was a pack of wild dogs that prowled the woods around the dump, and I'd forgotten about them, too. We'd seen them before, but only from a distance. At night, they must have come into the landfill to feed.

Now that I knew what to look for, I could see them openly, all around us, a slowly tightening ring. I'd never known dogs to be so silent, so subdued, but these animals were anything but docile. There was no barking, no wheezing, but twelve pairs of narrowed yellow eyes watched us, following our every move. A thread of saliva glistened in the flickering light.

A plastic grocery sack, brittle from the sun, crunched in the dirt under my feet. Was it true what they said about dogs—that they could smell your fear? If so, Trey and I were doomed, because I was terrified.

"Ignore them," Trey said, and he started forward through the grass. For once, there was no twitching from Trey's body, and his limp was momentarily gone, too. And somehow, the dogs sensed his purpose, the firmness of his step. Sure enough, one edge of the ring of dogs slowly opened like a swinging gate. When Trey pushed our way through, they did not follow.

"This way," Trey said, leading me not toward the pit where new garbage was being dumped, but eastward, to a part of the dump I'd never been to before—a cluster of buildings over by the entrance. Always before, we'd come here during the day, so we'd steered clear of the roads.

The complex of buildings was surrounded by a chain-link fence topped by barbed wire. No problem, I knew. We'd jumped dozens of fences like this before (the secret was to climb at a corner where the posts were stronger, and where you could climb over the wire using the two inner walls as hand and footholds). But somehow this felt different from our past adventures in trespassing—more reckless.

"You don't need to come," Trey said, still standing at the base of that fence. "You can wait here if you want." That's what he said, but it's not what he meant. He wanted me to come. I still didn't know why, but I knew he did. And I would. I'd already come this far. Besides, by that point in the summer, I was ready to follow Trey anywhere.

When we landed on the other side of the fence, Trey's T-shirt had snagged on the wire and pulled up over his back. That's when I saw the cuts.

"Jesus, Trey!" I said. "You're bleeding! Did you get caught on the fence?"

But even before he shook his head, I knew. Not the wire. His dad. He hadn't had his usual beating tonight. He'd had a full-fledged thrashing.

"That asshole!" I said. "What did he do to you?"

"It's nothing," Trey said, tugging his shirt down. But then to my surprise, he added, "His belt. He used the end with the buckle. He asked me again about you and me, and this time, I didn't lie. So he tried to beat it out of me. He said he wasn't gonna have no faggot son."

It was the first time he had ever spoken of the things his dad did to him. It made me realize how hot the night was, and how sticky it made me feel. Suddenly, I wasn't so sure I wanted to know where Trey was leading me. Somewhere behind us in the dark, a lone frog croaked, which surprised me, because there was no water anywhere near the dump. For a moment, there was silence. But then, from what sounded like miles away, a second frog answered.

"Trey," I said. "Let's go home. You can spend the night with me. We'll eat string cheese and talk till dawn." I tried to smile, but I knew it looked forced and phony, an ugly grimace, even in the dark.

"No," he said. "It'll be okay. It's just a little further." And he turned and walked toward the complex.

The building where Trey led me wasn't like any warehouse we'd broken into before. It was huge, but tall, not squat. There were no lights, but the door was open. He stepped into the darkness, and I followed.

For a long time, I couldn't see anything. It was too dark. Then I heard movement, something scraping, and I imagined it was the dragging of ghostly feet.

"What's that?" I whispered.

Trey flicked his lighter.

In the feeble light of a tiny flame, I stared around us, saw more yellow eyes, though much smaller than those of the dogs.

"Rats!" I said. They were huge, a foot long at least, not counting their tails. They were so fat that the fur had rubbed off their stomachs, exposing soft pink flesh. They glared at us defiantly. Their teeth were almost as yellow as their eyes.

There was garbage everywhere, trash that had gotten wet and soggy, then dried in shapes that conformed to the floor and walls, like papier-mâché. Trey picked up an elongated milk carton and Frisbeed it at the closest of the rats. The creature shifted just enough to avoid being hit, but it definitely didn't scatter. None of the other rats even budged. What if they were rabid? I thought.

"Just ignore them," Trey said, lighter upraised, turning toward the interior of the warehouse.

Finally, I saw the inside of that building. It was filled with some kind of massive machine, with bins and wheels and conveyor belts. If I'd been anywhere other than a garbage dump, I would have thought it was some kind of factory—an assembly-line machine that made auto parts or aluminum cans or soda crackers.

"What is all this?" I asked.

"It presses the garbage into cubes," Trey said. "Then they sell the cubes as fuel to burn, but only to third-world countries, where they don't have laws against toxic fumes." Sure enough, there were stacks of garbage cubes, almost like crushed cars except they were multicolored, lining the walls of the warehouse.

"That sucks," I said. "How do you know?"

"My dad. He invested all his money. This is the prototype. If they can make a profit here, they'll make more machines like this, all over the country. But their insurance doesn't kick in until midnight tomorrow."

"Oh," I said. "Oh!" Finally, I knew the reason we had come here. Suddenly, the whole evening—the single-mindedness, the urgency—it all made sense.

I stared at the lighter in Trey's hand. All it would take was one little spark. There was dried paper everywhere. The whole place would go up in flames. It would take out the machine for sure. But the fire station was less than a mile away; they could certainly put it out before it spread to the other buildings.

"Do it!" I whispered. God, did Trey's dad deserve it! After what the bastard had done to him tonight and so many nights before? They all deserved it. With one fell swoop, Trey could strike a blow for sullen sons everywhere, and for gay kids, too. "We can be out of here long before anyone sees us!" I said. "We'll be back in the woods before anyone even sees the flames!"

Trey thought for a second. The flame in his hand flickered once, but then did not waver. Then he nodded no. "I'm not gonna set it on fire."

"Why the hell not?" I swear it was the first time since I'd met him that Trey had made me mad. And suddenly, I was furious.

"Because I didn't come here to screw up my dad's life," Trey said.

I didn't understand. "Then why did we come here?" What the hell had this evening been all about?

"I came here not to." He turned toward me. "And I wanted you to come with me—"

"To see," I finished. In a flash, I finally, really, understood. Trey had come to this place not to destroy it, but to prove that he didn't have to get revenge. To know once and for all that he, the faggot son, was better than his dad. And he had brought me along as his witness. In that instant, it wasn't just that evening that made sense; it was as if that whole lazy, aimless summer, our whole odd-couple relationship, came into focus. Suddenly, it all had a point.

I stared at Trey for a long time. I saw the reflection of his lighter in his eyes. They looked wetter than before, like he was crying. The flame flickered again, twice, but then he let it go out, and we were both in the dark again.

"Hey, that's cool," I said softly. There was more I wanted to say to Trey, a lot more, about how much I admired him, about how I had never felt so close to anyone as I did to him at that moment on that night in that warehouse. But I didn't say another word. It wasn't needed anyway. Trey already knew what I was thinking.

"Let's go home," I said, feeling for and finding him in the dark. Then I turned him toward the door, and this time I led him, out into the August evening. It was cooler now, soothing even, as if the fever of the night had finally broken.

Melanie Braverman

Is this why I like girls?

Early fall, Iowa, leaves and humid
air just beginning to turn. My mother puts me
in too many clothes: dress, smock, laced shoes, white
socks. It is the first
day of school and I don't want her to let
me go, I want her to turn from the kitchen counter
where she is making our once-a-year hot
breakfast, the ash
from her cigarette dangling over the bowl
of batter like a threat, like the fragmentary, tenuous
thread that binds
my mother to me; if not then, I want
her after breakfast to throw
the heavy brown station wagon in reverse and flee
the Roosevelt Elementary School lot, I'm
quiet, I'm easy
to please, remember? But she

does not. She leaves me
weepy at the kindergarten door, stays
in the driver's seat eyes fixed
in the rear-view mirror sternly until I go inside. I do. I draw
my pictures of houses with jumbo crayons correctly: green
tree, red apple, brown roof, black
dog. Now
I am drawing pumpkins, the orange
crayon fits in my hand
like a friend, there's a lot of paper for me to use and for some
minutes I am free of thinking
about my mother until Mrs. Reger comes to stand by me
while I am working. She
is so old the skin
of her face looks like the fine
aged gloves my mother wears to drive when she's dressed up
and it's cold, and then I am missing
my mother again. I make it to lunch without crying, I sit
on the cafeteria floor with my milk and my bologna
sandwich and then, I still don't know what brings this on
but something
pushes something else in me to some edge and that's it, I can't
wait anymore, I need
my mother, crying
inconsolably, the one left with nothing
to be done, so many tears my cheeks grow quickly
chapped in the dry air of the school and sting as if

it is winter already, holidays upon us, some joyful
anticipation infused in our bodies until, stricken
and annoyed, the school
principal calls my mother at home, gets her to leave
whatever mysterious work she is accomplishing in the
air-
conditioned din of our house and get down there and
pick
me up. Poor
mom. When I see her face at the cafeteria door
I cry more.

Is this why
at nineteen, at a hippie fair in Oregon, drinking electric
lemonade, smoking pot all day, when crazy
August Hankla leaned over from her sleeping
bag and kissed me, I craned my face as if across some
great divide on the dusty northwestern ground where we
were lying for what seemed like hours watching
some nondescript planes we convinced ourselves were
really
UFOs blink their way across the sky, discussing
whether or not we would go
with them if they wanted us to, knowing I wouldn't
want to but if she
was going, I thought, why not, she leaned
over to me and put her full
mouth on mine and I

kissed her back, not shyly the way I had learned
to kiss men (as if
you were surprised, as if you were letting

them take something important from you) but as if
she was food, and I
was breaking some ridiculous
fast. All these years I've been afraid
of turning into my mother, I see now what I've really
been afraid of is staying
that five-year-old self, desperate, unquenchable,
alone. When I kissed
August Hankla that night, and after her Terra
Soluv and the few
other girls I've kissed since then the mending
of my long-unraveled seam began so that even
though I sometimes
feel like I'm running from one
overburdened woman to the next, I know the thing I'm
running to
in the end must somehow be me. When my mother
came to get me at school that day when I was five she
was
angry, I know, but she was happy
too, and why not?

Someone wanted her
more than anyone has ever wanted her before or

since. I talk
with my friends about having a child and we think
about this, what it must feel like to be desired
so completely, feared and loathed in equal
measure to be sure but wanted
utterly. My mother didn't breast-
feed me, is this why I like girls? August

Hankla had teacup breasts and when I touched
one the first
time the stakes that held me inside
myself came loose. When I put my mouth there the
whole
fucking tent went up and I have been sleeping
beneath the stars ever since. Lord help me, if I ever
have a child please keep me from turning
into a mother.
Let my gay boyfriends
make a baby with me and let me
be the mother I never had: the one who gets out
of the car, who makes
a little scene and cries in the parking lot when her child
for the first time leaves her, who stays
loose beneath her clothes, her broad
hips switching like grasses when she walks.
Let me make
a lantern of myself, like the lanterns in Oregon the night
of the country fair where August Hankla first
kissed me. Late

August now, and the plants on my deck need
water, perfect tomatoes turning fetid in the heat, over-
ripe
and dangling from their stalks like breasts.
Jesus, how can I have a child if I can't even water
the plants? When my ex-lover comes by to talk
about us I give her some tomatoes to take home. When
she says
she regrets having left me it isn't that I don't
believe her, I do, but when it starts to rain hard

as she talks I'm thinking not about her or her sorrow but
about
my new lover, the day we spent dozing on and off on this
couch while it rained
harder than I've ever seen it rain here before, how she
stayed
despite herself, having slept that night in my bed fully
clothed, boots
on because she was as nervous about staying as she was
about letting herself go. My ex is weeping and I am
thinking how
even though that new girl hasn't called me in days, and
may never
again for all I know, if someone belongs on that couch
with me now
it's not my ex, and I
am very confused: because I thought that what I wanted
was for someone
to stay, and short of staying to come

back, like all the stupid metaphors for constancy we
know: tides, seasons,
death.
When she says it's time for her to go
home I'm relieved. The sky has cleared, the couch
is mine, and I seem for the first time to have chosen
myself alone. Imagine. There must
be some other reason I like girls.

She Won't Bite
William Moses

"*Girls love scars.*" The nurse swabs my wound with alcohol pads. "*You'll have to fight them off.*" I am antiseptic.

I have dreamed of alley cats. Crawling all over me, claws catching my skin, tails stinking of trash. It will be like that. Girls snagging me, attaching themselves. Girls as thistles and thorns. Girls perfumed with Right Guard and Tic Tacs. Girls lynching me with enameled nails and their way of talking you into anything.

"*Uh, he's going down.*" The doctor's voice. "*We've lost him.*"

I am fainting. Into his lab coat, into the white world. I feel my descent, a satellite sinking to Earth. Will this Ken doll of a doctor break my fall? No, he rolls away on his stainless-steel stool. The nurse catches me, lays me down.

"*He's not good with pain.*" That would be my famously erroneous stepmom.

★

My mother died in August, the alchemical month when everything turns to gold. *"Don't worry, there's someone for everyone"*—her last words to me, not counting her letters with dollars for Hershey bars. I was nine. I'm gay because my mother died. My stepmom's theory. My point is that my mom knew about me but she died.

I met Zach that summer. If I'd known what to do with love, I'd have done it the night on the lake. Our bunk stole a bunch of canoes. Panty raid at the girls' camp. We paddled with the others, staying behind, though, and when our bunkmates hauled their canoes onto the girls' beach, no one noticed as Zach and I continued paddling, wordlessly, into the dark heart of the lake. Lewis and Clark.

We lay our paddles in the canoe and checked out the acne of stars above us. Zach assembled his clarinet. I fidgeted, combed my hair with my fingers, sighed like Romeo. Zach sucked on his reed a while, and we drifted toward a lesser-known shore. I discovered I loved the world like that, the night black as a clarinet and white as the silver stud in Zach's ear, gray fog filling my head, and the new-world potential of unexplored lakeshore.

Zach began playing his clarinet on the lake under a harvest moon, the moon a gold coin, the moon a conduit for romance or sewage. It was jazzy.

If I'd touched him, we'd have tipped—clarinet plummeting through the muck, turtles snapping at our toes. Would have been a good first-time story, though. But not as good as the concert for me.

✪

"Is she all right with kids?" I was on my knees. I was

smiling, making friends. Before my stepmom became my stepmom, she was vigilant about my care. Maybe that's not generous. Maybe no one wants to see a kid harmed.

"*Oh, yeah. She's been with lotsa kids.*" The she in question sat in the cripple's lap. On his hideous afghan. Cream of wheat stains on it. I leaned in to kiss her. Spread a little neighborly Christmas cheer. "*Go on, Taffy. Give your new neighbor a kiss.*"

★

Hard to eavesdrop on your parents. They get it wrong when they talk about you but you can't pipe up.

"*He's not to blame. The girls in his school are pathetic.*" My stepmom's voice.

"*Did you see him complete that pass?*" My dad.

"*I'm inviting the Sorensons for supper. The girl goes to Andover.*"

"*Don't go setting my son up with one of those lacrosse dykes.*"

"*Really now!*" My stepmom laughs, plays with her bulbous necklace. "*Who says anything about setting anyone up?*"

"*No dykes, you hear? And no sad sacks. I'm not having a faggot for a son.*"

A pillow thrown in jest and the two large people—he with his forty-inch inseam, she with her underwire brassieres—topple over one another onto the bed. I creep down the hall, turn off the oven, rescuing another of her tasteless casseroles. I don't wait for dinner. I flee like a faggot. I run. Nowhere to go, I head to the high school, I run laps around the field, I run until sweat breaks out on my chest, and I run until the sweat cools me, and still I continue around the track as the sun makes its magnificent wave farewell, so long, and I run until my diaphragm aches and my calves cramp, until I collapse and can't breathe, and I descend into my grave of tears.

★

The vampire bitch bit me in broad daylight. Quick close-up of yellowed teeth, blue tongue, then—*snap!* The fangs sink into my cheek. And they hold on, her muggy breath in my face.

More than anything else, I am stunned. And bewildered. *"Get your fucking dog off my face!"*

The guy in the wheelchair whomps the dog with his *Reader's Digest* and she whimpers, briefly, then snarls at me.

"Oh, sweet Jesus. Thank God she missed your eye—she could have blinded you. You have to be more careful. Don't antagonize her. What did you do to her? What did you do?" My stepmom sighs. We're going straight to the hospital.

"I ought to sue." And I'm thinking I've seen this filthy cripple get up and walk. *"And, sonny, don't get blood on my carpet."*

"A penetrating trauma with no pain on palpation." The doctor and his students investigate me as if I'm pretty damn interesting. And I'm feeling okay, even after the tetanus shot, until one of the medical students mentions the "fleshy protuberance," otherwise known as the cheek. My cheek. And you know what I'm realizing as that doctor is stitching me up? Know what my ten-year-old brain is doing? It's telling me if I were thinner, if I were less "fleshy," the dog wouldn't have been able to grab a hold of my face. This marks the

beginning of my induction into the statistical tables of rarities—the male anorexic. A statistic, there's one for everyone.

"*You're going to have yourself a nice little scar.*" The nurse again. I eye the doctor. No reaction. I notice he has a tic, a blinking tic. If it affects his suturing skills, I might come out of this a Quasimodo. And yet, how can I not feel tenderness for his tic, its spontaneity, its unabashed conspicuousness? The nurse continues to reassure me. I love the doctor. I'm going on a diet.

"*They attract the girls every time. Bees to honey.*" The nurse.

And boom, I go out.

★

What has become of me?

Do I have HIV, a lover, frequent anonymous sexual partners, leather jeans, a perfect haircut, or something pierced? Am I an interior designer with a gym membership? Do I have a favorite bar where I drink too much and eat too little? Can I make Lyonnaise sauce? Were my fingers broken by hoodlums on the waterfront? And aren't I ashamed of myself?

Yes. But you don't know a thing about me; you'd never recognize me. Try to find me. Point me out in a crowd. Do you know how common facial scars from childhood dog bites are?

★

Introductions are made. The Sorensons get sloshed. Tara works on her homework on the couch, while I fiddle with the pendulum on the coffee table.

273

"*Aren't you going to offer the young lady a drink?*" My stepmom raising her penciled brows.

"*Like something?*"

"*Whatcha got?*"

Smoothies. The adults in the living room try to yell over the blender but we keep it running until they stop and sit in embarrassed silence. Tara clears the coffee table. I place the tray, with sticks of carrots and celery—hints of every budding anorexic—on the table.

"*Well, go ahead. Sit next to your guest. She won't bite.*" My stepmom nudges me with her elbow.

I'm off-balance. I fall. The cheek of my ass berths itself on Tara's thigh.

The adults whoop with laughter. I despise the sound of ice in their highball glasses.

★

I live on the sea; I am wet-nursed by the sea, rocked to sleep by the sea and sometimes by a man with hair sprouting from his ears like turnips. This guy—you ought to meet this one. He's a giant of a man and stinks of redemption, of the ocean home to fish and seagull shit and dead sailors, and when he's done with me, I do, too. "My little mermaid," he calls me before he pushes off. A real live fisherman with black waders and wrists thick as hawsers. He's as ugly as his name, Gaston. His beard and hair, eyes and clothes are black and silver and shiny, like the fish he pulls from the sea. The Canadian flag is tattooed on his left biceps, the only bit of color on his entire gray body.

Gaston comes aboard now and again. I don't even wash the odor off me. Not even at the risk of being abandoned

274

by Tom. He's never said a word. He pouts. He doesn't ask me to take a shower anymore. Tom's too near death to care about fish rot or redemption.

"You're starting not to like me?" *Like me!* I really am very good to Tom: I clean him and kiss his pale forehead, and what am I to do with the love I hold in my belly and balls for Gaston? What harm is it doing anyone? I need affection. The old stepmom tells me to place Tom in a facility. She's afraid she'll catch his death through me. I begin to eat without doing the math. Indian pudding. Not that it counters the sadness. It's just time to stop making such a fuss over myself.

Of course it's safe sex. Once we used a fish skin, which Gaston tied at the base of his penis with a satin pink ribbon. What he was doing with a pink ribbon I don't know. Probably a trifle for his wife, though he isn't the kind of person to bring gifts. Other than fish.

Gaston, of all people, is repelled by my scar. He turns my cheek to the pillow when he mounts me—he won't look at it. "Ruins your pretty face." So says my Colossus. Never asked me how I got it. Is that a sign of indifference?

✪

I am asked to remember this by countless psychiatrists: "*He's a contemptuous, hypocritical bastard!*" Tara argues politics with my stepmom while I count calories. My stepmom nearly chokes on her white wine until my dad burps her with a thump of his great paw. My stepmom belches like a buffalo. Tara and I bond instantly. Tara doesn't insist on her femaleness and wears a silver ring on her pointer finger.

I drive to Andover a bunch of weekends. Doritos and brie and black forest ham on baguettes in the cooler. We watch a volleyball game. We listen to David Bowie. Talk our heads off. Her hair smells of sunlight. She puts her arms around me one night, the sweetest thing in the world, her skin as creamy as a proper crème caramel, and asks the horrible question. *Is it me?*

I do it.

I have sex with a few girls. It's fairly tolerable if you don't look. Tempted? Let me save you the trouble: It's a mouth! It can swallow rodents and small dogs whole. If you can do it, it gets you off. The one nice thing about every girl who's ever fucked me? They all ask me about the scar.

✪

So you haven't found me. And you're tired of guessing.

I live on my thirty-two-footer, a sloop named *Fassbinder*. Full galley and a Mac I use in my work. I design boat interiors. I dry-dock in Gloucester.

Tom dies in our apartment near Porter Square. He more or less sent me away when he got sick, but I'm there every week, feeding him mashed food, helping him to the toilet or changing his soiled sheets. I pray over him when he's not looking at me with his certain eyes.

I try to remember to water the plants. I leave him to our three-CD set of Benny Goodman. Irene comes by in the evening, sits by his feet softly singing calypso.

I like to think my mom heard Zach's playing the night she died. I like to think that every time I make love with a man I'm proclaiming my mother's unarticulated life. Love is exponential.

Forensics

Stephen Greco

The newspapers that spring had a field day with the guy who was abducting fag bashers from the streets of the city. The angle was that he didn't hurt his "victims." He would lure them into a van late at night, knock them out with a rag soaked in chloroform, and give them a makeover.

The next day the victims would be found unconscious but unharmed, in various spots around the city, styled in new looks—dressed in trendy clothing and accessories, and made up subtly as if for a fashion shoot. Their bodies showed no evidence of sexual activity or violence.

By July the abductor had been credited with fourteen victims. How he targeted them nobody knew. Some were arrested afterward—identified by gay men who had been attacked or by witnesses—and some just went home, accused of nothing. No "after" photographs of the victims were published because of legal concerns, but newspaper stories bubbled with details of the makeovers, as well as speculation about the methods and motives of the abductor, who was being called the "Velvet Kidnapper"—an ungainly term demonstrating how easily media coverage of the abductions drifted between formulaic horror and tabloid amusement.

There were few clues to the abductor's identity. He used a different van each time. Victims spoke of a lone white guy who was powerfully built, in his thirties or forties. The police distributed a sketch of a man with a crew cut and square jaw, but they did little else to pursue the case, since they were criticized for not doing enough about fag bashing in the first place. Then someone started a Velvet Kidnapper legal defense fund, which was collected in all the gay bars under signs featuring the police sketch and the tagline, "Get him out of jail if they catch him. Buy him a beer if they can't."

Art dealer Aaron Franck had been contacted by the association of bar owners to accept the fund as part of a benefit art auction he was planning in October for the city's leading gay legal organization. Aaron said yes, though even as a longtime community activist, the easygoing thirty-year-old didn't include bashing among his personal issues—until he was attacked one night in July on a quiet residential street in the West Village. It was one of those streets, narrow and tree-lined, that by day are charming and by night dark and lonely. Aaron had been on his way to buy some juice at an all-night deli when a stranger coming from the opposite direction bumped shoulders with him. It had felt deliberate.

"Whoops," said Aaron.

"What do you mean, 'whoops'?" the guy said, stopping and squaring off. "Don't you mean, 'I'm sorry'?"

"You bumped into me," Aaron said.

It was too dark to make out details, but Aaron thought

the guy might be Latino or Native American. He was thick, possibly muscular, but not too tall—maybe five foot nine. His clothes were baggy. His hair was a black mop. Above the treetops Aaron noticed the city's tallest building, the Dreadnought tower, glowing icily in the distance.

"What are you talking about?" the guy said. "You pushed me and I don't enjoy that kind of disrespect."

"Excuse me," said Aaron, looking down and calculating a retreat.

"Oh, you can't apologize?"

The guy pushed Aaron again, on the shoulder. Aaron began walking back in the direction he came from, but before he could run the other guy lunged toward him and knocked him to the ground. The guy was kicking Aaron and calling him "faggot" when two men came walking down the street.

"Hey! What's going on there?" one of the men yelled.

Instantly, the attacker took off. One of the men ran after him while the other knelt beside Aaron and helped him sit up.

"Are you okay?"

"I think so."

"Did you get a good look at him?"

"Sorta. Did you?"

"No, but I bet it was the same guy who's been beating up some other people we know."

The other man returned. "He got away."

Aaron checked his face and head with his hands. He was bleeding.

"Can you walk at all?" one of the men said. "We've got to get you to St. Vincent's."

Aaron was lucky—a few contusions, no concussion. All

he needed were a few stitches on his forehead. He told the police what he could remember. They said his description didn't fit any perpetrators they knew about, and in fact, there hadn't been any similar attacks in the neighborhood for weeks. But they said they'd look into it.

Two days later, the police had found nothing. Aaron felt angry and depressed, but kept his gallery open and went on with his life. He made jokes about the black eye that developed and continued working on the benefit.

On the third day there was a call on his cell phone. "Aaron, you don't know me but I heard you were attacked the other night." The voice was deep and serious. "I'm calling to see if you might help me nail the guy who did it."

At first Aaron was confused. Only friends had his cell phone number.

"Who is this? How did you get this number?"

"I'm a friend of a friend. I asked for the number when I heard you were attacked, because I want to help."

"Help? How?"

"I have a way of reforming bad boys."

It was the resonance of the statement that made Aaron understand it.

"You're the Velvet Kidnapper," he said.

There was silence at the other end of the line.

"Holy shit!" Aaron said.

"I'm afraid the press has made me into a cartoon bandit—but that's a whole other matter."

"What do you want from me?" Aaron said.

"You saw the guy. I want you to point him out to me so I can nail him."

Aaron laughed for a moment, then stopped. "Is this

legal?" Aaron asked. "Wait, of course this can't be legal."

"Look, think it over. I'll call you again tomorrow. If you want to do it, we can talk about how. If not, no problem, and I won't call you again."

The man called again the next day. He and Aaron agreed to meet at a coffee shop that afternoon.

Aaron arrived early and took a booth near the door. He couldn't deny a certain desire for retribution—though if the law couldn't get it for him he wasn't sure how far he was willing to go by other means. The man said he'd be wearing a blue blazer and white polo shirt, but Aaron would have recognized him anyway, the moment he walked in. He was the police sketch, only more handsome and wearing horn-rimmed glasses and a baseball cap.

"I use contacts at night," said the man, extending his hand.

Aaron realized he must have been staring. "Yeah, it's a different look," the art dealer said. The man's handshake felt like bronze. "You're…"

"Call me Joe."

"Not your real name."

"Not my real name."

They settled into the booth. *Gosh, he does look familiar,* Aaron thought. *Where might I have seen him? Food Bar? Fire Island? The art world?*

"I don't know what to say," Aaron said. "Are you in disguise?"

"No, this is me," said Joe.

They ordered coffee. After inquiring about Aaron's injuries, Joe explained how he operated. He was an attorney and an entrepreneur. His "interests" kept him traveling

all over the world. He sat on the board of several companies and anonymously funded numerous gay organizations
and initiatives. He shunned the fast lane but had friends in
high places—government, law enforcement, show business.
He also had other friends—the bartenders, shopkeepers,
and emergency room nurses who helped him identify and
capture those he called his "targets."

"It's not like a secret brotherhood with decoder rings,"
Joe said. "There are just a few of us who share information
and trust each other to be discreet. People help me because
they believe in what I'm doing and know I wouldn't hurt
anyone."

"But don't these guys deserve to be hurt?" asked Aaron.
"I thought we were talking about getting even."

"I believe they deserve to be changed."

Aaron chuckled. "Well, you certainly do change them,
don't you?" he said. "May I ask why you do it that way—
with the makeup and the clothes?"

"I guess I want them to look their best when they're
brought to justice," Joe said, cracking a smile.

"Velvet Kidnapper humor?"

"They get what anyone else gets from a makeover: a feeling of being loved and the possibility of a new point of view.
Some people can build more on that than on jail time."

Aaron told Joe everything he could remember about his
attacker. Joe listened intently, his hands folded, his steely
eyes focused on Aaron's.

"I've never seen him," Joe said, "but I suspect it's a
guy named Reuben. He's already beaten up a few people.
He's from New Jersey—Colombian, around twenty,
works in one of his family's businesses. He's had encounters with the Jersey troopers but no criminal record, and

the NYPD doesn't know anything about him."

"What do we do?" Aaron asked.

"That's up to you. We'd be taking the law into our own hands, but that's something I know how to do."

"What's involved?"

"You come out with me in the van for a few nights. I have some leads about how and where this guy operates. If we spot him, you get out and I take over. That's all, really."

"Do I help pick out the outfit? Just kidding."

Joe bowed his head momentarily instead of responding.

"So let's do it." Aaron said.

"Good," said Joe. "What about starting on Friday night? Only, you don't smoke, do you?"

"No, why?"

"Well, you know—driving around together. Big non-smoker here."

Aaron learned little more about Joe during two evenings when the two rode around Chelsea and the Village looking for Reuben. Joe wouldn't say what his business was, though he seemed quite knowledgeable about antiques, hotels, architecture, and physics. Aaron was surprised Joe knew of some of the artists he represented—though Joe changed the subject when any conversation threatened to become too detailed.

The van was new and spotless. It had Connecticut plates. In the back, neatly stowed, was everything needed for the abduction: clean rags and a package of antiseptic wipes, a roll of duct tape, a mattress pad and two pillows, a padded chest containing the chloroform, lights and a mirror, a large tackle box with makeup, and a well-stuffed canvas suitbag.

It was on their third night out, as they were travelling

north on 8th Avenue in Chelsea, when Aaron shouted suddenly. "That's him!"

Standing in front of Big Cup, talking to another young guy on the edge of the busy sidewalk, was Aaron's attacker.

"Yup," said Joe. "Fits the descriptions I have. So here's what we're going to do. We're going to go around the corner and you're going to get out and start walking in the opposite direction."

Aaron was about to agree when a commotion erupted in front of Big Cup. Reuben had pushed the guy he was talking to and the guy had pushed back. Scuffling ensued, onlookers scattered, and Reuben was suddenly running north, across 23rd Street and up 8th Avenue.

"Jeez, we better go with this," Joe said. "Sorry."

The van made the light and continued north slowly, following Reuben, who looked back a few times but not at traffic. Aaron was anything but sorry to be swept along with the chase. Happily, he helped strategize a path through the one-way streets. They were able to follow when Reuben turned west on 25th Street, because 25th runs west, but they had to loop around the block to keep Reuben in sight when he turned north again on southbound 9th Avenue.

"We've gotta get him before he gets on a subway," Joe said. "If he had a car he'd have led us to it by now."

They spotted Reuben turning east onto 29th Street, He was walking. Slowly the van went around the block again and drove past Reuben, who had come to rest on the stoop of a brownstone on 29th. Joe double-parked a few doors beyond. It was late; the block was dead quiet.

"I'm going to open the back doors, then go get him," Joe said, getting out and grabbing a shopping bag with a rag in it. "Sit here and be invisible until I knock him out. I can handle the body, but play like he's drunk if anybody comes."

Reuben was sitting, his head in his hands, when Joe approached.

"Hey, buddy, I wonder if you can give me a hand?"

Reuben looked up. He was handsome, with black hair, high cheekbones, and big brown eyes. But he looked expended, troubled. Joe smiled warmly. "My wife and I have seen you on the block, haven't we? Sure we have. My name is Joe." They shook hands. "Listen, I have to get this table out of my truck and into my house before she gets home." Joe pointed to a house a few doors away, opposite the van. "It's a surprise for her.

"It'll take five minutes. I'm parked right up there and I can give you fifty bucks, how's that?"

"Fifty bucks?" said Reuben. He looked up and down the block.

"Up front—here ya go," said Joe. He held out two twenties and a ten. "Please. It'll only take a second. Really."

Reuben stood up. He came down the steps to the sidewalk and started walking with Joe.

"Gee, thanks, man," Joe said. "Thanks a lot. This is so nice of you. I really appreciate it. My wife's gonna love this table. She's gonna be so proud of me for picking it up on sale."

They found Reuben the next day, near the 79th Street Boat Basin. He'd been given a new haircut and was styled in striped Paul Smith pants, a shirt by agnès b., and Nikes that were sold only in London. Aaron had not been allowed to see the transformation take place. After Reuben's body had been carefully secured in the back of the van Joe asked Aaron to get out, and he sped off.

The following day, the abduction was all over the newspapers. Some of the stories hinted at aliens and Satanism—everything, in fact, but the redefinition of justice, which is what Joe had told Aaron one night that his efforts were all about. Aaron got calls from friends, asking if he thought that the Velvet Kidnapper's latest victim might be the guy who attacked him. He said he didn't know.

Aaron had just gotten off the phone with a client when Joe called.

"How are you doing?" Joe asked.

"Fine, I guess. How'd it all go with you?"

"Fine. It was nice to have the help, so thanks. You're okay with the whole accessory-to-a-crime thing?"

"Piece of cake. They can't catch you, can they?"

"Will they catch me? No. Will the newspapers ever catch on to what I'm trying to do? That remains to be seen."

"Yeah, there was a lot of hot air about this one. But didn't I read that the kid and his family were pretty shaken up and that he was being shipped off to some kind of a religious rest home?"

"I hope it helps," said Joe. "Listen, I don't usually do follow-up phone calls, but you're an art dealer and I know you're interested in edgy work. I want to show my photographs."

"You take photographs?"

"I take photographs of the guys I abduct."

"Wow. Unconscious?"

"Yeah."

"So you're an artist."

"No. Well, I guess I kinda am, now."

"Honestly, Joe, I didn't think you were the type of person who'd want to profit from what you do."

"Oh, I don't want to sell my work, but I do want to show it."

"What do they look like, your photographs?"

"Lots of light, coming from all over. A little Mapplethorpe, a little Avedon, but also a little Nadar."

"Jeez. Just when I thought I could respect you as an outlaw, you go and get conceptual on me."

"Then say no. I'm just asking."

"Actually I'm interested."

"For me," said Joe, "it's not about creating objects of monetary value. It's about changing the climate."

"I see," said Aaron. He took a moment to reflect. "You may already know that I am planning a huge event next month that was supposed to center around an art installation."

"I had heard that," said Joe. He named the artist.

"The artist just pulled out due to quote-unquote creative differences."

"Aaron, let me show you my stuff."

Joe had nineteen portraits, which he showed Aaron over coffee the next day. They represented all his abductions thus far—the ones people knew about, plus four more that had escaped media attention. The shots were eerie and beautiful: figures inert but not lifeless, propped up lovingly in a wash of light radiating from all directions; clothing draped casually, suggesting poise; eyes closed yet still somehow expressive. Far from looking like a fashion spread from hell, the photos revealed a kind of beatific force circulating among the subjects. Joe's idea was to blow up the shots to five times life size, print thousands of each of them on cheap newsprint, and display them at the benefit auction in tall stacks, as decor. Guests would be invited to peel as many copies off the tops of stacks as they wanted, for free, as souvenirs.

Joe explained that even if the photographs were linked to real abductions they'd be untraceable, because they were going to be printed out of town using a standard process, by a printer who could be trusted.

"It might work," Aaron said. "Let me speak to my committee. But whom shall we list as the artist?"

"I don't know," said Joe with a grimace. "Do we have to say anything? Couldn't we say it's a secret collective of artists who sent an emissary to you in a mask?"

"Well, we can solve that. The pictures would certainly thrill everybody. You're paying for the printing, though."

"Of course. Just remember not to write me an acknowledgment for my generous tax-exempt donation."

During the following weeks, as they prepared the installation, they talked often by phone. Joe changed his cell phone number twice during that time. He didn't divulge his real name or where he lived. When the two met in person, it was in locations that were off the beaten path, so they wouldn't run into mutual friends—which Joe reminded Aaron could be touchy."

"I didn't start out as an artist," said Joe, on one occasion. "During the '80s and '90s, I started several businesses and then sold them all extremely advantageously. For a long time I was that typical gay success story—I collected art, I went to the ballet, I donated money to charitable causes."

"In New York?" asked Aaron.

"On both coasts," said Joe.

"So what changed you?"

"I watched someone bleed to death."

"I'm sorry. AIDS?"

"No, he got bashed. It was a couple of years ago. During those first big skirmishes over AIDS, I was in my twenties.

I got motivated but not what you'd call enlightened. Maybe that's my fault: I didn't have an empire to protect at the time. But losing Paul on Bedford Street one night after dinner—that woke me up. I understood that society wasn't necessarily set up to protect my interests."

"Was Paul your boyfriend?"

Joe nodded.

"Did they catch the guy?"

"No." Joe smiled. "Nowadays, I'm married to my work. I'm bored with the men of my generation, and all the younger ones seem to smoke."

★

The benefit auction was a huge success. It took place at a former factory space in the meat-packing district. Nearly 1,500 people showed up and over half a million dollars was raised. The mayor came, as did two senators, a gubernatorial candidate, and several stars of screen, sports, and pop music. Paparazzi shot guests all night, both inside the space and outside on the street.

Joe's pictures created a sensation. Word of the installation had been kept secret, for maximum impact, but as soon as people walked in they started chattering about the Velvet Kidnapper and his victims.

A reporter cornered Aaron after bothering clueless staffers all night.

"You should really tell us who took these photographs," she said.

"I've already explained," Aaron said, "This is the work of a newly emerged collective of artists who wish to remain unidentified."

"Are they dead or alive?"

"The subjects? The viewer is encouraged to make that call herself. No, wait. Of course they're alive. The models in the pictures are alive. Their eyes are simply closed."

"How do you know that?"

"One of the artists told me. He came to my office in a mask."

"Then you did deal with someone in the flesh. Didn't you suspect that it might be the Velvet Kidnapper?"

"That's such a ridiculous term, isn't it?" Aaron laughed. But the reporter's face remained wooden. "No, I didn't suspect that. I took the photographs as an interesting comment on the imprisonment of young men in a tyrannical system."

"What system is that?" spat the reporter.

"Oh, will you excuse me," purred Aaron, looking beyond her. "I have to say good night to the Schenks."

It wasn't long after the benefit that Aaron was summoned for an interview at police headquarters downtown. In a grim room with a view of the East River a detective told Aaron that an abduction victim had recognized himself in the background of a paparazzo shot published in *New York* magazine. The detective threw down the issue, open, on the table. The shot depicted a socialite gleefully unfurling her kidnapper blowup for the camera.

The victim was Reuben. That photo of him, eyes closed and angelic in the agnès b. shirt, was one of Joe's best. It would have been Aaron's favorite, except for the memory of his attack.

It was clear the detective had no knowledge of the attack. No, he said, the guy didn't have a criminal record and wasn't officially suspected of anything. Yes, it's true that he's been living in some kind of Catholic rehab facility. No, the detective didn't know why Reuben had come forward, except perhaps to see that justice was done.

"Justice?" Aaron said. But he offered little more. He spurted some art jargon and pleaded ignorance about the pictures' provenance. Per Joe's contingency plan, he gave the detective a phone number and address in Bethesda, Maryland—information he knew would lead to a dead end. He assumed he wouldn't be implicated in a crime and, in fact, was dismissed after an hour.

The detective admonished Aaron to notify him should he hear from the masked artist again.

"Good work," Joe said later on the phone. "Don't worry."

"I'm not worried," said Aaron. "In fact, I kind of like living beyond the law. I'd even want to come out and help you again, but I don't have the stomach for gassing people."

"You'll find a way to help me again, my friend," said Joe. "Fate always throws us a couple of brilliant options, along with the everyday shit. If you can suggest a way for me to get control of my public image, let me know."

The following morning Aaron sold a work by one of the artists in his gallery to Karen and Bernard Schenk. The Schenks were well-known collectors, prominent socially and in business. Bernie was the CEO of Dreadnought—the so-called biggest corporation in the world, aimed at the youth market, with fingers in everything—manufacturing, retail, recording, broadcasting—and Karen had a P.R. and marketing company that served high-end fashion and society clients. This is the kind of sale that helps a young artist's career take off, Aaron thought afterward. The work was a self-portrait depicting the features of the artist's face morphed into an iconic-looking, personal, corporate-type logo. The title of the work was *Brand (New) Me.*

That afternoon Aaron's land line rang.

"My name is Reuben. I'm the guy who attacked you. I stole your number from the police. I am deeply, deeply sorry for what I did and I want to apologize."

Aaron was stunned but calm.

"What do you want?" Aaron asked.

"I want to apologize," repeated Reuben.

"All right. Apology accepted. Now, I have to tell you that if you're planning something stupid, you're going to be caught. Or worse."

Aaron tried to sound authoritative. Reuben started weeping.

"Man, I am so sorry," Reuben said. "I'm not planning anything. Please let me come and see you and apologize like a man face-to-face."

The weeping startled Aaron. It sounded convincing, but he knew if he were to meet Reuben he'd have to take precautions.

"Can I see you today?" sobbed Reuben.

"I...don't know," said Aaron.

"Please, I am begging you. I am so sorry and I have to apologize."

"Let me put you on hold for a second," said Aaron. "I want to see if a friend I know is on duty at the SoHo Grand. We would have to meet in public."

Aaron returned to the line after a minute.

"Okay, Reuben? Come to the lobby of the SoHo Grand Hotel in two hours," Aaron said. "Do you know where that is? You can tell me whatever you want to tell me there."

Two hours later Aaron was sitting in one of several

plush, green armchairs clustered in front of a column and several potted palm trees, in the upper lobby of the SoHo Grand. In front of him was a low table with an iced tea he had ordered. Soaring windows over West Broadway flooded the broad, carpeted space with warm sunlight. Small groups of smartly dressed guests glided through the space serenely. Hotel staff and security hovered here and there in understated uniforms, looking genial. The place felt noiseless.

Aaron watched as Reuben stopped at the top of the stairs from street level, looked around, and walked straight over to him. He was handsomer than Aaron remembered, and his hair looked neater—perhaps a lingering benefit of his abduction. He was dressed in expensive Dreadnought-brand streetwear interpretations of chinos and a white shirt—neat but funky.

Out of habit Aaron stood when Reuben approached. Reuben extended his hand. "Thanks for meeting me," he said.

Aaron looked at the hand, then took it.

"I am so sorry for what I did to you, and I beg you to forgive me," Reuben said. He fell to his knees, beginning to sob again, repeating how sorry he was.

"Get up," said Aaron. "Have a seat. Do you want something to drink?"

"Everything all right, sir?" asked an attendant.

"Yes, we're fine, thank you," Aaron said. He sat back down in his chair and Reuben took the one next to him, under a palm tree.

"I was so angry when I woke up afterward," Reuben said. "I hated gay people even more. The police took the whole thing as a joke and warned me to stay away from

Chelsea. I was gonna come back as soon as I could, and strangle somebody with those clothes he put on me, only then my family put me in rehab and everything changed."

Reuben's family, comfortably middle-class as it turned out, owned several businesses—including a small but fast-growing streetwear label that had been started by Reuben's brother and that employed Reuben from time to time as "street-marketing strategist." He had been studying marketing at a local college. Reuben explained that being sent to the rehab center, a sort of halfway house run by the Catholic Church, had been his mother's idea. She was a devout Catholic and was sorry she had failed to turn Reuben into one. She knew about some of Reuben's previous attempts to antagonize gay people and told Reuben this time that it was either the home for him or another visit to the police, this time as the accused. He entered the center reluctantly. Day after day he participated in counseling and prayer sessions. He saw priests who were also psychologists. He went through the motions of praying to God and entreating the saints. And then something happened.

"I can't explain it," Reuben said. "One day I saw who I was and what I was doing, and I needed to put that person behind me. Nobody taught me to hate gay people. In school they taught us sensitivity, but still my friends and I would drive to the Village and ride around shouting, you know, 'faggot,' whatever. I wasn't poor. I wasn't secretly gay or anything. I have girlfriends. I was just stupid. But something happened in rehab. They have good people working there. My mother says the Holy Spirit came— I don't know about that."

Aaron nodded.

"So I had to find you and ask for your forgiveness," Reuben said.

"I forgive you, Reuben," Aaron said.

"Thank you. Thank you so much. But that's not all I have to ask, because something else happened while I was in rehab. While I was in there, I almost helped another kid get over his hatred, too. And that had an effect on me like you wouldn't believe. It felt so...good. I felt like I was using this new power I had. One priest said it was like I was discovering my calling. The priest let me be one of the people who counseled this kid, Jimmy. He was living in, like, total anger—for his parents, gay people, society. I know people like that, from the street. Anyway, I talked to Jimmy every day, I shared stories with him, I thought I was getting through...." Reuben went silent. He closed his eyes. "And then he kills himself. He cuts his wrists."

A tear rolled down Reuben's cheek. Aaron took his hand. They were silent for a moment.

"So I wanna meet your friend," Reuben said.

"What friend?" Aaron said softly.

"I know you know the guy who kidnapped me," Reuben said. "You have to. I want to help him. I want to learn from him."

"Help him?"

"One of the priests said, when I was helping Jimmy, that it would be so great if there was only some way of taking Jimmy away from himself for a little while—you know, like gently taking him out of his life of pain and putting him down somewhere else. I wish I could have done that. That's what your friend kind of does."

"Gosh, Reuben, what an idea," said Aaron. "The guy

you're talking about is technically a criminal, you know. Besides, he seems to be such a loner."

"C'mon," Reuben said brightly, "every superhero needs a sidekick. Besides, I have a couple of ideas for him—next-level stuff."

"Ideas? I can just imagine," Aaron said. "Tights and a cape?"

"You laugh, but image is everything, man. The look, the name, who you roll with, how you roll."

Aaron laughed.

"Seriously, man," Reuben said, "I could help that guy develop his brand. Look at these." He tugged at his chinos, showing the label known worldwide—the one with the tower on it. "Dreadnought: the hottest stuff on the planet. The image, my friend—not the quality of the cotton."

There was a rustle from behind Reuben's chair.

"Are you for real?" said Joe, stepping around from behind a potted palm. He was in a blazer and his glasses—looking like anything but a superhero. He had been sitting there all along, behind a newspaper. It was he whom Aaron had phoned while Reuben was on the line.

Reuben looked surprised but delighted. He and Aaron stood up.

"Reuben, Joe," said Aaron. "Joe, well, you know Reuben."

"Nice to see you again," said Joe. "I'm all ears, baby."

Reuben tumbled out a few sentences about street-level marketing, core values, and memorable taglines. He talked about the campaign he created for his brother's label. Then he said sheepishly that he hoped he weren't barking up the wrong tree.

Joe listened intently, not responding at first. Then he said to Aaron, "He may have a point. I've hired consultants younger than him to help with my companies." He turned to the boy. "Tell me, Reuben, do you smoke?"

Six months later, newspaper headlines blared the news of the next abduction. A kid was found unconscious in Tompkins Square, in a new outfit, looking fabulous. Only this time the abduction was credited to something called Forensics, which the newspapers said was the name of the Velvet Kidnapper's organization. A hangtag with the Forensics logo was found attached to the kid's wrist. The newspapers made it sound scary and exciting at the same time: a corporation that abducted people, a brand-name crime. Press releases from the organization had been faxed to the media from a temporary office in Baltimore. The release contained a brief bio of the kid who was abducted and statements from anonymous people who'd witnessed a bashing he committed, plus a one-page history of world justice and a recommendation that the authorities get the kid some therapy rather than jail time.

Later the victim said that there had been two abductors and that they had been very nice to him while knocking him out.

Contributors

Donna Allegra is a poet and dancer living in New York City. Her work has been published extensively in magazines, including *Essence,* and anthologies, including *Home Girls: A Black Feminist Anthology, The Persistent Desire, All the Ways Home, Does Your Mama Know?* and *Lesbian Travels.* Her arts reviews have appeared in, among other places, *Sojourner, The Lesbian Review of Books,* and *Colorlife!* as well as on WBAI radio. She is the winner of the Pat Parker Memorial Poetry Award and was a runner-up for the Audre Lorde Poetry Prize in 1994. Her short-story collection, *Witness to the League of Blond Hip-Hop Dancers,* was a Violet Quill Award finalist.

Melanie Braverman is the author of the novel *East Justice* (Permanent Press, 1996) and the collection of poems *Red* (Perugia Press, 2002), and the winner of the 2002 Audre Lorde Poetry Prize. She lives in Provincetown, Massachusetts.

Angela Brown is the editor in chief of Alyson Publications, the nation's largest publisher of books by, for, and about lesbian, gay, bisexual, and transgendered people. She is the editor of *Best Lesbian Love Stories 2003* and *2004* and the forthcoming *Mentsh: On Being Jewish and Queer*. Her work has appeared on NPR and Pacifica Radio as well as in *Out* magazine. A two-time Lambda Literary Award finalist, she lives in West Hollywood, California.

Christina Chiu has been the recipient of the Van Lier Fellowship, the Lannan Foundation Fellowship, and the Claire Woolrich Scholarship. Her stories have appeared in *Tin House, The MacGuffin,* and other magazines. She obtained a bachelor of arts degree in East Asian Studies at Bates College and a master's degree in fine arts at Columbia University. She is a cofounder of the Asian American Writers Workshop. She lives in New York City and is at work on her first novel.

Malka Drucker is the author of more than fifteen books for children, including *Jacob's Rescue* and *Frida Kahlo*. She lives in Santa Fe, New Mexico, where she is a rabbi as well as a Holocaust lecturer and writer.

Michael Thomas Ford is the author of more than fifty books in a variety of genres, including biographies and young-adult fiction. His books in the My Queer Life series have been national best-sellers and earned him two Lambda Literary Awards. He lives in San Francisco.

Stephen Greco is editor at large of the international style magazine *Trace*. A former editor at *Interview* magazine, *Stagebill, The Advocate,* and the New York weekly *7 Days,* Greco was editorial director and a cofounder of Platform.net, which for years was the Web's leading urban youth culture portal. A collection of Greco's erotic short stories and autobiographical pieces, *The Sperm Engine,* was published in October 2002 by Green Candy Press and was a 2003 Lambda Literary Award finalist. "Forensics" is from Greco's recently completed first novel, *Dreadnought.* He lives in New York City and is at work on a second novel.

Brent Hartinger is a novelist and playwright. His books include *Geography Club, The Last Chance Texaco,* and *The Order of the Poison Oak,* a sequel to *Geography Club* that will be released in February 2005. Brent's plays include *The Starfish Scream,* about gay teens, and the stage adaptation of his novel *Geography Club.* Brent lives in Tacoma, Washington, with writer Michael Jensen, his partner since 1992. Explore the author's Web site, Brent's Brain, at www.brenthartinger.com.

Gregory Maguire is the author of twelve novels for children, including the popular Hamlet Chronicles series, and four novels for adults. *Wicked: The Life and Times of the Wicked Witch of the West,* his first adult novel, has been adapted for the musical stage by Stephen Schwartz and Winnie Holzman. His most recent novel is *Mirror Mirror,* a retelling of the Snow White story set in the High Renaissance; it features Lucrezia Borgia as the wicked stepmother, a missing eighth dwarf, and a poison apple from the Garden of Eden. Gregory lives in Massachusetts with his partner, the painter Andy Newman, and their three children.

Pam McArthur's work has been published in the anthologies *Bushfire, Afterglow, Woman in the Window, Out Rage,* and *Testimonies.* She lives with her partner of twelve years in Framingham, Mass.

Transplanted Australian **Claire McNab** has written nineteen best-selling mystery novels. Fourteen of them feature the highly popular Detective-Inspector Carol Ashton, while four feature the undercover agent Denise Cleever. With *The Wombat Strategy*, Claire began a new series starring Aussie knockabout Kylie Kendall. She has served as the president of Sisters in Crime and is a member of both the Mystery Writers of America and the Science Fiction Writers of America. She lives in Los Angeles.

William Moses is a naturalist from Champaign, Illinois.

Lesléa Newman is the author and editor of more than forty books, including *Heather Has Two Mommies, A Letter to Harvey Milk, Girls Will Be Girls, Good Enough to Eat,* and *She Loves Me, She Loves Me Not.* Her literary awards include fellowships from the National Endowment for the Arts and the Massachusetts Artists Foundation. Six of her books have been Lambda Literary Award finalists. A native New Yorker, she lives in western Massachusetts.

Judd Powell is an actor and writer. "Crossing Lines," written in 1994, was his first published story.

Nan Prener has taught at every level from prekindergarten through master's (educational technology). Her writing has appeared in *Instructor* and *Cat Fancy*. She has written several novels and more than 200 short stories, published and distributed privately through the counterculture audience.

Bonnie Shimko is a retired second-grade teacher living in upstate New York with her husband, Robert. They have two children. Her novel, *Letters in the Attic,* won a Lambda Literary Award in the Children's/Young Adult category.

Brian Sloan is a renowned independent filmmaker whose work has been screened to the delight of audiences around the world. His writing has been published in various magazines, including *Genre* and *Christopher Street.* His play *The Boys Who Brunch* received the top prize at New York's 1999 CenterStage One-Act Play Festival, and his play *Sex and the One-Act* won the festival's top prize in 2000.

Judith P. Stelboum is the author of *Past Perfect,* a novel of lesbian life. Her essays, fiction, and poetry have appeared in a variety of anthologies and journals such as *Common Lives/Lesbian Lives, Sinister Wisdom, Sister and Brother, Resist: Essays Against a Homophobic Culture, The Oxford Companion to Twentieth Century Literature in English,* and *The History of Homosexuality: Vol. 1: Lesbian Histories and Cultures.* In addition, she is a reviewer and essayist for *Lesbian Review of Books* and *Lambda Book Report.*

Laurel Winter is an accomplished sci-fi and fantasy writer and poet. She won the 1999 World Fantasy Award for her story "Sky Eyes" as well as the Science Fiction Poetry Association's Rhysling Award for the trenchant meditations "Why Goldfish Shouldn't Use Power Tools" (*Asimov's* December 1997) and "Egg Horror Poem" (*Asimov's* 1998). Her first young-adult fantasy novel, *Growing Wings,* received runner-up for best children's fiction from The Society of Midland Authors and was one of five finalists for the Mythopoeic Award for children's fantasy.